2019

Chattering Blue Jay
A Gabriel Hawke Novel
Book 4

Paty Jager

Windtree Press
Hillsboro, OR

This is a work of fiction, names, characters, places, and incidents either are the product of the author's imagination or are used fictitiously, and any resemblance to actual persons living or dead, business establishments, events, or locales, is entirely coincidental.

CHATTERING BLUE JAY

Contact Information: info@windtreepress.com

Windtree Press
Hillsboro, Oregon
http://windtreepress.com

Cover Art by Christina Keerins
CoveredbyCLKeerins

Published in the United States of America

ISBN 978-1-950387-64-9

Special Acknowledgements

I'd like to thank the Oregon State Police Fish and Wildlife division for allowing me to ride along with an officer to learn all the ins and outs of the job. Special thanks also go out to the Ada County Sheriff's Office and Mercedes Christesen.

Author Comments

While this book is set in Wallowa County, Oregon, I have changed the town names to old forgotten towns that were in the county at one time. I also took the liberty of changing the towns up and populating the county with my own characters, none of which are in anyway a representation of anyone who is or has ever lived in Wallowa County. Other than the towns, I have tried to use the real names of all the geographical locations.

This book also has southern Idaho as the area that Hawke is working in. The towns were all kept the same, but any references to the characters in the area in the Idaho State Police, Ada County Sheriff's Office, Boise City Police, and the Idaho Search and Rescue are all people and events made up by me. There is no correlation to anything factual.

Chapter One

"And then when I spotted a small limb had been snapped off at the right height…"

Gabriel Hawke tuned out one of the other instructors at the National MRA Spring Conference in Boise, Idaho. Hawke would have preferred working over giving a workshop at the Search and Rescue Conference. However, his lieutenant, at the Oregon State Police, told Hawke at the beginning of the year, he would appreciate Hawke's cooperation in attending more Search and Rescue conferences to learn more about the latest technology that was being used, and he wanted Hawke to make contacts with the search and rescue groups on the Idaho side of the Snake River. The lieutenant's exact words, "You never know when we'll need to ask for help from across the river."

"I bet Hawke would have found that missing family faster than you did," James Newton, with the Wallowa County Sheriff's Department and head of the county's Search and Rescue team, said.

Hawke rolled his eyes and sipped his beer. A small contingency of the conference presenters had ended up in the bar after registering with the conference coordinator. Most attendees arrived Thursday night to be ready for the first workshops in the morning. He'd wanted a beer before heading up to his room and had found a table away from the growing crowd standing around the bar.

"Is that so?" Sean Sheridan, a master tracker with the Idaho Search and Rescue, shoved away from the bar and sauntered over to Hawke's table. Sheridan had been the one talking up having found a family by his tracking prowess. He pulled out a chair at Hawke's table and plopped down without asking if Hawke wanted company. "I remember not that long ago a little girl outsmarted Hawke, the great Indian tracker." The man had already had more than his share of liquor. Sarcasm dripped from his comment.

Hawke didn't flinch at the accusation he couldn't track a child or the slur on his heritage. He'd met other trackers who couldn't claim the heritage he could who were as good or better than him. His teacher had been his Nez Perce grandfather who knew old ways of tracking. The old man had also taught him qualities that the trackers who were taught at conferences, like this, didn't learn. And it had been a cunning child who'd outsmarted him several times and who made him smile every time he thought about her.

He ignored the jab at his ancestors and said, "Kitree didn't want to be found and tried multiple times to cover her tracks." Hawke sipped his beer. He stared into Sheridan's glazed over eyes. "A good tracker knows to not drink more than he can handle to be ready to go at a moment's notice."

The others who'd gathered around the table, laughed and commented. "Oooo, he got you there," and "You might want to ease up on the juice if you're teaching in the morning."

"I could out track you even with a hangover," Sheridan boasted, peering at Hawke with glassy eyes.

Hawke finished off his beer and stood. He'd had enough chitchat for the night. He preferred to stay to himself, give his workshop, and sit in on the subjects of interest. Dropping a tip on the table, he started for the door.

The head of the Idaho Search and Rescue and chair of the conference strode into the bar. His height gave him an advantage as he scanned the conference attendees. His gaze locked onto Hawke, and Henry Childress covered the distance between them.

"I need to talk to you," Childress said, motioning for Hawke to come with him.

Without a glance around, or a comment, Hawke followed the man to a seating of three chairs in the hotel lobby.

"Wait here." Childress disappeared into the bar and returned with Sheridan in his wake.

Hawke didn't care for the other tracker, but out of respect for Childress, he kept his thoughts to himself and his face remained blank.

Sheridan smiled smugly as he plopped into a chair.

Childress leaned toward Hawke. The man's broad shoulders loomed over his beach ball stomach stretching the button-up shirt. He glanced at Sheridan as if he remembered the man was there. "You're both going to have to bow out of your workshops tomorrow."

His comment didn't hurt Hawke's feelings, but Lt. Titus wouldn't be happy. "Have you called my Lieutenant?"

"I spoke with him. He's cleared you."

"Cleared me?" This meant they needed his help as a State Trooper. He glanced at Sheridan. The man had better sober up quick if they had to work together. He didn't care to babysit a drunk. He'd done that enough in his life with his stepfather.

"We had a murderer escape our maximum-security prison near Boise. We have reason to believe he is headed to Hells Canyon. It's where he grew up, and where he committed the murders that put him in prison."

Sheridan leaned forward. "No shit! White got loose?"

Hawke noticed the gleam in the other tracker's eyes. This would be another story he'd embellish at a future conference.

"When did he escape?" Hawke calculated the distance from Boise to the canyon. "Was he on foot or did he get a vehicle?"

"We believe he escaped sometime this morning. No one noticed until the mid-day meal and then it was an hour or so after that before they'd confirmed he was missing." Childress shook his head. "We think a woman he'd been corresponding with is involved. She didn't turn up to work this morning and no one can find her, either. A description of her car is out statewide."

Childress held out a map. "This is the area where we believe he will try to hide."

"I know where it is," Sheridan boasted. "I was with the team that found the bodies."

Hawke studied the area that was circled. He gave a low whistle. "That's rough terrain." He studied it some more. "This is where he grew up?"

"Yes. There's a small valley, gap, whatever you want to call it, with a spring and an old homestead. The Goodwin family purchased it five years ago while White was in jail on assault charges. When White got out, he headed back to the homestead, killed the family and a man who'd come to the homestead to visit with the Goodwins."

"There was blood everywhere and bodies..." Sheridan stood and hurried toward the restrooms.

"Nasty piece of work, it sounds like." Hawke thought of all the boaters and hikers in that area who, if they came across a madman like White, could end up dead. "I take it you're pairing me with Sheridan?"

"He does know the area, but I want you to keep a handle on him. He tends to do stupid things, thinking he's a hero."

"Thanks a lot." There was nothing worse than babysitting a rogue cop when there was a job to do. This time it was a rogue tracker who didn't have to obey orders from a law enforcement officer. "We'll drive to Saw Pit Saddle and start from there. Any chance a command center can be set up in that area?"

"We were hoping you'd pick that point. There is a team already headed that way," Childress said.

Hawke stood, glancing toward the restrooms. No sign of his partner on this job. "Do you think the woman is in danger?"

"I haven't heard from the authorities what they

think about that." Childress stood. "Be careful, White is dangerous. Just find him and the woman. Let the rest know where they are and they will move in and apprehend. Do you need supplies?"

"I'll have my dog flown to Big Bar airstrip along with my pack. I'd prefer to go after this guy with just me and my dog. White sounds unstable."

Sheridan stumbled out of the restroom.

"And so does Sheridan." Hawke strode to the hotel elevators and rode up to his room.

He called Lieutenant Titus, filled him in, and asked him to contact Dani Singer of Charlie's Hunting Lodge and ask her to fly her helicopter to Prairie Creek airport in the morning to pick up his backpack and dog and fly them to the Big Bar airstrip. Then he called Herb Trembley, his landlord, and asked him to grab the already packed backpack in his apartment and Dog and deliver them to Prairie Creek airport early in the morning.

"Why do you need me to take them to the airport?" Herb asked.

"I need them for a tracking job." Hawke didn't want to tell his landlord what he was doing. Wallowa County was like most small communities. What you said to one person could spread to the whole county in a matter of a few hours.

"Who am I meeting?"

"Dani Singer. The woman who owns Charlie's Lodge."

The man chuckled. "You sure you aren't just using this conference as an excuse to run off with that pretty lady?"

Hawke groaned. If only he were running off with

Dani and not going after a killer with an overzealous tracker. "Sorry, but you can't start a rumor like that. She's just transporting the items I need. Talk to you when I get back." He ended the connection and shoved the few toiletries he'd set out on the bathroom sink into his duffel bag, made a quick scan of the room to see if he'd taken anything else out, and exited.

Out in the hall, Sheridan stepped out of his room, a large pack over his shoulder. It was curious the man had the right gear for the job.

"Guess we'll find out who is the better tracker." Sheridan's eyes had lost some of the liquor glaze as he stared at Hawke.

"This isn't a contest. We're to find an escaped convict and let the authorities know." Hawke kept on walking.

"Sure, sure. But it will be interesting to see who picks up his trail first." Sheridan thudded down the hall behind him.

Hawke ignored the man as he waited for the elevator.

"Don't you feel the adrenaline of being the only two out of the fifty other guys here who we were picked over?" Sheridan placed a hand on Hawke's shoulder.

"We aren't partners or better than the other trackers here. I'd say our workshops were less needed than the others." Hawke shoved the man's hand off his shoulder.

The elevator doors dinged and Hawke stepped in. Sheridan followed. It took all of Hawke's control to not put out a hand and stiff arm the man off the elevator. He'd already made up his mind they weren't driving together. He couldn't put up with the man's mouth and attitude for two hours.

Hawke pressed the lobby button and drew in a deep breath. The faint mint of mouthwash lingered between them. It was evident the tracker didn't want to lose his chance at this operation by having the person in command smell booze on his breath.

The only thing going for Sheridan was he knew the area and where the man might be hiding. If he were by himself, there was no telling how long it would take him to find a man who knew the area better than him. Hawke knew a lot about the Oregon side of Hells Canyon but this would be his first time actually exploring the Idaho side. If it had been for any other reason, he'd have relished the time spent walking the craggy tops of the rocky canyons and sliding down basalt and shale tailings. If he were alone. With the attitude and mouth on Sheridan it would be a trial.

"You take your vehicle and I'll take mine. I'll meet you at Saw Pit Saddle. From there I'm meeting up with my gear and dog at Big Bar air strip."

"That will put us off track of heading to the homestead," Sheridan said.

"I'm not going after White without my gear and my dog." Hawke climbed into his pickup and turned the ignition. He didn't care if his getting the proper equipment stalled their going after the man. This hike could be a matter of life and death and he planned to be prepared.

Chapter Two

Lt. Titus called Hawke before he lost cell service. He'd contacted Ms. Singer and his pack and dog would be picked up at the Prairie Creek airport and delivered to him.

At the end of the road at Saw Pit Saddle there were half a dozen vehicles and tents set up. He cringed, thinking this was a sure way of letting the man they were after know they were on his tail.

Hawke walked over to the group who appeared to be the ones in charge. "Hawke. Childress said I was to coordinate with you."

"I'm Sheriff Barnes and this is Deputy Mathews. He and his group will be tailing you. You'll stay in contact with him and let him know when you have your eyes on White and the woman." Barnes was a tall, thin man of around Hawke's age. Mathews was in his thirties, fit, and had a no-nonsense attitude about him.

Sheridan arrived right behind Hawke. "Barnes,

Mathews." He slapped the two officers on the back and started talking with them.

Hawke returned to his truck and pulled out a small daypack he always carried when traveling. He checked the contents: water bottles, jerky, flashlight, knife, and a first aid kit. Opening the vehicle's glovebox, he grabbed his holster and Glock. He strapped that on over his T-shirt and pulled on a long-sleeved shirt. He grabbed an old denim jacket that was stuffed behind the seat. It was the beginning of June and the nights could still get cold. A quick shake tossed the worst of the dirt off the garment. He shoved his arms into the jacket and slipped the backpack over his shoulders.

His worn, dusty, brown felt cowboy hat hung from a rifle rack across the back window of his pickup. He flicked the dust off by slapping it against his leg and shoved the hat on his head.

He walked back over to the group gathered at the makeshift command center. "I'm headed to Big Bar airstrip to pick up my pack." He leaned over the map they had spread out on the table. "Sheridan, you can meet up with me here. The rest can follow you in and be behind us as we near the homestead."

"That sounds like a plan." Barnes nodded to Sheridan, who started to open his mouth and clamped it shut.

Mathews agreed, they'd be there.

Hawke walked over to the trail that would take him toward Myers Creek. From the map Childress gave him, it looked like the best route to Big Bar airstrip. He'd watched small prop planes and helicopters land on the airstrip several times while patrolling the Snake River in his capacity as Game Warden, keeping an eye on fishermen.

It was the middle of the night. If the quarter moon had shone more light, he wouldn't need the flashlight to illuminate the trail. The lights of the command station would have kept White away from this path into his hideout. That meant White could have driven farther north, perhaps to throw the authorities off his trail or he didn't plan to head to his childhood home.

What little he knew of the man, Hawke had a suspicion White would go back to the home he knew and where he'd committed murder. If the Idaho criminal system believed he'd go home, they had to have a good reason. Knowing so little about White made trying to outguess him hard. All Hawke could do was hike the two-and-a-half miles to the airstrip, get Dog and his pack, and read everything Titus sent him before he took off toward the homestead and met up with the others.

He kept a steady downhill trek on the faint trail. If he was lucky, he'd get to the airstrip with a couple hours to sleep before Dani arrived.

《》《》《》

The thump of helicopter blades roused Hawke. He slid his hat back on his head, letting the sunshine slowly seep into his eyes. His body twitched awake as he stretched and watched the helicopter make two circles above the airstrip.

He stood, showing his upper body above the bush he'd used as cover while he'd slept. The airstrip was a good fifty yards from his sleeping spot. Picking up his daypack, he strode toward the rough strip used by sport fishermen and hunters as well as people who lived in the canyon.

The helicopter gently settled on the cleared path and the rotor blades slowed to a stop.

Hawke walked up to the aircraft as Dani opened the door.

Dog leaped out, landing on Hawke's chest. "I don't blame you boy, she's a scary pilot." He wrapped his arms around the tri-color, wire-haired mutt for a moment then set him on the ground.

"What kind of lies are you telling that dog?" Dani asked, standing on the ground in front of him wearing a jumpsuit that covered her compact body.

As usual, her presence flustered him as if he were a teenager instead of a fifty-three-year-old. That was one of the reasons he hadn't pursued her. That, and the fact he'd survived just fine the last thirty years on his own after his wife divorced him because he'd arrested her brother for possession of drugs.

"I'm not telling any lies. I saw how wide his eyes were before he jumped into my arms." Hawke joked. He'd finally discovered under that military gruffness Dani had a good sense of humor.

"His eyes were wide because he couldn't believe it was you." She opened the back door of the helicopter.

"Here, let me get that." He reached around Dani, bumping her as he latched onto his backpack. His body came to life. Ignoring it, he opened the pack, acting like he was inspecting the contents. "Gotta love 'em," he said, tying the top closed.

"Love who?" Dani asked from behind him.

"My landlords. Herb grabbed the right pack and Darlene put cookies in it." He faced the woman staring at him with a wrinkled brow and pursed lips under her short-cropped dark hair.

"They take good care of me and my animals." Hawke set the pack away from the helicopter and faced her. "Did a trooper bring something as well?"

She nodded to the still open back door. He leaned in and found the file Lt. Titus sent with information about the man he was tracking.

"Are you going after the murderer who escaped here in Idaho?" Her tone was soft, tinged with worry.

He pulled the file out and stood in front of her. "It's what I was asked to do."

"But you could have turned it down. You were at a conference with how many other trackers? Twenty? Thirty? Couldn't one of them have gone instead? One from Idaho?"

He didn't know what to say. Her being worried about him had his chest expanding. He had hoped she'd someday have some feelings for him other than exasperation, but now wasn't the time to think about it. "I was asked to do it. And there is another tracker, from Idaho, going with me. The command station is only three miles that direction."

"But you would rather do this by yourself. You and Dog, wouldn't you?" Now her tone was confrontational, like so many of their conversations.

He put a hand on her shoulder. Nothing more than he would do to a friend. Touching her face like he wanted, would make the moment to intimate. "Yes, I would prefer to do this by myself, only to keep others from being harmed. But I'm stuck with a know-it-all tracker, and I'll deal with it."

"You better be careful. What am I supposed to tell Kitree if you don't come back?" She peered into his eyes.

"She'll understand, I do what I must to keep others safe." He dropped his hand to his side. "You better go. I need to meet up with the other tracker."

She held his gaze for a moment and slammed the helicopter's back door before climbing into the pilot's seat. "You better be careful," was her order before she closed the door, waited for him to get out of the blades reach, and started the helicopter up.

Hawke stood beside his packs with Dog at his feet and waved until she was a dot on the horizon. Damn! He didn't need or want anyone worrying about him. Shoving the daypack into the larger backpack, he had to admit it was kind of nice having someone worry about him. However, he didn't want to dwell on it and become a victim of the dangerous man they were tracking.

"Come on, let's get hiking. If we don't show up, the others will think I'm lost," he said to Dog. He wanted to be good and tired when he stopped for the night. Sleep would keep any yearnings, he had for the woman or a life other than what he had, at bay.

≪≫≪≫≪≫

Hawke groaned when he came upon Sheridan leaning against his pack at the area where they had planned to meet. He'd secretly hoped the man had gone rogue and headed out without him.

Mathews and his group of six were waiting in the same area.

According to the map, the homestead the authorities believed White would head to, was six miles away near Elk Horn Spring. There were several craggy mountain ranges Hawke and Sheridan had to climb to get to the area, all while keeping an eye out for other hikers and the escaped convict and woman.

He let Sheridan take the lead as they headed toward the first mountain they had to cross.

Mid-day, Hawke suggested they stop to eat. He pulled out the report Lieutenant Titus had sent along.

"What are you reading?" Sheridan asked, tearing the top off a bag of trail mix.

"The report on White." Hawke continued to read and eat his jerky.

"How did you get that?" Sheridan stood and walked toward him.

"My lieutenant sent it to me." He glanced up. "You said you found the bodies. What can you tell me about White?"

The man shrugged. "What's to know? He killed five people, went to jail, broke out, and now he'll get what's coming to him." He added. "When we find him."

It was clear the man knew nothing about the escaped convict. Hawke flipped through the pages. There were photos of White and the woman, Tonya Cox. At least he would know them before they figured out who he was.

The convict's file read like a typical antisocial psychopath. He'd been in and out of jail since he was eighteen. Each instance was an escalation of the prior conviction until he murdered the Goodwin family. Husband, wife, and two daughters. And a Mr. Theodore Shoat, who had been visiting the family. Photos of the crime scene were in the file. The cabin was a bloody mess. The bodies appeared to have been stabbed and sliced like White had been on something. What kind of animal would do this to five people?

Reading on, White was picked up by Idaho Fish and Wildlife when he'd walked to the edge of the Snake River and knelt to wash dried blood off his face and hands. He'd rambled about people and blood everywhere. Eventually the bodies were found, and he was charged with their murders. His counsel had tried to plead insanity, but the man had passed all the evaluations that might have put him in a mental health facility rather than prison. The jury had found him mentally competent.

Hawke closed the file and shoved it back in his pack. This was one messed up human he was tracking.

"Come on. I'd like to get on the south side of Triangle Mountain by dark." Hawke shouldered his pack and headed along the side of a rock outcropping.

Sheridan fell in step behind him, for once not trying to run the show or even talk. It was a nice hike.

A couple hours later, Dog stopped. The hair along his spine stood up. His lip raised, baring his teeth as a low growl bubbled in his throat.

"What do you see?" Hawke whispered and watched Dog's ears twitch as he curled his neck to look behind them. "Someone sneaking up behind us?" Hawke asked, noticing they'd lost Sheridan. The man must have stopped to take a dump or a leak.

They'd been traveling with the man for hours. Hawke wondered that Dog would have such a reaction to the man coming back up behind them.

He placed his pack on the ground and pulled out a water bottle and granola bar. He opened the bar and placed it across the top of the water. "Come," he whispered to Dog. They walked up a rocky area and sat down behind a boulder, watching his pack.

Fifteen minutes later Sheridan came into view. As soon as he spotted the pack, water, and snack, he stopped and scanned the area. The man's familiar shape, short legs, long torso with wide shoulders and pack, should have eased Dog's reaction. The animal continued to growl deep in his chest.

Hawke cursed under his breath and stood up from behind the boulder. He really didn't like whatever game Sheridan was playing.

Dog ran down the rocky slope, snarling.

"Hey!" Sheridan pulled his pack around in front of him as a shield. "You know me."

"Dog, sit," Hawke commanded.

Dog plopped down on his haunches, still showing his teeth at Sheridan. Seeing his dog's reaction to the man solidified how he'd always felt about the obnoxious tracker. Someone to not trust.

"Where did you disappear to?" Hawke asked, bending over and picking up his water and granola bar.

"Stopped to take a dump. Didn't think you needed to know what I did every minute." The man wore sunglasses, making it hard to read if he was being sarcastic or angry.

The hair on Hawke's nape tingled. This was not a man to trust. He had a feeling Sheridan didn't make any excuses for always wanting to win. Hawke just wanted to keep people safe and would have preferred to find White on his own. He'd not worked with Sheridan before. Only knew the tracker from his boasting. So far, the man had acted as Hawke had feared.

"We're supposed to stay together. You know this man is a killer." Hawke unscrewed the top of his filtered water bottle and drank.

"I've chased after other killers before and lived to talk about it."

This was the attitude that could get them both killed. Hawke preferred to sneak up on the subject he was following and have surprise on his side.

"Besides, we know he had a head start and he's headed for the homestead." Sheridan shrugged and pulled a water bottle from the side of his pack and drank. "We'll find him there and take care of things."

"We don't know for a fact he is at the homestead. He could be anywhere." Hawke stared at the other man. They had no clear knowledge White was at the homestead. He could be following them for all they knew.

Sheridan replaced the water bottle and pulled out a map. "I was part of the search and rescue who went looking for the bodies after White was found washing at the river. We're only about a mile from the homestead." He placed his finger on a spot on the map.

Hawke didn't even look. "If we're that close, anyone we come upon could be the man." He shouldered his pack. "Best to not even talk about an objective." He continued in the direction he'd mapped out. It would take him about a hundred yards above the area where the homestead stood. He'd rather not have Sheridan with him, the man was a loose cannon. But he had no choice.

Dog trotted ahead. Hawke heard Sheridan breathing and kicking a rock now and then behind him. The man's sounds made it hard to focus on the sounds of nature. He not only relied on what he saw but what he heard to make sense of a situation.

Dog placed his nose to the ground and started to move down the side of the cliff.

"Come," Hawke said only loud enough to catch Dog's attention. The animal returned to him. It had to be the trail of a person. Dog had learned not to follow the scents of animals. Had White and the woman crossed here on their way to the cabin?

He decided to see how well Sheridan would work with him. "Dog caught the scent of something. You check that way. I'll look this way for the tracks of a person." Hawke had suggested Sheridan go the direction the person or persons may have come from.

The man narrowed his eyes. "The homestead would be downhill from here. I'll take the tracks that way."

Hawke grabbed his arm. "You go the direction I tell you. If they should be this direction, I don't want them to know we are here. Our job is to locate and call authorities. That's all."

"Are you saying you think I'll give us away?"

"I'm saying I don't trust you to just find them and back off. Your boastfulness makes me think you would try to engage. That's not why we're here." Hawke pointed. "See if you can find which way they came from."

He told Dog to heel and searched the ground for tracks leading downhill. It took some searching on the rocky surfaces to find a spot that finally showed a boot heel mark on a small patch of dirt between rocks. The print did show the person to be heading down into the small gorge below. The map and file weren't clear as to whether the homestead was in the bottom of the gorge or up the other side.

Following the telltale evidence of tracks for fifteen minutes, he could discern there were two people. This fit White and the woman, but it could also be hikers, though why they were off the trails would be interesting to know.

Dog growled quietly.

Hawke glanced behind him and knew why the animal was talking. Sheridan followed.

"I figured you'd found their tracks when you didn't come back right away," the man said, accusingly.

"I don't know whose tracks they are. I was following to figure out which direction they are headed."

"Right." Sheridan said, sarcastically.

Hawke faced the man who'd butted heads with him from the beginning of the assignment. "There is no way of knowing if these are White and the woman."

"But you think it is because of the direction they are headed." Sheridan studied him.

He had never lied to another person, especially one he was working with. "I do believe these could be their tracks. But we can't rush down the hill and either get caught or compromise the woman he has with him." Hawke glared at the man as the sun hovered just above the western horizon. "It's going to be dark soon. Make camp. We'll continue in the light tomorrow."

He walked over to a spot that was relatively flat and unrolled his sleeping bag. He placed his pack at the head end of the bedroll and sat, watching Sheridan wander about studying the ground.

"You aren't going to find any soft rocks," Hawke said, laughing to himself over his joke.

Sheridan glared at him and finally rolled out his

sleeping bag and sat down.

Hawke smirked and pulled out a bag of jerky. It appeared all the other man had was a sleeping bag. Hawke had an inch-thick mat. Darlene, Herb Trembley's wife, had made a pocket on one side of his sleeping bag several years ago that allowed the mat to slip in and had a Velcro lip that kept the mat in place. It saved time to roll it all up and out at the same time, plus the added padding. He'd have a bit of cushion from the rocks, but Sheridan wouldn't have any.

Hawke radioed Mathews to let him know they'd stopped for the night and would have an eye on the homestead in the morning.

He glanced over at Sheridan, shimmying around on the ground as if making a bed in the dirt. While he would have rather spent this night with just Dog, at least he knew he had another person to keep an ear out for anyone sneaking up on them.

Chapter Three

The skittering of rocks and cold air through the open zipper from Dog rising off the sleeping bag roused Hawke. Stars twinkled in the inky sky. The sliver of moon barely lit the tops of trees. He shifted to his side, glad it was so dark. His eyes didn't have to adjust from darkness to light. His gaze landed on the empty spot where Sheridan had spread his bedroll.

Damn! The boastful tracker had headed to find White in the dark. Hawke sat up. Sheridan not only put his life at risk, but Hawke's as well. Maybe even the SAR officers as well. He scrubbed his hands over his face, thinking. It was senseless to try and follow Sheridan or find the homestead in the dark.

He studied the sky. At least three hours before the sun would come up. Might as well get more sleep. He called Dog back, and they settled down to sleep a few more hours.

《》《》《》

Chattering Blue Jay

Hawke discovered Sheridan's trail easier than the tracks of the two he'd found the day before. To Sheridan's credit, he was following the faint tracks of the two headed into the gorge. Hawke kept Dog at his heels, not wanting the animal to rush forward and make their approach known.

An hour after rising and eating a couple of granola bars and downing a bottle of water, Hawke stopped behind a rock formation and studied what appeared to be a shack across the narrow rocky gorge.

He pulled out a small set of binoculars and scanned the area around the building. Someone was presently at the homestead. A pack, that wasn't Sheridan's, sat beside the door and freshly chopped wood was stacked under the only window he could see. The inside was dark, and no matter how hard he tried, Hawke couldn't see the interior.

Using the binoculars, he surveyed the area between him and the shack. Sheridan had to be somewhere in between. There weren't any trees and only a few bushes besides the ragged teeth of basalt that sprang out of the hard rock ridges.

Movement caught his attention. Honing in on the area, he spotted a small herd of mountain sheep. They didn't look disturbed. Sheridan must be closer to the shack.

He did a careful back and forth sweep of the far side of the gorge below the shack. There was the boastful tracker.

Damn! He was slipping out of his pack and heading toward the shack. Hawke had feared this behavior when the man had been asked to join him on this assignment. Sheridan was like the chattering Blue

Jay. He wasn't happy unless he had a story to tell. Especially, if he came out looking like a hero.

Hawke had planned to sit here, watch for movement, and see if the couple were in the shack. After verification, he'd call Mathews and wait for help to apprehend White and the woman. Or, if the man and woman took off before the authorities arrived, to follow them, relaying their whereabouts.

If Sheridan made contact, there was no telling what White might do.

Hawke's only recourse to keep from losing his objective was to wait and see what happened.

His gut churned as he held the binoculars to his eyes and watched Sheridan sneak up to the side of the shack. The way he crouched, approaching the building, there must have been a window. Yep, Sheridan slowly raised up, looked at the building, and froze.

What did he see?

The blast of a shotgun dropped Sheridan to the ground. Hawke stood. His instincts bunched to go to Sheridan's aid, but the door of the shack flew open.

A woman, fitting the description of Ms. Cox, and a man, resembling the description of White, ran to the side of the shack. White had a shotgun in his hands but it wasn't aimed at Sheridan.

The woman was talking, her arms swung wildly as if she was either in hysterics or chewing out White.

Sheridan sat up. He had some bloody spatters on his face, but no signs of a large amount of bleeding.

What he wouldn't give to be closer to hear what was being said.

White and the woman grabbed Sheridan under the arms and hauled him into the shack.

That answered his questions about if the two were there.

Hawke dug into his pack and pulled out the radio.

He dialed in Mathews. "This is Hawke, can you read me?"

"Copy," Mathews said.

"I found the two. They are in the homestead." He hesitated to say, he'd lost Sheridan and the fool was now a hostage. He'd wait on that until backup arrived. "I'll wait here for backup. Should they move out, I'll follow and let you know."

"Copy."

Some static was followed by silence.

"Looks like we make camp here," he told Dog and found a rock formation to place his pack against and then sit, using the two as a back rest. He studied the building and area through the binoculars and wondered how long it would take backup to arrive and what the two in the shack were doing to Sheridan.

He knew not to try and take on the convicted killer, but Hawke's curiosity and need to move and not sit still, got the better of him. He waited until just about dark and headed down the gorge with Dog on his heels. He hoped to have a better chance of looking into the shack up close without getting caught like Sheridan.

He'd kept his pack with him and found a spot beside a bush where he stashed the backpack and pulled out the binoculars. As darkness filled the wide crevice and shrouded the shack, he waited for a lantern to illuminate the inside.

An hour passed with the structure remaining dark. Rocks rumbled from the top of the cliff. The ground tremored. Boulders crashed into the back of the shack and shattered the roof.

Hawke grabbed his flashlight and aimed the beam of light at the shack. The back wall and the roof were nothing but rubble. Dust plumed in the air around the structure.

"Dog, stay!" he ordered and ran toward the building. It had to have been White who rolled the rocks down on the building.

He shoved the door open and ran the flashlight beam around the inside of the small one-room shack. Sheridan was tied to a chair, on its side on the floor. A craggy edged rock had the man crushed up against the side wall. If the wall gave way, he'd be buried.

A quick scan of what was left of the building revealed only Sheridan had been in the cabin before the boulders fell. The other two must have snuck out the back somehow and then caused the rock slide onto the building.

"Hawke, that you?" Sheridan asked.

"Yeah. What were you thinking making contact with them? Our orders were to find and keep track of them, not make contact." He pulled the knife out of his boot sheath and sliced through the parachute cord binding Sheridan to the chair. Then he wound the line around the rock and pulled the hunk of basalt back far enough to get the tracker out.

"I thought I'd find them and report back to you." Sheridan moaned as he sat up, holding his side with his right hand.

"I had the perfect spot to do the job, and you got yourself blasted with a shotgun." Hawke felt the man's legs and arms for breaks.

"It's just my ribs. Stand me up and wrap them with

something." Sheridan reached out his left arm.

Hawke hauled him to his feet, Sheridan's groans echoed in what was left of the shack. The flashlight beam revealed the one front wall that was left standing. "I've got vet wrap in my pack. Come on. As soon as I get you stabilized, I'm going to look for their tracks."

"They're headed north, I know that much."

Hawke beamed the flashlight toward the door. "Did you tell them I was out here?" He was skeptical about stepping out the door and being met by the blast of a shotgun. If the two stuck around to see what kind of damage they did, they would have seen his flashlight beam bobbing toward the shack.

"I told them I was a hiker who wandered off from my group. I think they bought it."

"Why did they have you tied up and try to kill you if they believed you?" Hawke was skeptical Sheridan hadn't told them the cops would find them. He was too boastful to not have said something.

"They said they were going on and that someone would come along and find me. But to make sure I didn't follow them, they tied me up."

"And tried to kill you." Hawke wasn't pleased with himself. His thought was to send Sheridan out the door first. The boastful tracker's showing up had to have made the two change their plans. The fact they tried to fake an accidental death meant they weren't above getting rid of anyone they came across.

"Come on." Hawke turned off the flashlight, exited the rubble, and led Sheridan over to the bush where he'd left his dog and pack. Both were still there.

"Good boy." Hawke praised Dog then dug in his pack and came up with the vet wrap he always carried with him. The way the four-inch wide stretchy fabric stuck to itself when stretched, made it the perfect all-purpose item. It covered wounds, compressed sprains, worked to splint breaks and ribs, and would even work to hold items together with a few wraps.

"Get your shirt up, and I'll wrap your ribs." Hawke scanned the skyline of the ridge above the cabin. Had the pair gone straight up after causing the slide or did they take off east or west?

He wrapped Sheridan's ribs. "Let's get your pack and find a spot for the night. I'll have to let the authorities know we've lost them."

"We haven't lost them. I told you. They are headed north." Sheridan hissed as he twisted, staring into the darkness. "I think my pack's over there."

Hawke followed his line of sight. "It isn't."

"How do you know?" Sheridan started the direction he'd noted.

"Because I watched you take it off and nearly get your head blown off." Hawke headed to a rock thirty feet to the right of the one, Sheridan was circling. He picked up the pack. "I'll carry it tonight, but your ribs better be on the mend tomorrow."

Hawke headed up the ridge behind the shack. The couple had to have come this way to cause the rock slide. He didn't care what Sheridan overheard, he wanted to find solid proof of the direction they went. Even though it was dark, he could still find where they'd dislodged the rocks. That would be his starting point in the morning.

"You don't have to carry my pack," Sheridan said, but his words were interrupted by catches of breath.

Hawke ignored the man who was making this

mission more difficult.

At the top, overlooking the shack, he discovered where the rocks had been dislodged, Hawke radioed Mathews and told him the birds had flown the coop, supposedly heading north. He'd know more in the morning when he found their trail. He rolled out his sleeping bag, leaving Sheridan to roll out his own, and tried to sleep.

He wished there was more moonlight. Then he could find the couple's tracks and give the Search and Rescue more of an idea where to find them. The tracks always showed the truth. Just because the couple told Sheridan they were going north didn't mean they were.

Chapter Four

As the sun bathed the basalt rock in pale light, Hawke stretched, made sure Sheridan was still with him, and wandered to a rock to relieve himself. Dog used the same rock. The animal winked at him, and Hawke chuckled.

He peered down the cliff toward what was left of the shack. He could envision White releasing the rock and watching to see what damage had been caused. That meant, the convict knew there was a second person on his trail. And, quite possibly, that Sheridan had been saved. If that were the case, White wouldn't be heading north, knowing the intruder would tell authorities that was what he had said.

Hawke returned to the small camp and pulled out jerky and his water bottle that would need refilled when they came across a stream. "Did White take the shotgun with him?" he asked Sheridan, who sat up against a rock, sipping on a water bottle.

"Yeah. They each had a pack. White had the

shotgun and I thought I caught a glimpse of a handgun." Sheridan winced as he reached in his pack and pulled out a packet of freeze-dried food.

Hawke pulled out the radio, dialed in Mathews and waited for a response.

"Mathews," a male voice replied.

"I don't know which direction they are headed yet. I doubt it's north, and they are armed. They tried to kill Sheridan last night with a rock slide." Hawke released the button on the radio.

"Copy. We are about two miles from the homestead."

"I'm on the ridge north of the homestead. You'll find the building under a rock slide and Sheridan, who was injured."

The cocky tracker shook his head, stood, and walked over to stand above Hawke. "You won't find me. I'm going with Hawke."

Hawke glared at the man. "You need medical care, not hauling your pack all over Hells Canyon."

"I'm either going with you or following you." Sheridan glared back at him.

Shit! "Sheridan won't be waiting for you. He's too bullheaded to wait for medical care. I'll try to keep you posted where I'm going so you can stay close behind."

"Copy."

Hawke turned off the radio and shoved it into his pack. He rolled up his bed and tied it on. "If you're so insistent on going, shoulder your pack and let's find their tracks."

He wouldn't cater to the annoying tracker. Sheridan should stay behind and get medical attention. If he refused, it was better to have him where Hawke could see him rather than lagging behind or worse trying to get in front of him and getting caught, again.

Walking slowly back and forth and moving a foot farther and farther from the edge of the ridge, he found traces of what he suspected to be the tracks of the two. He knelt and studied the rocky surface, noticing the faint trace of dirt leading across a three-foot by four-foot slab of rock.

"They're going that way." He pointed west, toward the Snake River. The thought of the two armed people headed to the more populated river added to his urgency to find them before they met up with innocent people. They hadn't known Sheridan was anything other than a lost hiker, and they'd tried to kill him.

"How do you know that?" Sheridan crouched next to him, staring at the rock.

"See the way those bits of dirt make a trail across the rock?" He put a finger beside the first almost triangular shape. "It isn't dirt put there by the wind. They are in a pattern, like the bottom of a shoe."

Hawke stood, following the trail that was like a beacon now that he knew what to look for.

"I knew that," Sheridan muttered behind him. Then started proclaiming he had once followed a trail across a thirty-foot, solid rock, bluff looking for a lost hiker.

A smile twitched Hawke's lips. The man would never admit he hadn't seen the trail. Sheridan also couldn't stop trying to make himself out to be better than Hawke. Having learned long ago the more you boasted the farther you fell, he ignored Sheridan's words and concentrated on the trail.

He continued across the rock slowly, keeping his gaze on the faint dirt patterns. It disappeared at the edge of a nine-foot-wide rock flow. The pieces in the flow were anywhere from a few inches to nearly a foot in size. The abstract sizes and shapes would be hard to discern where they'd walked. The pieces could have also slid as they were stepped on.

"You go down this side, looking for where they came out. I'll go down that side." Hawke and Dog crossed the flow and walked along the side of the rock slide, studying everything that looked out of place to figure out where the two had left the rocky version of a river.

Twenty feet or so downhill, Hawke noticed crushed plants. "Dog, sit," he commanded and crouched, studying the area around them. Something with feet larger than a hoof or a paw had flattened the lichen growing on the rocks.

He stood and whistled at Sheridan.

The other man stopped and stared at him.

Hawke waved for him to cross the flow and join him. When the man started across, Hawke returned to studying the ground. By the time Sheridan joined them, he'd figured out which way White and the woman had headed.

"Are you sure about this?" Sheridan asked. "This isn't north."

"They won't go north. That's what you heard. White probably stood on the ridge and watched me bring you out of the shack. He's not going a direction he mentioned."

"That makes sense. But what if he didn't watch and is headed north?" Sheridan opened his water bottle and drank.

"He watched. From what I read in his file, he

would have wanted to see his destruction." Hawke drank the last of his water and followed the sparse trail. Two hours later, he stopped and pulled out a map. "It looks like they are heading for Kirby Creek."

Lowering his pack to the ground, he dug in the side pocket for the radio. "Hawke to Mathews."

Static crackled. "This is Mathews." His voice came in clear.

"I'm approximately two hours from Kirby Creek. I believe that is where the fugitives are headed. Either for the night or to get to the Snake and steal a raft."

"Copy. Are you familiar with the area?"

"No, why?"

"Kirby Creek Lodge is at the Snake. I'll notify them there is the possibility of the fugitives coming their way."

Hawke's chest tightened with dread. "Tell them not to try and be heroes and to stay out of the way. White has killed before, and I'm sure he would do it again to remain free."

"Copy. We're about two hours behind you. We picked up your trail on the ridgeline."

"I'll go straight to the lodge and see if I can't keep people safe."

"Copy."

Hawke turned the radio off and shoved it back in his pack. He didn't like White heading to a lodge. Someone would get hurt, he could feel it in his bones. "Either keep up with me or wait for the others," he told Sheridan, shouldering his pack and whistling for Dog.

"If everyone stays in the lodge, I bet White will go straight for the boats docked at the river," Sheridan said, keeping up with Hawke.

Hawke didn't look for tracks. He was seventy percent sure the fugitive would head for the nearest place he could find a boat. And that was the lodge. "You know as well as I do that there is always one person who tries to be a hero." He stared over his shoulder at the man who'd gone to the homestead on his own and been caught.

"It's the first of June. I bet there's not any families at the lodge yet." Sheridan said. "But there could be fishermen. The Snake is good fishing all year long."

He had thought of that. Whether it was only the people who lived there or guests, he had to keep them all safe. With the homestead in pieces, he had a feeling White would try to vanish. To do that, he'd need to get to civilization to either get supplies or to get a new identity. "We can't do anything for anyone until we get to the lodge."

Chapter Five

At a creek, Hawke crouched at the edge of the stream, filling his water bottles. Sheridan knelt beside him, filling his bottles and washing his face and hands. The last half mile the other man had lagged behind and was dripping like a fat man in a sweat lodge.

"You sure you don't want to wait here for Mathews? I bet they have a medic with them." Hawke added the purification drops to his three water bottles, wishing he had one ready he could drink. He popped a hard candy in his mouth.

"I'm not stopping. I want this bastard more than you do. He tried to kill me." Hatred flashed in Sheridan's eyes before he glanced down at the bottle in his hand and added purification drops.

Hawke saw more than anger for a man who'd made an attempt on his life. Hawke became suspicious of Sheridan's sneaking off and barging into the shack by himself. Was there history between White and

Sheridan?

There had been little mentioned about White's family in the files given to Hawke. He'd dig into that when they had the lodge secured.

"If they are following Kirby Creek, we should get to the lodge before they do. That is if you can keep up this pace." Hawke shouldered his pack and headed straight down the rocky gulley the small creek followed.

Less than half a mile and the water disappeared. Hawke veered to the left to head in a more westerly direction. They topped a rocky peak. The lodge buildings were clustered along the bank of the impressive Snake River. Whether he rode in a boat on the wide swift river or walked along the shore, he felt the life and energy of the water.

He'd traveled many times up and down the river and had passed by the lodge. Until Mathews had mentioned it, he'd forgotten it would be a place that White could find a boat.

He pulled out his binoculars and scanned the area from the lodge toward the rocky peaks behind. He spotted two people walking along what had to be Kirby Creek.

"Come on. I see them. We're going to have to hurry to get there before they do." As he started down, he spotted people hurrying toward the boats. It looked like everyone was evacuating the lodge and taking the boats with them. Good. Then he could sit back and see what White and the woman did.

"What are they doing?" Sheridan asked.

"Taking the boats to safety. I hope everyone left." Hawke and Dog took the direct path down to the lodge.

The new spring grass was softer on dog's feet than the rocks they'd been scaling most of the day. Hawke navigated around bushes and rocks on his way to the bottom.

Once there, Hawke waited for Sheridan to catch up as he surveyed the best place to watch and see what White and the woman did when they reached the lodge.

He decided to stay up on a slight rise to the northeast of the buildings.

"This way," he said to Sheridan, moving to their right.

"Where are you going? White will be down at the buildings." Sheridan stopped, in full sight of anyone trying to sneak up on the lodge.

"Get your ass down and over here!" Hawke glared at the man. "We aren't to apprehend, only keep tabs on them."

"But there's two of us. We can take White." Sheridan walked to the spot Hawke had picked to watch the lodge.

"There are one and a half of us. You're injured. White has two weapons which means we could have two people shooting at us." Hawke shrugged out of his pack and sat at the base of the tree, holding the binoculars to his eyes.

"They're just coming out of the trees along the creek."

The sound of a jet boat drew his attention and the binoculars to the river. A patrol boat was throttling down and drawing up to the dock.

"Shit!" Hawke muttered. He yanked the radio out of his pack and dialed in the frequency for the river patrol. "This is Hawke, jet boat at the Kirby Lodge dock, move off before they see you and rabbit."

The boat idled back away from the dock and drifted downstream with the current.

He refocused on the area where he'd last seen White and the woman. Nothing moved.

"Did they get to the buildings while I was on the radio?" he asked Sheridan.

"I didn't see anything."

"Damn! I have to make a visual to know what to tell the patrol." Hawke stared through the binoculars, checking out the area he could see in front of and between buildings. He didn't see anyone.

"Maybe they saw the boat before it moved off," Sheridan said.

"If they did, then they headed back up in the hills." He scanned the hillside on the opposite side of Kirby Creek. There were bushes and trees but enough space between he should see the two.

He spotted what must have been the group Mathews was leading at the top of the hill he and Sheridan had descended.

"What's that?" Sheridan asked.

"Our backup. I have a feeling White and the woman are either hiding in the trees until dark or headed back up the creek, having seen us, the boat, or the group coming down the hill."

He was tired, thirsty, and hungry. He'd thought they'd catch White here and he'd be back home tomorrow. It didn't look like that was going to happen. White had the instincts of a wild animal, knowing when he was in danger.

《》《》《》

Hawke and Sheridan sat on chairs on the deck of

the lodge waiting for Mathews and his party to arrive. He'd made a search of the outbuildings and was certain White and the woman weren't hiding in any of them.

"You here for a holiday?" Mathews asked, his gaze landing on Sheridan. "What happened to you?"

Hawke sat back in the chair watching Sheridan and wondering what the man would say.

"I had an altercation with a rock."

From the frown creasing Mathews' brow, Hawke had a feeling the deputy had worked with Sheridan before. "How'd that happen?"

Hawke was glad that Mathews didn't seem to like the tracker either. Maybe he could get Sheridan shipped out of here.

When the unwanted man didn't answer, Mathews shifted his attention to Hawke. "Where's White?"

"He either saw the patrol boat before I contacted them to move out of sight, or he saw us or you coming down the hill. I spotted them about a hundred yards from the lodge, coming out of the trees, heard the boat, focused on getting it out of sight, and then I lost sight of White." He nodded to Sheridan. "Keep him here. I'll go see if I can figure out if they're still in the trees waiting to come out at dark or if they took off."

"You're going alone?" Mathews asked.

"No." Hawke whistled. "Dog's going with me."

He stood, shouldered his pack, and strode down the steps and along the side of the building. Not having Sheridan dogging his footsteps was a relief.

"Come on, let's see if we can do a better job on our own," he said to Dog as they entered the trees where he'd last seen White.

《》《》《》

It was almost dark when Hawke and Dog spun around at the same time. Someone or something followed them. The hair down Dog's back stood up and his lips curled. Hawke wrapped his fingers around Dog's muzzle and whispered in his ear, "Quiet."

He crouched beside Dog in the shadow of a tree and reached under his shirt, resting his hand on the handle of his Glock.

A slight snap now and then was the only sound that gave him an idea of the direction the person or animal was coming from. The sound of stumbling feet and a muffled groan revealed it was a person.

He didn't think it was White. The man moved through the woods like a cougar. He hoped it wasn't Sheridan. If he got away from Mathews and was stumbling around, he could get himself caught again, or worse, killed.

A shadow moved among the trees. From the body shape it appeared to be Sheridan. How the hell had he followed them?

Hawke tightened his grip on the Glock as the shadow moved closer.

He released his hold as the man came into view. It was the boastful tracker.

"What are you doing out here?" Hawke said in a loud whisper.

"Hawke? Did I find you?" Sheridan asked.

"Yes, and you probably brought White with you." Hawke stood, wishing he had let Dog attack the man. He was getting tired of dragging him around everywhere. "Why did you come out here?"

"I didn't want you chasing White alone. He's a ruthless killer."

He noticed Sheridan wasn't wearing his backpack. "Where's your pack?"

"I had to leave it behind to get away from Mathews."

"I'm going to put all your reckless behavior in my report. You're an idiot to follow me and come unprepared. I've a notion to tie you to a tree and tell Mathews where to find you."

"You wouldn't do that. White could find me before Mathews." Sheridan didn't have any fear in his voice.

The chance of being found by White was something Hawke feared. Why didn't Sheridan fear the man? Why did he keep getting involved in the apprehension of White?

"Which way is he going?" Sheridan asked.
"I think back up the creek. But it's too dark to follow the trail without using a flashlight and I don't want him to know I'm looking for him." Hawke dropped his pack to the ground. "I'm sleeping." He rolled out his sleeping bag and lay down with Dog beside him. He didn't give a rat's ass what Sheridan did as long as he didn't bring trouble.

Chapter Six

The call of a chukar woke Hawke. He opened his eyes and studied the man sleeping with his back against a tree and his arms wrapped around him as if he were cold. Served the dumbass right, heading out without gear. Hawke was beginning to believe that Sheridan's boasts were just that. So far, he hadn't proven that he was the tracker he'd bragged about. All chatter and no substance.

Hawke sat up, stretched, and dug in his pack for granola bars. He tossed one at Sheridan. It landed in the man's lap. He jumped, making squawking noises.

"Not funny," Sheridan said, picking up the bar.

"You can give it back and go without anything to eat." Hawke stood, ripped the wrapper off his meal, and started eating. When that was gone, he drank some water, rolled up his sleeping bag, and picked up his pack. "Let's go. I can't report anything until I know how close I am."

49

"You wait too long and Mathews will come looking for you."

"Then he'll have a good trail to follow with the way you were breaking a path through the brush last night." Hawke found the tracks he'd been following before dark and strode along, hoping to find where White and the woman camped during the night. It might give him an idea of how far behind they were.

After an hour of following their path along the creek, the tracks made a veer to the right and out of the creek bed. There it appeared as if they had eaten and waited for it to get light enough to climb the rock cliff. Up a good two hundred yards, there was a gap in the rocks that looked like a cave entrance.

Hawke backed Sheridan into the trees and pulled out the radio.

"This is Hawke. Mathews, you have the radio on?"

"I've been waiting for your call."

"I believe they are in a cave about two hundred yards up a cliff, three miles up Kirby Creek. Then south of the creek. Sheridan is with me."

"I wondered where the dumbass went."

Sheridan made a noise in his throat.

"We'll sit tight until you get here." Hawke sat down next to his pack and put the radio away. "Take a nap, we aren't moving unless I see White come out of that cave headed somewhere else."

"How do you even know he's up there without looking?" Sheridan eased his body to a sitting position.

"The tracks say he is."

"What if he didn't go to the cave but went to the right or left halfway up? He could be at the top and taking off who knows where while we're just sitting down here."

Hawke shook his head. "Air support knows where we are. If he pops out up on top, they'll have a visual."

"You know for being an Indian, you sure do seem more like a coward."

Hawke stared at the man who had messed up this assignment every chance he had. "My heritage gives me the patience to not walk into trouble. If being smart is being a coward, I will consider the title with honor." He pulled out his water bottle and drank. Even though he did believe his words, it was hard to swallow the water and his anger at the man watching him. It was as if Sheridan wanted him to go into a rage. But he'd learned while in the military, using his fists hurt him more than the person he beat up. Because afterwards, he had his conscience to live with.

After fifteen minutes of silence, Sheridan had to say something. "I still think I can out track you."

Hawke didn't say anything. There was nothing to say. Tracking wasn't a competition. It was a means to find someone or something.

"By not saying anything are you agreeing with me?" The smug expression on the man's face really needed to be wiped off with a fist.

Hawke tilted his head and studied Sheridan. "Why do you want to get White so bad? Or should I say keep me from getting close enough to bring him in?"

Sheridan's eyes flicked wider before he stared down at his hands. "I don't know what you're talking about."

"There was no sane reason for you to sneak away from me and go to the shack. You had a motive. Whether it was to warn him or to try and kill him, I don't know, but I will find out."

Sheridan jerked his head up and glared at Hawke. "Whatever you're thinking is something you made up, and you'll never be able to prove anything."

Ahhh. Hawke studied the man. He'd just given himself away. Hawke now knew for certain there was something between Sheridan and White.

"Are you a relation to White? A cousin?" Hawke didn't take his gaze from the man. People talked in more ways than words. Their actions and reactions could tell as much as a sentence.

The other man didn't glance his way or say anything.

"That's it. You are related and either you despise him for what he's done, or you idolize him." Hawke continued to watch, hoping to catch a movement that would help him figure out the man's connection.

Dog growled low in his throat and peered into the trees to the right of them.

"You may get your chance to meet up with White again," Hawke whispered. "You can either hide in the trees with me or stay here in the open."

He didn't wait for the man's reply. From the way the hair stood up along Dog's backbone whoever, or whatever it was, couldn't be more than twenty feet away.

Hawke grabbed his pack. He and Dog retreated deeper into the trees, crouching behind a currant bush. He had a good visual on the area where Sheridan remained. That the man wasn't hiding and letting who or what was coming see him, only convinced Hawke more that Sheridan was a cohort of the man they were following.

Dog growled.

"No," Hawke whispered and put an arm around the animal's body, keeping the dog at his side.

A brown snout and then a big furry head appeared.

Sheridan shot to his feet and took off running the opposite direction Hawke had hid.

The brown bear's fur jiggled and swayed as the animal walked over to the tree where Sheridan had sat. The bear was in good health by the shine of his cinnamon colored coat. It smelled the ground at the base of the tree and the trunk. The animal tipped his nose in the air and shook his whole body. A low mumble rumbled from its partially opened mouth as if the bear were arguing with himself on whether to go after the human. The beautiful animal shook his head again and continued toward the mountain cliff.

Hawke wondered if the creature was headed to the cave. If so, it would be interesting to see if White and the woman came running out with the bear after them. Or White could shoot the bear. The sound of a shotgun would tell them if the couple had holed up in the cave.

Figuring Sheridan was following him to help White, it was probably a good idea to find the tracker and keep him away from the fugitive. Hawke rose, whistled low to Dog, who was smelling the bear's tracks, and headed the direction Sheridan had bolted. If he was lucky, he'd find the man hiding a short distance away.

The tracks Hawke followed were headed to the cliff and the cave. Damn! He'd hoped to keep Sheridan away from White.

He had to make the decision of going after Sheridan or waiting for Mathews and his bunch.

Knowing there were three people possibly holed up in the cave and none of them would appreciate his presence, he decided to sit at the bottom and wait for backup.

Dog had caught the scent of something that made him stop, glance all around, and then heel.

"What's ahead? Did you get the bear's scent again?" Hawke lowered his pack to the ground. They were on a rock ledge that one lone fir tree had the tenacity to cling to. Where its roots went for dirt and water, Hawke wasn't sure, but it provided them with cover as he kept surveillance of the cave.

He pulled out the radio and twisted the knob. Static crackled. "This is Hawke. Mathews, can you hear me?"

"Loud and clear. We're about a mile away. Know anything more?"

"Sheridan took off up the cliff toward the cave. I'm beginning to think he's a fan of White's."

"Damn! We don't need one of our own helping White." Mathews tone, revealed he didn't think much of traitors.

"I agree, but it seems that way. Either that or he's being stupid to try and be a hero." Hawke squinted up at the cave. "They also might have a visitor. A big old boar bear came by me headed toward the cliff. I caught sight of him on a trail up to the cave."

Mathews chuckled. "That should be entertaining. Hope we get there in time to see the show."

"Copy."

Hawke set the radio down and pulled out a granola bar and dog biscuit. They snacked and waited.

Dog perked his ears and stared up the cliff.

Hawke caught sight of his backup as a boom

echoed through the cliffs. He peered up at the cave entrance. A man and woman hurried out, headed around the north side of the cliff on what appeared to be a narrow rock ledge.

"Shit!" They would have to go up and see if the two shot the bear or Sheridan.

"What was that?" Mathews asked as he and the six others scrambled up the cliff to the lone tree.

"White and the woman came out of the cave after the shot and traversed a ledge around the cliff." Hawke shouldered his pack. "You all don't have to come, but I'd prefer not to go up there alone in case the bear is still alive."

Mathews and another deputy drank some water and followed him on the trail the bear used to get to the cave. Claw marks striped the rocks from many trips, indents in grass the size of a dinner plate, and scat revealed this to be a bear path.

"What happens if the bear is only injured?" the other man asked.

"We'll have to finish it off." Hawke wouldn't let an animal suffer. A bear had great strength and the ability to survive the harshest weather. He deserved a quick release from pain.

As they approached the cave, Hawke held onto Dog's collar. He didn't want his friend trying to protect him from a bear. The dog wouldn't be a match for the massive animal.

With his free hand, Hawke grabbed his flashlight and shone the beam into the dark interior. The beam travelled from one side of the cave to the other and up and down. No eyes glittered in the shaft of light.

"Dog, stay!" he commanded, released the collar,

and stepped into the cave. There wasn't any sign of a bear. Maybe when the bear stuck its head in, they shot, scaring it off. He walked a few more steps and saw a body.

"There's a person down!" he called.

Mathews was beside him. He shone his light on the body and the third man reached out to turn it.

Hawke already knew who it had to be. It wasn't wearing Sheridan's clothes.

They put both beams of light on the man's face.

"I'll be damned. It's White," Mathews said.

"That means either Sheridan or the woman killed him." Hawke sighed. If only the bear had taken the fugitive's life, then he could be headed home. Now he'd have to find Sheridan and the woman so they could stand trial for murder.

Chapter Seven

Mathews stepped out of the cave to call a helicopter and forensics. Hawke followed him, picking up his backpack.

"Where are you going?" Mathews asked.

"After Sheridan and the woman." He had a vendetta with the chattering tracker.

"I can't follow. I have to stay here until the scene is cleared."

Hawke nodded. "We'll be fine. I'll stay in contact." He whistled to Dog and headed to the rock ledge he'd watched the two use to leave the cave.

The ledge was nothing more than a mountain goat trail. Dog, being the size of a half-grown mountain goat, managed to gingerly walk ahead of him.

Hawke pointed his feet in opposite directions to fit on the uneven, five-inch-wide outcropping. His face was inches from the rocky cliff. Two times he'd thought about letting his pack go to keep it from pulling him backwards. Each time his fingers dug into the rock crevices, he hoped he didn't put a hand on a rattlesnake.

After what seemed like hours, the ledge went between two rock pillars and the top of the cliff was an easy walk along the edge of a small patch of snow that hadn't melted. Dog stopped and ate snow as Hawke dropped his pack. His limbs shook as he drank from his water bottle. He scanned the ground for traces of the two he followed. A blob of mud on a rock had to have come from a shoe.

Too bad he'd shown Sheridan ways to avoid being tracked. That was going to make following the two a little harder.

When he'd quenched his thirst and his legs no longer shook from his feet pointing the unnatural direction, he followed the bits of mud across the rocky top of the mountain until they disappeared into a marshy gulley of snow run-off.

The two had to know they were the suspects of a murder. Would they head back to civilization, pack up and disappear, or would they keep this wilderness chase going? Knowing how highly Sheridan thought of himself, Hawke had a feeling the man would remain out here until he ran out of food sources. It was the beginning of summer. A rain storm was easy to sit out under a rock overhang or in a cave. The nights were cool but nothing a person couldn't survive.

He sighed. Hiking all over Hells Canyon and the Seven Devils wasn't his idea of a fun summer. Now if he had his horse and mule with him, it would be different. Camping and riding all over this area all summer long would be a vacation. Hiking and figuring out how to get more supplies, wasn't a vacation.

He followed the green grass, slick mud, and broken

limbs on the bushes, downhill for a good mile before the tracks veered to the right. They were now far enough south he didn't think they were headed back to Kirby Creek Lodge. Where would Sheridan go?

Hawke pulled out his radio. "Mathews, copy?"

"Copy."

"I'm headed south following Sheridan's tracks. See if you can get information on him and relay it to me. Specifically, how well he knows this area."

"Copy."

Hawke turned off the radio to save the batteries. Thunder rumbled in the distance. The air had the scent of rain. He and Dog followed the tracks until he came to a rock outcropping large enough to keep them both dry. Watching the lightning crackle through the sky, growing closer as the thunder rumbled around them like being inside a drum, Dog ate a biscuit and Hawke a bag of jerky. Rain poured from the sky as they bedded down. The rain would either help them or hinder them, they wouldn't know which until the morning.

《》《》《》

The sun lit up the rocky cliff wall across the gorge from their dry bed. Hawke rolled up the sleeping bag, wishing he had a hot cup of coffee. The damp air and drop in temperature during the night had his bones aching. If he didn't enjoy the outdoors so much, he'd say he was too old for this. As the oldest Game Warden in Wallowa County, he should have been taking all the easy assignments. Like giving talks at conferences. He snorted. Look what that got him into. But he wouldn't give up this job until he was too old to sit a horse and follow tracks.

He tossed a biscuit to Dog and ate a granola bar.

Even a greasy breakfast at the Rusty Nail sounded good this morning. The granola bars and jerky were getting old. He had enough to last him two more days. After that he'd have to find a way to get more supplies.

"Let's see if we can find them," he said to Dog as he shouldered his pack. He didn't have any idea how far behind the two they were. Judging by the mud yesterday, he believed to be only an hour behind. The unknown was whether they'd stopped as soon as he had to wait out the storm and sleep.

He continued the direction the tracks had been headed before the rain. Any place that formed a gulley, water had rushed through, wiping away any trace of who or what had traveled ahead of them.

Dog sniffed the ground and dug with a paw. A wrapper appeared. Hawke grabbed the plastic, dumped the crumbs of jerky into his palm, and fed it to Dog. "Good job." This had been ground into the dirt to hide it.

He studied the ground and spotted tracks fading in the mud. The tracks led to a rocky area.

Hawke crouched beside the rocks and studied the surface. Water sat in small puddles in indentions in the rocks. Some of the puddles had water splashed around the edges with muddy drops.

Following the trail was slow until the sun began to dry things up. At noon, Hawke sat on a rock and pulled out the radio.

"Hawke to Mathews," he spoke into the radio.

"Mathews. Location?"

Hawke glanced around. "I'd say four miles southwest of you. I haven't looked on a map, just been following tracks. They've gone up to the tops of ridges and back down in gulleys."

"That doesn't help us find you." The man sounded tired.

"I'll let you know exactly where I am when I have them in sight. Any information about Sheridan?" Hawke knew there had to be a connection between White and Sheridan, and now, possibly the woman, though she could just be a hostage because she saw Sheridan shoot White.

"They are still digging into Sheridan. You should have everything they know about the woman in the files given to you."

"Copy." Hawke switched the radio off and pulled the files out of his pack as he drank water and snacked on more jerky.

The files on Tonya Cox said she was an honor student at her high school and later at college where her major was journalism. Hawke peered the direction the tracks pointed. Had she befriended White to get a story and now was being held hostage by Sheridan? He wouldn't know the truth until he caught up to them.

Hawke pulled out the map to see where he was and how he could get more supplies. They were heading south. They were close to Saw Pit Saddle and his vehicle. Though it would do him little good. He didn't keep food in the truck, and he didn't have time to run to a store. The command station was probably still set-up there, but he doubted they'd have supplies for someone backpacking. If the two continued south, he might be able to make a detour to the Sheep Creek Cabin on the Snake that the Fish and Wildlife Troopers used to stay overnight when patrolling the river. There would be some provisions there.

He folded the map, finished off a bottle of water, and shoved to his feet. Shouldering his pack, Hawke whistled to Dog and they continued following the tracks.

Chapter Eight

The gray of dusk settled over the small gorge Hawke picked to spend the night. He'd discovered several scuffed marks as if the two he followed had fought. The thought Sheridan would be physical with the woman, Hawke now believed was a hostage, made his anger boil.

If there had been more moonlight to use to follow the trail, he would have continued. But trying to sneak up on them with a flashlight would be hard to do.

He would get up as soon as there was light in the morning and push hard to catch up to the two. Once he and Dog ate the last of the food, he turned on the radio.

"Hawke to Mathews or anyone on this frequency."

"This is Mathews. We are down on the river by Hells Canyon Dam waiting to hear from you."

"I'm beginning to believe the woman is a hostage. There have been signs of the two struggling. I plan to get close enough tomorrow for a visual. They are staying away from all trails and places where they might be seen." He sighed. They had been going up and down the mountains when they could have been travelling the ridges.

"Do you know your location? There's still a helicopter flying in daylight."

"I'm on the west side of McCatron Ridge. I'd appreciate a copter dropping rations to me tomorrow, including dog biscuits, if they see me."

"Copy."

Hawke turned the radio off and stared at Dog. "We have to catch them soon. We can't keep following them all over Hells Canyon."

He settled in for the night with Dog by his side. He set his watch to wake him at four. There would be enough light to see the tracks and possibly catch up to Sheridan.

《》《》《》

Golden rays of sun lit the side of the gorge as he and Dog crept up toward the pair he'd been following.

"Stay!" he whispered to Dog as he slipped out of his pack and used the cover of boulders to move closer to the two arguing people.

"Just let me go. That guy you say is following us will get me out of here," the woman, Ms. Cox, said.

Sheridan laughed. "He'll call in someone to come take you, but he will keep following me. I'd rather have you with me as leverage."

"You mean to kill if the need arises? I saw what you did to Felix. I know you'd rather kill me than drag me around."

Hawke moved closer. The woman's hands were bound in front of her. Interesting. They hadn't been when the two were scaling the ledge. What had changed between them since the cave? He'd believed she was working with Sheridan the way the two had scurried away.

Sheridan picked up the shotgun. A revolver was shoved into the waistband of his pants. "If you keep holding me up, I wouldn't hesitate to leave you here for the bears and cougars to eat."

The woman stared at him before grasping the straps of a pack with her bound hands and carrying it in front of her.

Hawke put a hand on his Glock. He didn't like shootouts. Hadn't been in one for years. The woman was between him and Sheridan. The man had shown no remorse about anything, which meant he'd have no qualms in shooting the woman to get Hawke.

The thump of a helicopter approaching captured Sheridan's attention. "Get in the trees!" he shouted at the woman.

She took her time.

Hawke knew the copter was looking for him to drop his supplies. When Sheridan headed to the trees, Hawke stood up on the boulder and waved his arms. It not only signaled the helicopter but it gave him a chance to see that the woman was not near Sheridan.

He jumped off the boulder and headed to the woman.

Her eyes widened and she opened her mouth. He clamped a hand over her mouth while circling her waist with his other arm. "I'm a friend. Come." With a hand on her elbow, he led her back the direction he'd come.

"Tonya? Where'd you go?" Sheridan called just above a normal tone. His voice was only about ten feet away.

"Hurry," Hawke whispered. He grasped the woman's arm and pulled her around behind a boulder.

"Boom!" The echo of the shotgun ricocheted off the walls of the gorge. Rock on the top of the boulder shattered and rained on them.

Tonya shrieked.

"Shh." Hawke whispered and pressed her against the boulder. "You stay here. I'll see if I can get around him."

She stared at him wide eyed.

"Stay." He stepped to the side of the boulder and peeked the direction the shot came from.

Sheridan peered down the barrel of the shotgun pointed at Hawke.

A bundle fell from the sky five feet in front of Sheridan. The gun went off, blasting the bundle of supplies. He glanced up and headed for the trees.

Hawke ran to his pack and pulled out his radio, dialing in the helicopter. "This is Hawke. Did you get eyes on Sheridan?"

"Copy. He's headed down the gorge like something's chasing him."

"Keep him in sight and let the others know his coordinates. I have the woman. I'll bring her to Sheep Creek Cabin for pickup."

"Copy."

Hawke flicked the switch and tucked the radio into his pack before grabbing it and walking to the boulder where he'd left the woman.

She stood, flat against the boulder, Dog baring his teeth in front of her.

"Dog, sit." Hawke walked over to Ms. Cox. "Hold

out your hands."

She did.

He pulled his knife out of his boot and cut the parachute cord wrapped around her wrists. It was an item he kept in his pack for the occasional need to belay down to someone who'd fallen. It appeared Sheridan was using White's well-provisioned pack.

"You saw Sheridan kill White?" he asked, walking over to the supplies the helicopter had dropped.

"Why else do you think he was dragging me all over these mountains?" She walked over and stared down at him. Her expression held nothing but contempt.

"He wasn't dragging you when you two left the cave. You were following him just fine. It wasn't until yesterday, I noticed you weren't getting along." He unbuckled the canvas pack and looked up.

Her arms were crossed as she glared at him. "I wasn't going along with him because I wanted to. He kept threatening to kill me, and I have no idea where we are."

He raised an eyebrow. "From your file it says you grew up in Riggins and hiked these trails a lot with your uncle."

She spun around, wiping her eyes. "I don't like to talk about my uncle."

While Hawke didn't like to deal with women when they were crying, he wasn't a pushover either. "Why didn't you try and get away from Sheridan?"

Ms. Cox glared at him over her shoulder. "Because he threatened to kill me."

He studied the woman before he pulled supplies out of the canvas pack and shoved them into his backpack. No more jerky. They sent him freeze dried food that needed water to be cooked. He shook his head. The only things that didn't require preparation were the granola bars and crackers with cheese. He shook his head. Who put this together?

"Hand me your pack." He held a hand out toward the woman.

She glanced at the open bundle at his feet before walking over and placed the small pack next to his. "How did they know to find you here?"

"The same way I knew where you were." He wasn't going to tell her he had given them directions. Best she thought the air surveillance knew their every move. He closed the packs and handed hers back to her.

"Come on. I'd like to get to the Sheep Creek cabin before dark." He rolled up the canvas the supplies had been in, tied it to the top of his pack and slid his arms through the pack's straps.

"Dog!" he called. The animal burst around a boulder and Ms. Cox flinched.

"Did the bear come in the cave the other day?" he asked, heading down the side of the cliff. He'd be glad to go straight to the cabin and not trek up and down every canyon, gorge, and crag they came to.

"Bear?"

He glanced at the woman. She handled the pack with ease. Definitely a seasoned backpacker as her file had stated. "The bear that was headed to the cave White was shot in."

"I didn't see a bear. Only Sean. He stepped into the entrance and before I knew what happened, a gun went off, Felix fell, and Sean yelled at me to get my pack and dragged me out of the cave and along that ledge."

Hawke stared forward, watching his step and replaying what he'd seen and heard that day. He hadn't processed whether it was the shotgun that went off or another gun. But if what the woman said was true, Sheridan had to have a gun with him when they were tracking. While it wasn't uncommon for a tracker to have a carry permit, why had Sheridan kept the weapon hidden from him?

Now Sheridan had the shotgun and a handgun. He'd seen the two. From what Ms. Cox said, the handgun Sheridan said White and the woman had must have been left in the cave with the body. If not, either Sheridan had three weapons, or his traveling partner had one of the handguns.

If that were true, why hadn't she used it on Sheridan to get away?

《》《》《》

The first rest they took, Hawke snatched Ms. Cox's pack and dug through it.

"What are you looking for?" she asked. "You know what food you put in my pack."

"I'm not looking for food." He finished his inspection and handed the pack back to her.

"Did you think I had a gun? If I had, I would have used it on that bastard Sean. He's a backstabbing…" Her voice faded.

"It seems you know him better than just being his hostage." Hawke handed her a granola bar.

She shook her head. "No. I know his type. All he did was brag about how he could lose you and that he was a better tracker." She studied him with narrowed brown eyes. "He acted like you were some kind of tracking guru."

69

Hawke shrugged. "Don't know anything about that." He sipped from his water bottle and put it in the side pocket of his pack. It appeared the woman didn't know he was in law enforcement. Best to keep it that way. "Let's go."

"Will there be someone to take me out of here when we get to the cabin you're talking about?" Ms. Cox walked alongside him down the ridge angling toward the Snake River in the distance.

"Yes. I'm hoping by the time we get there the authorities will have picked up Sheridan." Unless the man had evaded the helicopter earlier in the day. If that happened, then he and Ms. Cox could be targets. The only eyewitness to Sheridan's killing of White was walking alongside him. And he was the only one who knew Sheridan had gone to the cave. Mathews only knew what Hawke had told him. It wouldn't hold up in court. He and Ms. Cox had to make it out of here alive to testify against Sheridan.

Chapter Nine

They had less than a mile to reach the Sheep Creek Cabin when Dog growled.

"What do you hear?" Hawke asked his vigilant friend.

Dog looked to the right. The hair down his spine stood up and his tail quivered.

"Get behind me," Hawke said, pulling his Glock from the holster under his open shirt. He scanned the sides of the gorge where they followed Sheep Creek down to the Snake River. The Larkspur and Paintbrush were in bloom farther up. Here they'd been trudging through brush and around poison ivy. They'd had one encounter with a rattlesnake, but once he'd discovered they didn't plan to harm him, he'd moved on.

It would be easy for someone to sneak up on them crouching in the brush.

He listened.

Nothing.

Not a sound from any birds or scraping of branches on clothing.

It was eerily quiet.

"What's wrong?" Ms. Cox whispered.

The hair on the back of his neck tingled. The woman scrubbed at her arms as if her hair was also bristling.

He'd only felt this feeling one time before in his life. "Put your back to mine. If you see anything move, tell me."

She backed up to him. Hawke snapped the leash he had dangling from his pack to Dog's collar. "Easy boy."

A flash of tan between the bushes confirmed his reaction. A cougar was checking them out.

"I'm going to fire my gun. We've got a big cat playing with us."

"A cougar?" the woman said on a gush of air.

"Yeah." Hawke pointed his Glock in the air and pulled the trigger twice. The shots rang through the gorge for several seconds. He spotted the cougar a hundred yards up the side of the cliff.

Dog's hair relaxed on his back. Hawke unhooked him from the leash and pivoted to the woman. "It's gone."

She rubbed her arms. "In all the years I've hiked the Hells Canyon, I've never had my hair stand up on my arms."

"Then you never came this close to a cougar before." Hawke holstered his Glock. "Come on. Let's get to the cabin by dark."

They hadn't gone a quarter of a mile when the cracking and snapping of more than one person hurrying through the brush grew in volume.

Hawke stopped and waited.

Mathews and two other men came into sight.

He waved and they slowed their pace.

He and Ms. Cox continued toward the three men.

"We heard the shots and thought we'd better come see what was happening," Mathews said.

"We had a cougar tailing us. I warned it off." Hawke continued. Mathews fell into step beside him. The other two walked alongside Ms. Cox.

"Did you pick up Sheridan?" Hawke asked.

Mathews shook his head. "He disappeared about two hundred yards from where they dumped your supplies."

"Damn!" Hawke had hoped the man was in custody. "Ms. Cox is a witness to his killing White. We need to get her out of here tonight."

"Can't do that. The boat is coming back in the morning. They had to deal with something up river so they dumped us off here." Mathews led them to what was called the cabin.

It was an old rundown single-story house that had once had a life of its own. Hawke had heard stories of the families who'd lived in this area and how they had endured the rattlesnakes, weather, and terrain to grow crops and raise cattle and sheep to live. The two-bedroom home was made of weathered boards, had a pitcher pump, an old spindle-legged table with four chairs, and four old spring cots with cotton ticked mattresses. The land and building were purchased by the Forest Service as part of the Hells Canyon Recreational Area.

Hawke dumped his pack inside the door of the

cabin. Ms. Cox would get one of the bedrooms. Since the Search and Rescue group had pitched tents around the cabin, he'd take the other bedroom. Then again, to make sure Sheridan didn't get to the woman, he'd have Mathews pitch his tent under her window and he'd put a cot in front of her bedroom door.

He didn't like the idea of Sheridan out there somewhere, possibly trying to get close enough to kill the woman. Or, if they were lucky, Sheridan could be headed out of here.

Ms. Cox sat down on one of the chairs at the table. "What now?"

"Pick the room you want and make yourself to home. I'll put you on the boat in the morning with Mathews." Hawke gave the old hand pump water spout a pump. From the wet spots in the basin it was in working condition.

"What about you? Aren't you leaving, too?" She peered at him. Her blonde hair had come loose from the band, holding it into a ponytail, a long time ago. The honey colored locks hung over her shoulders, bits of grass and weeds poked out like insects clinging to branches.

"I'm going to hike back to my truck and go home." He hadn't had a shower in a week and was sick of eating jerky and granola bars. He wanted a cup of coffee, bacon, and a large stack of pancakes.

"Where's your truck?" she asked, fiddling with a bottle of water.

He studied her. Why would she care where his truck was? "Where I left it." Hawke walked to the door and stepped out, taking in the bustle of the search and rescue crew making meals and settling in for the night.

He walked over to the small campfire surrounded by Mathews and a couple other deputies. "Mind if I heat up some water for coffee?"

"If you have a cup, we have a pot brewed," one of the deputies said.

"Be right back." Hawke returned to the cabin and his pack. The door to one of the bedrooms was open. Ms. Cox stood by the bed, digging through her pack. He ignored the woman and retrieved his tin cup from his pack along with a small aluminum pan and two packages of freeze-dried stroganoff. He'd eat well tonight.

Back at the fire, he sniffed the coffee after the deputy poured and wondered at how just the scent awakened his senses.

"Keep a lookout for anyone wandering around here tonight," Hawke said, before sipping the coffee.

"You don't think Sheridan is long gone?" Mathews asked.

Hawke shook his head. "Ms. Cox is an eyewitness to his killing White. After listening to him for several days, I don't think he'd like her to get out of here to testify against him." He peered at Mathews. "When she goes to bed, I'll set my cot in front of her door. It would be a good idea for you or one of your men to set a tent outside her window. It's the one in the south east corner."

Mathews nodded. "I'll do it. Get your belly full and a good night's sleep. We'll be out of here in the morning."

He didn't bother to tell Mathews any different. The deputy would find out in the morning that he was headed to Saddle Pit for his truck. And as much as he'd like to wipe his hands of this assignment and murder, he knew, he'd be checking out the background of Sean Sheridan right after he took a shower.

《》《》《》

Hawke's stomach hadn't felt so full since leaving Boise a week ago. Even Dog was stretched out, content and full, on the floor beside the cot. The coffee hadn't been a good idea, considering he had a soft place to sleep.

His mind raced over the events of the last week. Something was nagging at his brain. Something he should be grasping and wasn't.

Dog's soft snore, the springs creaking as the woman rolled on the bed in the room behind him, and the muffled sound of the Snake River churning through the canyon as it had for thousands of years, slowly relaxed his mind, allowing him to forget his thoughts and fall to sleep.

《》《》《》

The creak of the rusty hinges on the outside door woke Hawke. He didn't move, only stared at the door. It wasn't open as if someone had walked through. Had the creak stopped whoever planned to come in? He rolled to the edge of the cot, trying to keep the springs from squeaking. The bit of moonlight filtering through the dirty windows revealed Dog's silhouette, sitting, facing the door.

Hawke eased to his knees on the wood floor and slowly stood. One foot lightly placed in front of the other, he crossed to the door and pulled it open.

Nothing but moonlight and the shadowed mounds of the search and rescue team's tents. He knew he hadn't been hearing things because Dog had been alerted. Nothing moved in the shadows. The sound of the river and the rustle of leaves from the slight breeze were the only sounds.

He closed the door and faced the room. Shit! The bedroom door behind his cot was open. He knew before he stepped over his cot that the room would be empty.

How had the woman maneuvered over him and Dog without waking them up? Damn! Damn! Why had the woman left the safety of the search and rescue team?

So much for getting a shower. He dug through his pack for a flashlight, shoved his feet into his hiking boots, and laced them up. A grab for his pack, and he headed for the door.

"Come," he said to Dog and left the cabin.

Chapter Ten

The early glow of dawn allowed Hawke to turn off the flashlight and still see the tracks the woman made. She didn't seem to be worried about hiding her trail. He knew he wasn't very far behind her even after telling Mathews the woman had fled and he was going after her.

But he couldn't seem to catch up, no matter how hard he pushed. Her prints revealed she was jogging. She was half his age. Stronger lungs and legs. If he jogged, he wouldn't be able to keep his eyes on the tracks and he'd be out of breath when he did catch up to her. What surprised him was the fact she hadn't headed to the peaks. She traveled upriver just high enough to not be seen from the water.

If she wanted to hide from Sheridan, she would have taken off over the peaks to civilization. Her file had said she knew this country well. Why she was staying low and heading upriver, had him wondering if she knew where Sheridan was headed. There was a definite purpose in her strides. They weren't the frantic splayed dirt and debris of someone running to get away. They were even, balanced strides of someone moving at the pace they wanted. She knew the direction she wanted to go and was covering the ground quickly. If she did know where Sheridan was headed, she appeared to plan to meet back up with him at some point.

Which made Hawke think, once again, that she and Sheridan had planned the murder of White together.

What he wouldn't give for a file on Sheridan. The bits and pieces he'd garnered from brief radio contact and what Mathews knew didn't explain the man at all.

Hawke stopped to drink and eat a granola bar. He pulled out the radio.

"Mathews, are you listening?" Hawke asked the radio.

"I'm here. What's your location?"

"She's jogging upriver out of sight of the water. Can you take a boat, head toward the dam, and pull in at McGaffee, maybe try and intercept her?" It was the only way he knew to stop the woman from meeting back up with Sheridan and for the officials to question her.

"Copy."

Hawke clicked the radio off, ate his bar, tossed Dog a biscuit, and finished off the water.

"Let's go." Hawke stood and continued over the rocks and grassy patches Ms. Cox was traversing.

He heard several boats out on the river but didn't always have a good view of the water to see if one was Mathews. As he walked, he contemplated why Sheridan killed White. If it had been self-defense, he would have probably come away with hardly a blemish on his record. But Ms. Cox said Sheridan shot right after stepping into the open cave.

What was the connection between the three?

Dog stepped in front of him, his ears perked.

Hawke stopped, grabbed Dog's collar, and heard the sound of an agitated rattlesnake.

"Easy, Dog," Hawke backed himself and Dog up, listening to the sound to determine where it came from.

Down the cliff.

He leaned out and peered down. Twenty feet below them, on a rock outcropping, Ms. Cox stood still as a tree. A rattlesnake, head up, facing her, coiled five feet in front of her.

"Stay," Hawke ordered Dog and worked his way down the side of the canyon, kicking debris and rocks, which rolled down ahead of him.

The snake had stopped some of the debris. The rocks and sticks had confused the creature. It no longer reared back with its attention on the woman.

Hawke picked up a long stick on his descent. When he was within reach of the snake, he scooped the creature with the stick and flung it farther down the canyon wall, stick and all.

He grabbed Ms. Cox's wrist before she could take off in the other direction. "Why are you hurrying away from safety?"

She raised a hand to push her wild hair out of her face and grimaced. "I wanted to get home."

He grinned and shook his head. "You're headed the wrong direction. I read your file. You live and work in Pullman, Washington. That's north, not south."

"But my vehicle is in Boise. That's south."

He laughed. "I know it was your car that drove White to this area. And I would guess it's parked somewhere north of the homestead where I found you. Going with Deputy Mathews this morning would have gotten you to your car faster than jogging alongside the Snake River." He studied her, waiting for a response.

She glared at him before her gaze turned speculative. "Do you want to find Sean?"

He released her wrist, scrutinizing her. She had something on her mind. "Law enforcement would like to find him to discover why he shot White."

Her eyes narrowed. "Not law enforcement. You."

It was his turn to narrow his eyes. She didn't appear to know he was law enforcement. Sheridan must not have told her he was Oregon State Police. "Why would I want to find Sheridan?"

"He was with you when he shot the person you were tracking. Don't you want just a little bit of the satisfaction of finding him?" Her posture relaxed. "After all, you could be named an accomplice in Felix's murder."

Hawke returned the woman's smug gaze. "If anyone is an accomplice, it's you."

She didn't drop her gaze. Ms. Cox held his gaze as if it were a staring match like he'd played as a child. He'd be damned if he'd look away first. He wasn't the one who was running from the law.

He did feel he'd let his boss and Mr. Childress down by having the person he was tracking get shot before they could bring him back. That it was the boastful Sheridan who'd slipped away and killed him had been grinding in his craw ever since it happened.

The woman finally squirmed. "I'm not his

accomplice either. That means both of us want to find him to make sure he pays."

"He's long gone. It's going to take more than me to find him." Hawke said it as if he didn't care. But in his gut, he'd love to bring the smug, talkative man in. He was pretty sure the woman had other motives for finding Sheridan than making sure the law got a hold of him, but he'd keep that to himself if he could get her to help him.

"What if I told you, I know where he is?" Ms. Cox nodded her head.

"How would you know that?" He studied her. Was that where she'd been headed when the rattlesnake trapped her? She'd been backtracking, heading back down the river. That was why she was hurrying to get ahead of him. She'd planned to sneak past.

"He told me his plans. But I won't tell you anything other than I know where you can find him." She held out a hand. "Want to work together?"

He had a feeling working with her would be the same as working with the cunning coyote, but his curiosity had been piqued. Why would this woman want to go back to Sheridan when he had her hands tied and would have shot her given a chance?

Hawke knew better than to shake hands. Even if you shook hands or even signed papers, it was a given that the other person wouldn't keep their word. His ancestors learned it the hard way, and he always kept that in the back of his mind in any dealings.

"You can take me to Sheridan? And why do you want to find him?" Hawke whistled for Dog to join them.

She glanced up at Dog, running down the side of

the canyon. "We have unfinished business."

"What kind?" Hawke put a hand on Dog's head, watching the woman. She was good at concealing emotions.

"The kind women don't talk about but men brag about." She stared at him as if he were the man who'd done wrong by her.

"I take it he's downriver, since you were sneaking around me?" He motioned for her to go ahead of him.

She didn't say a word, just headed back the way they'd traveled half the night and half the day.

They would have been at McGaffee in another hour. Now he'd have to wait and see where they were headed to contact Mathews again.

《》《》《》

It was dark when Ms. Cox finally stopped and acted like she was ready to end the day. They'd covered more ground in the last eight hours than they had the first eight hours.

Hawke was tired, hot, and hungry. He opened his pack and stared at the freeze-dried meals that needed hot water to be edible. He should have specified jerky and granola bars for supplies.

Ms. Cox set out a small backpacking camp stove. She glanced over at him. "I'll share the stove, but all you put in my pack were granola bars."

He tossed her two packs of freeze-dried stew. "I have food to share and no way to cook it."

She grinned, walked to the creek flowing nearby and filled a small aluminum pan with water. Back at the stove, she lit the burner, placed the pan on, and sat back. "This baby doesn't take long to boil."

"You have a small pack for staying out for very

long," Hawke said, hoping to get her to talk about her uncle and growing up hiking this area.

She wrapped her arms around her drawn up legs. "I love it out here. If I could find a way to live here and make money, I'd do it in a heartbeat."

"You're a writer. I thought writers could work anywhere?" He leaned back on his pack, sipping on his last purified water. He'd refilled his other two bottles and added purification drops as soon as they'd arrived at the creek.

Ms. Cox shook her head. "If I wrote novels. I write for newspapers. You have to be where the stories are." She stared across the canyon to the Oregon side. "One of these days, I plan to write a book, but I have to have enough money saved up to live on before that can happen."

"What called you to writing for newspapers?" he asked as the water in the pan started to boil.

She ripped the tops off the two freeze-dried packets, poured water in, and stirred them with a fancy spoon that had fork tines on the opposite end.

Hawke watched her, wondering if he should invest in the fancy packing items she had for cooking. The small stove would be easier to make a cup of coffee when the woods were too dry to build a campfire.

She handed him one of the packets. "Hope you have your own spoon."

"I do. Thank you." He took the packet, dug in his pack for a spoon, and scooped up a mouthful of the stew. It wasn't as good as his mother's or the canned brand he liked, but it filled his empty stomach.

"You aren't planning to sneak away during the night are you, Ms. Cox?" Hawke asked when he'd finished his meal.

Her eyebrows rose. "You may call me Tonya. No one calls me Ms. Cox. And no, I won't sneak away. You've proven to be helpful. My uncle always told me not to hike alone."

"Your uncle sounds like he was a smart man." Hawke watched as she poured the leftover water into a tin cup.

She glanced up. "Have a cup for whatever hot beverage you have?"

He nodded, pulled out his tin cup, and she poured the remainder of the water into his cup. Hawke pulled out a packet of instant coffee.

Tonya dumped hot chocolate in her cup.

He sipped the coffee, relaxing a bit, hoping he could trust her to not run off. His handcuffs were in his pack. But bringing them out would clue her in that he was law enforcement.

"Sean called you Hawke. Is that a nickname?" she asked.

"No, it's my name."

She studied him. "That's an interesting name for a tracker. It fits, since you seem to be able to see tracks where no one else would see them. At least that's what Sean said."

Hawke wasn't sure whether to be flattered the fellow tracker he'd allowed to kill a man seemed to be in awe of his skills or to be disgusted that Sheridan thought so highly of his skill, and yet, he'd allowed the man to get away.

"Was your uncle a tracker?" he asked to find out more about her and talk less about him.

"No." She set the extinguished camp stove to the

side, pulled out a wad of shiny material that rolled out into a sleeping bag and crawled in.

That was the end of his trying to learn anything from her.

Chapter Eleven

Rain drizzled all morning as they hiked up the side of a mountain and started out along the ridge. Hawke continued to follow Tonya. Hoping she wasn't taking him and Dog on a goose chase.

He'd checked the map this morning before she'd awakened. They were passing around the Pittsburgh Landing by staying on this ridge. They would at some point have to cross the road from Whitebird to the landing. Unless she planned to hike the road out to the town of Whitebird. That could have been where she'd left her car.

The rocks and vegetation became slick as the rain continued to fall.

"Let's find a tree or rock outcropping to hole up under for a while," Hawke said.

"You can hide out if you want. I'm continuing." She didn't even stop, just trudged into a grove of trees.

Hawke and Dog followed. "Is there a specific day

you're to meet up with Sheridan?" He'd stared at the woman's tall, slim frame all day as she'd stayed at a steady pace.

"No. But if we don't hurry, he'll leave. Then we won't know where he's going next." The irritation in her voice told Hawke she was in a hurry because she was afraid she'd get left behind.

"I'm sure the police are looking for his vehicle and staking out his place. After all, he did shoot a man." He wanted to remind the woman they weren't looking for a boyfriend who didn't want to be found. They were following a murderer.

"That's why he'll be where we're going." She glanced over her shoulder. "If you did less talking and more hiking, we'd get there sooner."

Hawke narrowed his eyes. She was either trying to lose him or make him mad enough he'd stop following her. Neither would happen. He planned to find Sheridan. The man had messed up his assignment from the moment the tracker was assigned to him. Then to shoot White and flee… This woman wasn't going to get away from him. She knew something. Something he had a feeling the authorities didn't know.

Dog followed Tonya, keeping on her heels. It was as if the animal also sensed she would lose them if given the chance. The night before, after the woman had fallen asleep, Hawke had placed a ring of small sharp rocks and twigs around her. That way he would hear her if she tried to sneak away.

She'd cussed that morning when she'd slipped out of her sleeping bag and stepped on the small stones.

He'd grinned. That was what he'd have heard during the night had she tried to leave.

The road to Whitebird sat in an open area in front of them. Tonya stopped, peered both ways, and jogged through the opening and across the road.

Not wanting her to get out of sight, Hawke and Dog did the same. Just as they entered the trees on the far side, the sound of a vehicle rumbled through the air. A Dodge pickup. Diesel from the sound. What he wouldn't give for a vehicle or even his horse, Jack.

Tonya continued, but was moving lower on the hill, getting closer to the river. That would make walking easier.

When they were down close to the river, Hawke noticed Tonya peering out at the water as if watching for something.

"Is Sheridan floating the river?" Hawke asked when they stopped to rest and snack.

"No." She didn't elaborate.

"Why do you keep looking at the water?" He hadn't had a chance to pull out his radio and update Mathews or anyone else on the law enforcement frequencies.

"Just watching." She finished off a granola bar, shoved the wrapper in her pack, and started downstream.

Hawke was never one for conversation, but he was chatty compared to this woman. He found it odd that she didn't talk that much. Every woman he'd ever known, including the retired Air Force Officer, talked when given the chance. That was another thing that made him suspicious about Ms. Cox. She didn't like to talk about her family or herself. Odd. Man, he wished he had more information on her.

Knowing they were heading north and presumably

would come to Dug Bar where his ancestors crossed the river to avoid going on a reservation, he decided to chat her up and see what he could find out.

"I crossed this river several years ago following the trail of my ancestors."

She glanced over her shoulder, a hint of interest on her face. "Ancestors?"

"My family are Nez Perce and Cayuse. They roamed this area for thousands of years."

"Really. Then they probably ran in to my family," she shot over her shoulder.

Something. "Your family homesteaded here?" he asked.

"They ran sheep along the river and had one of the first ferries." Pride rang in her words.

"I would think as a writer that would make an interesting book." He was always fascinated by history whether his people or those who came afterwards.

"Not really. The only scandal was a great, great uncle being with the group that slaughtered the Chinese miners. Not something I want to write about." She hitched her pack a little higher on her back and stepped onto an animal trail that ran alongside the river about fifty feet up.

"You could write about how your family survived in this canyon. They must have been heartier than most to have lived here." He'd thought about the families whose dwellings had clung to the sides of the canyon and the flat areas where they'd planted hay and raised gardens to sustain them through the winter months. How hardy the sheep and cattle had to be that had grazed these unforgiving slopes.

"They were." She glanced over her shoulder. "I

am."

He nodded. She'd been hiking as if her life depended on it, stopping only briefly until nightfall to rest and refuel. "Up ahead, at Dug Bar, my ancestors crossed the Snake River in June, this time of year. Men, women, children, horses, and cattle to try and be free in Canada with Sitting Bull."

"What do you mean try?" She slowed her pace.

"The army caught up to them at Bear Paw in Montana, short of the Canadian Border. The women, children, and the old were cold and hungry. Many warriors had been killed or wounded. Young Chief Joseph surrendered." His gut swirled at the fate of the people. "And they were sent to Oklahoma where many more died. The lucky ones survived the eight years away from their beloved country only to be brought back and put on reservations that weren't with their people." He'd heard many angry words about how the government had made an example of what happened to Indians who disobeyed them. He'd also heard the story of the separation from both his non-treaty family members and his treaty family members. Even now, there was still a bit of contention between the two groups.

"That's cruel," Tonya said. Her consideration for his family made him wonder if he'd been too skeptical about her.

"Hurry," she said, sliding down the side of the canyon toward the river.

Hawke heard the sound of a boat and wondered if that were Sheridan. Tonya was determined to get to the water by the time the boat came to them.

"Stay back!" she told him and walked to the edge

of the river.

He stayed back, crouched by Dog, and watched.

She dropped her pack beside her and pulled her shirt off. In her sports bra and shorts, she dipped the shirt in the water and started washing.

The boat revved and cut a curl toward the river bank and Tonya.

Two men with fishing poles stood up in the boat. They appeared to be in their late thirties.

"Hey, you lookin' for a lift?" one of the men called.

"Maybe," she called back and wiped her shirt across her bare belly.

Hawke hoped he didn't have to intervene in a boat hijacking. It would spoil his chances of getting to Sheridan.

"How far north are you two going?" Tonya asked, pulling her shirt back on.

"We're headed to Cat Creek Ranch." The boat nudged up to the bank and one of the men hopped out.

"Any chance you would have room for two more?" Tonya waved to Hawke.

He stood up. He and Dog walked toward the boat.

The man on land, started to reach for the pistol strapped to his hip.

"We're not taking your boat or anything," Hawke said, raising his hands. "We're just tired of walking and need to meet up with someone."

The man sized him up and glanced at Tonya who smiled and nodded her head.

"Kind of a sneaky way to get us over. You could have just waved your arms and yelled," the man in the boat said.

Hawke shrugged. "I didn't know what she was doing until you changed course." He studied the man in the boat. He looked familiar. Had he given the man a ticket? He hoped not, if the man remembered where he'd seen him.

"Come on aboard. But my friend, here, will keep an eye on you." The man driving the boat stood up. He held out a hand to Tonya, helping her into the boat.

"Go," Hawke told Dog, and the animal jumped into the boat.

As Hawke stepped over the side, the boat rocked and the driver reached to steady him. His hand landed on the Glock under Hawke's shirt.

Their eyes locked.

Chapter Twelve

Recognition hit. Hawke knew where he'd seen this man before. He was one of the Idaho Game Wardens.

Relief swamped Hawke as he sat down next to Tonya. The driver had to know that he was on the trail of White's killer. As long as the boat driver didn't let the woman know his true identity, Hawke had a person who could report their whereabouts.

"Jeremy, get our guests something to drink," the driver said, backing the boat away from the bank.

The other man opened a cooler and handed them each a bottle of cold water. Hawke thanked the man, and drank it so fast, pain pinged through his brain. He should have known better, but after sipping warm water for days, the cold water was refreshing and sweet. Kitree would have laughed at his impatience. He grinned thinking about the girl who now lived part of the year at Charlie's Hunting Lodge. He was glad the Kimbals, Dani Singer's employees, were able to adopt the girl.

As he reminisced, he watched the two men talk. Jeremy, the one who brought them the drinks, came back and motioned for Hawke to get up. Taking this as his cue to chat with the driver, Hawke stood and motioned for the man to take his seat.

He stepped over Dog and wandered to the front of the twenty-foot boat. "You know how to navigate these rapids?" Hawke asked by way of conversation and so Tonya wouldn't catch onto what he planned to convey to the man.

"Been doing it for fifteen years," The driver replied loud enough for the two in the back to hear. Under his breath he said, "You Hawke, the trooper from Oregon?"

Hawke nodded. "Tell authorities we're headed north. She says she knows where Sheridan is but won't tell me."

"Hold on, we're coming into some class four rapids," the driver said, loudly.

Hawke gripped the side of the windshield and held on. The boat tossed and rolled, but the driver kept it in the right pocket and they slid out the other side.

"Nice job," he said.

"She doesn't know you're law enforcement?" the man asked quietly.

Hawke stared down the river. "She doesn't seem to. Thinks I'm a tracker like Sheridan."

It was the driver's turn to shake his head. "I'll pass along where we drop you off and see if we can keep you in sight."

"Appreciate that." Hawke raised his voice. "Any chance you caught some fish? I wouldn't mind having fish for dinner tonight instead of freeze-dried food."

The man who'd been sitting with Tonya stood up and walked over to a cooler. He raised the lid and six steelhead lay on ice.

Hawke whistled. "Nice ones. I have a few dollars if you'd let me purchase a couple of those."

The driver eased them through another small rapid. "Jeremy wrap up a couple steelhead for the man. We'll get to catch two more if he takes those."

"Thank you." Hawke said, watching Jeremy wrap two of the twelve-inch fish in newspaper, then put them in a plastic bag with ice.

"Hope that keeps them good until you cook them," Jeremy said.

Hawke tipped his head toward the woman. "She's calling all the shots." Hawke glanced at her. "Will we stop long enough tonight I can cook these?"

"We'll see." Tonya stared at the landscape on the Idaho side.

He figured she knew it well. Yet, she'd taken the men up on their offer of giving them a lift to Cat Creek Ranch. That was on the Oregon side of the river. Was Sheridan heading into Hawke's territory?

Hawke shrugged and sat down beside the woman, making sure he didn't touch her or make any intimate looking actions. He didn't need these two thinking he was with her in any sense other than finding Sheridan.

《》《》《》

Thirty minutes later the boat veered left. The engine was cut, and Jeremy jumped out of the boat, wading through the knee-high water to secure the boat's line to a pile of rocks.

"Thank you," Tonya said, stepping off the boat and into the water, wading to the shoreline.

Hawke walked to the front of the boat and used the open bow to get less of his pant legs wet. "Thanks," he said to the driver and Jeremy as he slid into the water and whistled for Dog.

The animal dove into the water and splashed to the shoreline.

Hawke hurried after the woman that hadn't even stopped to shake the water from her shoes. Dog shook himself, spraying more of Hawke with water.

"Thanks a lot," he mumbled at the dog and caught up to Tonya. "I take it we aren't camping here tonight?"

"Not with those two spending the night." She sniffed. "The one asked too many questions I didn't like."

"Like what?" Hawke had wondered if the other man had tried to pry information out of her.

"What was I doing hiking with such an old man? Where had we come from? Where were we going?"

Hawke would have taken exception to the man's comment, but he understood the officer had been trying to act like a fisherman and not the official he was, and that he knew she was the woman who helped a murderer escape prison.

"What did you tell him?" Hawke was curious how she'd answered the questions.

"I said I found you on a trail acting turned around and offered to take you where you wanted to go."

Hawke's face heated. From anger and that she'd turned the tables on him. "What about where you'd been?" He knew it would have been easy for her to say she was on vacation hiking the area.

"I told him it was none of his business." She glared at him over her shoulder. "You were pretty friendly with the boat driver."

"Just asking him about the boat and fishing." He waved a hand. "Catching that boat saved us time. Are we getting any closer to Sheridan?"

She'd hiked north along the shore. They came to a gulley Hawke knew as Bob Creek and she ducked into the gulley. This meant they were going deeper into Wallowa County. Now they were in country he knew. Bob Creek would take them to Deep Creek and either Lord Flat or Mormon Basin. He wondered if Sheridan had plans to use the airstrip at Lord Flat. That could be the reason for Tonya's urgency to get there. She didn't want left behind.

Following the creek, they were under the cover of mahogany and mountain ash trees. The berry bushes along the creek were just sporting buds. Too bad it was June instead of August. Then they could have grabbed berries as they walked.

Before long the creek grew louder and deeper in narrow beds of solid rock as the climb became steeper. They would have to go up and over several ridges before they'd encounter anyone. This part of the county was mainly occupied by cattle and elk this time of the year. If it were fall, there would be deer and elk hunters all over the place. Now, he could hope for a cowhand checking on cattle to relay where they were to authorities.

Darkness crept over the ridge.

Tonya finally stopped.

Hawke had been salivating the last hour as his stomach grumbled thinking about cooking the fish. "Help me round up some dry branches," he said to his traveling companion.

She dropped her pack and stared at him.

"If you want one of these fish, you'll help get wood for the fire."

"Joke's on you. I don't have a pan to cook them in." She sat down and pulled out her small pack stove.

He grinned. *No lady, the joke's on you.* He built a stone ring to put the fire in. After gathering a pile of dried limbs from the trees and bushes along the creek, he started a small fire in the middle of the ring.

"You get that smoking too much and we'll have Forest Service on top of us," Tonya said, watching him.

"I know how to make a near smokeless fire." He steepled the sticks getting them good and hot. While gathering the dry wood, he'd also found a green willow bush. He used the limbs he'd cut from the willow to spear through the filets of the steelhead, he'd gutted and cleaned. Leaning the fillets, skin side down, over the fire with the long ends of the willows held under rocks on the outside of the fire, he cooked the fish.

The aroma made his stomach squirm with joy. Finally, a food that wasn't processed or tasted like cardboard.

"That smells good," Tonya said, eyeing the fillets.

"I thought you weren't interested in fish for dinner," he said, pulling out his metal plate and fork. He checked the fish. The meat flaked off onto his plate. He did this with three of the fillets and handed the fourth one to the woman. He could have eaten all of it, but knew she could use the extra protein from the fresh food.

"Thank you," she said, before eating the meat straight from the skin skewered on the willow sticks.

Hawke wondered what made a woman who

seemed to have good manners and had a decent upbringing as far as he knew, want to be friends with a known murderer. "Why did you help White escape?" he asked, before realizing he'd said it out loud.

She studied him. "Why would a nice girl like me get involved with someone like him?"

"Yeah. You seem normal, though driven."

"I told you. I'm a reporter. When I realized there wasn't going to be a story by just interviewing him, I figured, why not help him break out. And after he was captured, say I was kidnapped and then write a story that would get me better jobs than human interest stories."

It was his turn to study her. "You made yourself an accomplice to get better stories?" He didn't believe it for one minute. "Why are you chasing Sheridan? Will this trek across country also be a story?"

"Sheridan promised me he'd tell me why he killed White. Then every time I tried to question him, he'd start off on some tracking thing, until I decided to forget him and that's when you showed up. He said he was taking me with him as a hostage." She didn't look at him. Her gaze was on the fire between them.

He could tell she wasn't telling the truth. Whether it was her truth, what she believed, or she was lying to keep him from discovering why she was really going after Sheridan, he didn't know.

"If that's all true, you're done with him. Why are you leading me to him?" Hawke studied the way her hand clutched the eating utensil and her gaze slowly raised to his.

"Because he killed Felix. I have an eyewitness account of the killing and the man being found by a tracker like himself." Her eyes lit up. "Justice will have been served. And I'll have the firsthand account of it all to report." The second comment was almost as if she thought it should be said, not that she cared to report what happened.

He finished off his fish. Dog sat beside him, starring at the skins still on the sticks. Hawke tossed the cooked fish skin to Dog before throwing the guts and sticks into the fire. While all of that burned, he washed up, made his bed, and used his pan to haul water over and douse the fire when all that was left were ashes.

His eyelids grew heavy, but he remained awake until Tonya had bedded down and was breathing steady. Then he placed the thorny branches from the berry bushes around her sleeping bag. It was nature's security system to let him know if she decided to head off without him during the night.

Chapter Thirteen

The sound of hooves pounding the ground, sat Hawke straight up. The sun had barely lit up the ridge.

"What is that?" Tonya asked from her bedroll.

"Sounds like we have a herd of elk headed this way." Hawke jumped up and started rolling his bed up. Everything other than his boots were in his pack.

"Ouch!" Tonya yelped, hopping on one foot and then crying out as she stepped on another stickered limb.

Hawke shoved his feet into his boots and kicked the thorny limbs out of her way.

"Thanks," she said, shoving her sleeping bag into her pack.

The sound of the stampeding elk grew closer.

"What do we do?" Tonya asked, fear evident in her wide eyes and high-pitched voice.

"They're coming from that direction," he pointed east. "Get behind the west side of the largest tree or boulder you can find and don't stick anything out to the sides until the herd goes by."

"Dog, come!" he ordered his friend. They ran for a boulder large enough to cover them both. Hawke glanced the direction Tonya had darted. She was standing still behind a mahogany tree. She would have been safer up the gulley a bit, behind a boulder, but she'd made her choice.

He peered to the east. A large bull elk with a spread of antlers more branched than the tree Tonya hid behind, came crashing through the gulley. He was followed by a herd of about seventy-five cows, calves, and younger bulls.

Whatever had spooked them had them running as if their lives depended on it. They crashed through the bushes and antlers clanked on branches adding more chaos to the roar of their hooves.

When the last brown and tan body passed and the thunder was little more than his stomach grumbling, Hawke glanced across the gulley, through the settling dust, to where Tonya had hidden.

She pressed against the tree, her fists clenched, eyes shut tight.

Hawke stood, shouldered his pack, and walked over to her. "They're gone," he said, putting a hand on her arm.

Her eyes shot open. "I've never. They were so close I smelled their stench and felt their breath. The ground moved under my feet." Her head turned. She peered into his eyes. "Why were they running?"

He shrugged. "A pack of wolves, a cougar, men. It's hard to say." Hawke wandered back over to the scattered ashes and rocks from the fire.

The sun warmed the gulley. "Get something to eat, and we can get going." It felt good to be the one giving the orders for a change. If she'd just tell him where they were headed, he could get her there on an easier route than up and over all the ridges.

He pulled out his water bottle and two granola bars. He tossed a biscuit to Dog and sat eating while the woman gathered herself together, joined him, and nibbled on a protein bar.

"Do you know your way around this side of the Snake River as you did the other side?" He sipped water and watched her from under his eyelashes.

"No. I hiked the High Wallowas once, but I've never been in this area." She looked up from her protein bar. "What about you?"

"I know my way around. Where are we going? I might know a better way to get there." Hawke shoved the last of his granola bar in his mouth.

Tonya picked at the bar in her hand as if contemplating giving him any information.

He could wait. Patience was something he had in spades when waiting on someone to tell him what he wanted to know. He'd learned from years of getting information out of fishermen and hunters that just waiting, not pushing, got the answers quicker, and with less hassle, than badgering.

"Do you know anything about an area called Lord Flat?" she asked.

He'd been right. "Yeah. We go over the next ridge, drop into Deep Creek Canyon and follow the right fork up and over to the flat. Should be there by late afternoon if we get going." If he could get a chance to get on the radio, he could call and have backup meet him there.

"Why are you so ready to get going? You seemed to balk when I was giving orders." Her eyes narrowed.

"Because now I know where we are going. I didn't like the way you didn't seem to know which way to travel." It sounded like a good response.

"Typical man! Didn't like taking orders from a woman."

He'd let her think that. "Sure. You ready?" He shouldered his pack and headed up the ridge. He'd have to find a way to contact the Oregon State Police soon, if he wanted help when they reached Lord Flat.

《》《》《》

"I need a break," Tonya said from behind Hawke.

He stopped and twisted to glance at her. "We can take a break." He'd been keeping the pace as fast as he could to hopefully get her to rest. Now that she had, he needed to get on the radio. A few more hours and they'd be at Lord Flat.

The woman dropped her pack and sat down, taking her hiking boots off. She'd ran to the tree with them tied to her pack this morning. He wondered if she still had a thorn from his security system in her foot. Guilt crept over him for a split second until he remembered she had helped a killer escape and was after another killer.

"I'll be back." He kept his pack on and headed away from the woman. Dog started to follow. "Stay," he commanded. The animal sat on his haunches, watching.

Hawke walked a good quarter of a mile through the trees and stopped. He pulled out the radio and dialed in the Wallowa County Sheriff's Office.

"Hawke contacting Wallowa County dispatch." He waited. Someone at the Sheriff's Department should hear his call.

"This is Hawke. Do you read me?" He repeated several times, then switched to the frequency the OSP officers used among themselves when trying to catch a poacher. "This is Hawke. Anyone on this channel?"

A crackle and his fellow officer's voice rang clear. "Hawke, this is Tad. Where are you?"

"We're coming from the east, headed to Lord Flat. Should be there in three to four hours. Could use backup if Sheridan is there like the woman with me says." Hawke's body relaxed knowing there would be help.

"I should be there in two hours. We've been combing the area after getting word from the Idaho Fish and Wildlife where they'd dropped you off."

"Stay out of sight. I'm not sure where Sheridan will be. Aircraft could be coming in to pick him up." Hawke wondered at why the man had picked this particular area. "Anyone know why he'd be here?"

"He grew up in the Imnaha area."

Tonya's voice carried to him. "Are you done?"

"Copy. See you at Lord Flat." Hawke spun the dial, turning the radio off, and shoved it deep in the pack. He shouldered the pack and headed back toward Dog and the woman.

If Sheridan had grown up in Imnaha, why would he be headed to Lord Flat?

He didn't have time to think about it. Dog lunged at him, and Tonya glared at him when he walked into the area where he'd left them both.

"What took you so long?" she accused.

"Not enough water intake." His comment did what he'd hoped, shut her down and reddened her cheeks. "Let's go."

He led the way up Deep Creek until it veered right. Then he followed the west fork.

"Are we going the right way? It doesn't feel right," Tonya said.

"You said Lord Flat." He hoped she hadn't told him wrong and now would go a different direction.

"Where are we now?" She made a slow circle.

"We just left Deep Creek Canyon and are headed to Lord Flat. It's on top of this ridge." He pointed to the ridge to the right of the gulley he planned to take to avoid climbing straight up the side of the ridge. There was a road that came in on the south end of the flat. It would be the road that Tad Ullman would take to enter the flat. If Sheridan was on foot, there was no telling which direction he would come to the flat from. Or where on the flat he'd instructed any aircraft to pick him up.

He continued up the gulley, listening to the woman behind him muttering and her heavy footfalls. She hadn't been walking that heavy before. Was she trying to make sure anyone in the area heard them coming?

He glanced over his shoulder. "You might want to watch slamming your feet down."

She narrowed her eyes at his comment.

"You can curse me all you want, but do it in your head." He smiled as she sneered at him.

Hawke resumed walking and noticed Tonya walked with lighter steps and no longer mumbled. The underbrush became denser. He worked his way to the edge of the tree line continuing in a westerly direction to avoid scraping noises from the thick underbrush. It not only made walking easier but he could look up if any aircraft flew over.

He stopped to get a drink and turned around to see how Tonya was doing. "Damn!" The woman no longer followed him. Had she hurried off to catch up with Sheridan, or had getting to Lord Flat been a ruse to get her closer to? What else was in the area other than the roads and the landing area on Lord Flat?

There were a couple of cow camps.

Wondering where she went or backtracking and looking for her tracks wouldn't get him to the flat. He wanted to see if anyone showed up, and if they didn't, he'd catch a ride home and sleep in his own bed before trying to find the woman and Sheridan.

"Come on," he said to Dog. He planned to get to the road and catch a ride with Ullman to the landing site.

Chapter Fourteen

Hawke sat on his pack beside the road leading into Lord Flat. He drank the rest of his water and turned on the radio. "Hawke to Ullman."

"Ullman."

"Location?" Hawke asked, hoping the man hadn't already passed this point.

"Ten away."

"Copy." Hawke left the radio on and leaned it against his pack. Dog lay on the ground at his feet, chewing on a biscuit. "We'll be home tonight. Never thought I'd be so glad to go home to our place over the arena." He lived a simple life. Renting a one room and a bath studio apartment over the Trembley's riding arena. It worked out well for him, Dog, his two horses, and mule. While his mother would like him to find a house and settle down with a wife and children, he'd tried the wife thing once before and it hadn't worked. Children— he wouldn't mind. Especially if they were all as quizzical and precocious as Kitree, the young girl he'd tracked through the Eagle Cap Wilderness after her parents had been murdered.

The sound of a vehicle approaching drifted through the trees. He stood and a State Trooper truck appeared on the road. The vehicle stopped beside him.

"Thought you were with a woman?" Ullman said, moving things in the back seat to make room for Dog.

"Me too." Hawke opened the back door. Dog jumped in, and Hawke dumped his pack on the seat before closing that door and climbing in the passenger seat. "She ditched me an hour ago."

Ullman stared at him. "You didn't have her in custody?"

"She didn't know I was a cop. I wouldn't have gotten anything out of her if she'd have known that." He pointed ahead. "Go to the airstrip and see if there's any activity." The more he thought about it, he was pretty sure they wouldn't find anything at the strip. It had been a general landmark Tonya had used to get her in the vicinity of where she wanted to go.

"You look like shit," Ullman said, giving him a sideways glance.

"Thanks. That's what over a week in the same clothes will do to you." He rubbed a hand across his face. Even after a week, he didn't have the hard, scruffy beard his counterparts sported. His whiskers were soft and patchy. Like he'd eaten honey, wiped some across his face, and then rolled in rabbit fur. With the fur only sticking in patches.

Ullman drove the half a mile to the airstrip. It was wide open, not a soul around. "What do you think?"

"We sit and wait a bit. Are there any of our guys in

the air?" Hawke peered up into the blue sky.

"Should be a copter around somewhere. I called it in after talking to you." Ullman turned the vehicle off and sat. "Whew, you are ripe."

"I told you I've been in these clothes and hiking miles every day for a week. What do you expect?"

Ullman rolled down his window. "I should have brought some air freshener."

"Funny." Hawke was more worried about where Tonya Cox had disappeared to. "Did you happen to notice any activity at the cow camp on your way in?"

"They haven't put any cows up here yet."

Snoring from the back seat made Hawke grin. "I think Dog is as tired as I am."

"You two covered a lot of ground. Tell me how you ended up becoming hiking companions to a woman who helped a man escape prison?"

Hawke settled back in the seat and started from sipping his beer at the hotel to sitting alongside the road waiting for Ullman.

"You have had a busy week." Ullman scratched his head. "But if this woman helped White escape, how will a jury believe she saw Sheridan kill him?"

Hawke shrugged. "I'm not the one who has to make a jury see her truth." He groaned. "I just have to find her and bring her in."

"I know Spruel has her file on his desk. That might help." Ullman reached for his radio. "I think I'll see if he wants us to stay here longer or head back."

"Good idea." Hawke pulled his hat over his eyes and leaned back in the seat. While following the woman and then getting here, he'd kept moving even when he'd been exhausted. Now, knowing he was headed home and in good hands, he fell asleep.

《》《》《》

"Wake up! There's smoke coming from the cow camp!"

The words banged around in Hawke's head as he tried to break the veil of sleep.

The vehicle sped up and bounced over the rough road, slamming Hawke's shoulder against the door and causing Dog to yip.

The bouncing and Dog's whimpering brought Hawke out of the deep sleep he'd fallen into.

"What the hell!" He stared in disbelief as smoke curled into the air and flames shot out the window.

Ullman slammed on the brakes and bailed out of the vehicle. Hawke was behind him. They kicked in the door.

Hawke spotted a body sprawled on the floor. He grasped it under the arms and pulled. Closer to the door, he glanced down and could see it was a man. He hauled the man out of the burning building.

Ullman was back at the truck calling in the fire.

Before he rolled the man over, Hawke knew what he was going to find.

Sean Sheridan had what looked like a bullet hole in his chest. Someone had shot him and started the fire to make it look like an accident. Only one person knew where to find Sheridan.

"Who's that?" Ullman asked, walking up to where Hawke knelt beside the body.

"Sheridan."

"No way! The man we were waiting to get on an airplane?" Ullman pulled on a pair of latex gloves and handed a set to Hawke.

"The very same." Hawke started searching the man's pockets as Ullman pulled out his phone and took photos. "It's too much of a coincidence that both men have Ms. Tonya Cox in common."

Ullman stopped taking photos. "The woman you lost?"

"Yeah."

Ullman whistled. "Shits gonna hit the fan over that."

"Don't I know it." He had to find proof the woman had been at the shack. "You finish here. I'm going to look for tracks."

"Sure you're up to it? You were deep in La-la land when I saw the smoke." Ullman studied him.

"No, I'm not sure, but I have to find her tracks and prove she was here." Hawke grabbed a water bottle and his phone and started at the front door, looking for the track he knew as Tonya's hiking boots.

About five feet from the entrance that he and Ullman had compromised by running into the burning building, he found the tracks while defending himself from the heat of the out of control burning building. He found the tracks of her leaving the house headed east. She was going back to the country she knew.

He was too tired to follow her, but he could let the Idaho authorities know she was headed their way. Hawke took photos of her tracks. A thought came to him. Where did she get a gun? He knew for a fact there hadn't been one in her pack. But Sheridan had run off with the shotgun and handgun. He'd come back up here tomorrow and dig through the ashes and see if he could find both guns. If Ms. Cox didn't leave it in the burning building, he might be able to find the gun and prove she killed Sheridan.

What he really wanted to know was why? Was it because he'd killed White, who she'd fallen for and helped escape prison, or was it for some other reason? His head began to hurt. These were questions to ponder after a long sleep and a decent meal.

He walked back to the truck and climbed in.

"Forest Service is headed this way to keep an eye on it overnight," Ullman said.

"Tell them not to touch anything. I'm coming back tomorrow and sifting through the ashes. I want to know if both guns Sheridan had are in the house or if the killer took one with them." Hawke leaned his head back against the seat and closed his eyes.

《》《》《》

"Hawke, you look like and smell like a homeless dog." Herb Trembley's voice roused Hawke.

"You want me to help you get him to his apartment?" Ullman asked.

Hawke pried his eyes open and saw they were at the Trembley Ranch. Where he lived. "I can make it to my place."

"But will you stay awake long enough to take a shower?" Herb asked.

"I'm sure I can."

At the sound of his voice, nickering and braying started in the area of the paddock where he kept his horses and mule. He walked over to the stall gate. The animals snorted and stared at him. "Yeah, even you hay bags don't like the sight and smell of me."

Herb had his pack.

"Just dump that at the bottom of the stairs. I'll deal with it tomorrow." Hawke whistled for Dog who was in sniffing noses with Jack, the horse, his buddy.

"Want me to bring you over some food?" Herb asked, standing at the foot of the stairs leading up to the apartment.

"Yeah, a shower will wake me enough to eat. Thanks." Hawke ascended the stairs, his tired legs feeling as if he were climbing Mt. Everest. He'd scaled ridge after ridge the last week and they hadn't made his legs feel like mush.

Chapter Fifteen

The aroma of freshly brewed coffee woke Hawke. Funny, he didn't remember setting his coffee pot last night. He inhaled, allowing the scent to pull him out from under the covers.

A cold nose poked his thigh. He automatically patted Dog on the head. "I'm getting up." Even though he said the words, his body had a mind of its own. It had been a long time since his limbs ignored messages to get moving.

"We're getting too old to hike like we're on a mission," he said, continuing to pet Dog and allowing his muscles to engage with his brain. Finally, after the pot had spewed its last blast of hot water through the coffee grounds, he sat up, swinging his legs over the side of the bed.

"We're taking Jack and Horse with us today. If we're going to track, I'm riding." Hawke filled a cup with coffee, sat down in the one chair at his small table, and sipped the dark, satisfying brew. He sighed. While he didn't down coffee like a lot of other officers did, he had to admit, a good cup to start the day was something he didn't like going without.

His stomach grumbled at the same time neighing and the staccato bray of Horse started down in the paddock. "Guess we should say good morning to those three and feed them before we go to the Rusty Nail." He finished off the coffee, pulled on clean jeans, T-shirt, long-sleeved snap shirt, socks, and boots.

Dog bounded down the stairs ahead of him and straight to the room where the grain was kept. He loved catching rodents among the sacks of feed.

Hawke walked to the paddock and patted his horses and mule on the foreheads. "Hey, boys, did you miss me?"

"They did." Darlene's voice came from down the alleyway.

Hawke watched his landlord approach, leading her favorite mare. "You going for a ride?"

"I was thinking about it. Jezzy and I haven't been on a trail ride for a while. We both could use the change of scenery." Darlene stopped in front of Hawke. "Herb said you were so tired last night he hoped you didn't fall asleep in the mashed potatoes I sent along with that meatloaf."

He smiled. "I don't remember starting my coffee pot, but I do know I didn't fall asleep in the mashed potatoes."

Darlene laughed. "Herb started your coffee pot. He said the shape you were in you'd need the caffeine this morning."

"Ahh, that explains why I couldn't remember

doing it. Tell him thanks. And thank you for the food. Soon as I get these three fed, I'm headed to the Rusty Nail for breakfast, then to the office." He nodded toward the stall. "I'll be taking Jack and Horse out when I get back. Probably be gone a few days again. Can you keep an eye on Boy?"

"Not a problem." Worry lines wrinkled her brow. "I heard the escaped convict was found killed. Why do you need to go back out?"

"There's been another homicide. And I believe I know who did it. I just have to find the person." After a good night's sleep, he was convinced Tonya Cox had killed Sheridan to get back at him for killing White. It made no other sense. He just had to prove she did it and find her.

"Good luck." Darlene led her mare away.

Hawke grabbed the wheelbarrow leaning against the feed room and filled it with hay. He pushed it to the end of the horse run and tossed it into the feeder. Then he topped off the water tank that was clear and clean. He'd have to pay more rent this month for the good care Darlene took of his animals when he was away.

After the animals were tended to, he left Dog with the horses and headed to Winslow and his favorite breakfast place, the Rusty Nail.

《》《》《》

At the café, Hawke took his usual seat at the counter. It was late enough that the breakfast crowd had gone, leaving only the mid-morning gossips having coffee.

"Heard you didn't make it to your conference," Justine, his favorite waitress and friend, said, pouring him a cup of coffee.

He studied her over the cup as he sipped. "Who told you that?"

"The other half of the Hawke Fan Club." She winked and tossed a dark braid over her shoulder. "Want your usual?"

He nodded and wondered if it had been a good idea for Justine and Dani to have become friends. It was good for the two women. Dani was new to the area and didn't really fit in given she was a retired Air Force officer and not from a county family, and Justine, while having grown up in the area, didn't seem to have any friends. If not for him, the two would have never met. Yet now that they had, they seemed to have become good friends.

His phone rang. Spruel.

"Hawke."

"It's Sergeant Spruel. Are you coming in today? I wouldn't blame you if you didn't. Ullman said you were dead on your feet when he picked you up yesterday."

"I'm coming in. I want to read that file you have on Cox and head out to Lord Flat and sift through the debris."

"Hawke, you need to take at least two days off. After the week you had, you should take the days you'd marked off for the conference as well." Spruel was always on his butt about taking time off.

"We'll talk about it when I get there." He ended the connection. For the first time in the last fifteen years that he'd been a Fish and Wildlife State Trooper in Wallowa County, he was thinking a month long vacation sounded good.

"Here's your food." Justine set the platter-sized

plate in front of him. Two eggs, three hotcakes, ham, and hash browns. His mouth watered as he shook salt and pepper on the eggs.

"You should call Dani and let her know you made it back." Justine's quiet comment grabbed his attention.

He stared into her hazel eyes. "Why?"

His friend's face scrunched into anger. "Because she is worried about you." She studied him. "Are you that thick skinned you haven't noticed she cares?"

His throat tightened as he tried to swallow the pancake he'd been chewing. Could the woman who kept entering his thoughts at the all the wrong times actually feel something for him other than annoyance? He wasn't getting his hopes up. Besides, he didn't have a life that boded well for any kind of relationship. Like now. She'd worried about him, and he thought they were just friends.

He swallowed the bite. "You care about me. Have you been worried?"

Her cheeks darkened a bit. "Not until Dani called and asked if I'd seen you in the restaurant lately and said she'd hauled Dog and your pack to you to chase down an escaped killer."

Hawke cut the ham viciously with a knife and hissed for only her to hear, "See! That's why it's best for you and Dani to not care about me. It's why I like being single. No one has to worry about me."

He dug into his breakfast, eating fast to get away from the narrowed gaze Justine sent him every time she stopped at the counter. The food wasn't as tasty as he'd remembered. But he knew it was only because Justine had put thoughts into his head. Ones that were both interesting and worrisome.

Tucking money for his meal and a tip under the edge of his plate, Hawke left the café. Work was what he did best. What had he been thinking, taking a month-long vacation? If he did that, his "Fan Club" would be wondering what happened to him. He huffed and drove to the building in Winslow that the Fish and Wildlife shared with the State Police.

Spruel grabbed him as soon as he walked in the door. "Get me up to speed."

Hawke relayed his last week's activities. "I won't get it all typed up today. I want to get up to Lord Flat and sift through the debris."

"The incident crew is already up there. What are you looking for?" Spruel asked.

"If a shotgun and a handgun are found. I know for a fact the Cox woman didn't have a gun with her. I went through her pack. If she killed Sheridan, she had to have used one of his guns. I want to know if they were in the fire or if she took one with her. If she did, we might be able to prove she killed him." Hawke studied his superior. The man was thinking awfully hard.

"How do you plan to find her?"

"Her tracks were headed back to Idaho. That's area she knows. She admitted her uncle had taken her on many hikes in that area."

"I bet he had. Her uncle was Theodore Shoat, an Idaho Forest Service employee, and the man Felix White shot along with the Goodwin family." Spruel studied him. "Are you sure Sheridan shot White?"

Hawke shook his head. "No. That's what Ms. Cox said. But why else would Sheridan have run if she'd killed White? And why would she kill Sheridan if she'd killed White? I mean, it sounds like she helped White escape to kill him." He rubbed his temples. He was still running on too little sleep to think clearly.

"Get someone to drive you to Idaho to pick up your vehicle. I don't want you on duty today or tomorrow." Spruel picked up a file. "Read this and get your report typed up before you go get the vehicle."

Hawke knew better than to argue with the sergeant when he used that tone. He took the file and wandered to his work station. It was part of a long counter with several other computers. Each trooper had their own station, though it was rare for more than one or two to be in the office at the same time. Only five troopers, three of which were also Fish and Wildlife, patrolled the over three thousand square acres of Wallowa County.

He sat down at the computer and started typing the week's activities as he'd told both Ullman and Sergeant Spruel. Two hours later, he rubbed his eyes, hit save on the report, and stared at the file the sergeant had given him. He wasn't sure he could read this right now. Hawke grabbed the file and headed for the door. He'd go home, take a nap, and then figure out who to call to take him to Idaho. He was sure Herb would give him a lift, but he hated to always ask his landlord to drop everything and help him.

His next thought was Dani. He wouldn't mind spending several hours in a vehicle with her. Then he remembered his conversation with Justine that morning. Shit! He didn't want to ask either woman after that conversation.

His phone rang as he pulled up to the barn and arena at the Trembley's.

Dani.

He hated that his body reacted to the sight of her name. "Hawke."

"About time you answered your phone. I had to call Justine to find out you were home." The reprimand in her voice didn't upset him like it would have from any other woman. From her, he knew it as her way of saying she cared.

"I've been busy. Had to write a report, talk to my superior, make arrangements to get my truck." Shit, he shouldn't have said that.

"Your truck's still in Idaho?"

"Yeah."

"I'm in town to pick up supplies. I could take a day and run you to Idaho." The wistfulness in her voice was something he'd never heard from her before.

Hawke opened his mouth and snapped it shut. He'd just told himself he wasn't going to have either Dani or Justine take him to get his truck. But that would mean relying on Herb. Again.

He sighed. "If you have the time, I could use a ride."

"What time tomorrow do you want to leave?" Her tone was all business, with a bit of a lilt he'd not heard before.

"Might as well get this out of the way. You said you were in town. We can leave in an hour if you don't mind driving over there. I'm pretty sure, I'll fall asleep." He hoped he did. That would keep him from staring at her or saying anything that might give Dani any ideas he was looking for a woman.

"You know, leaving this time of day, we'll have to spend the night." There was the officer tone that had set his hackles up when he'd first met her.

"I'm sure we can find rooms in Riggins or Whitebird. I'll pay for your gas and your room. I'm asking you for a favor." He wanted to make it clear they wouldn't spend the night together and this was purely a friendship thing. Though... he wouldn't mind spending the night with the uptight ex-officer. He was pretty sure she'd take control. And damn if that didn't excite him.

"Then I'll check out of the Wagon Wheel and see you at your place in an hour." The connection went silent.

He shook his head. "What have I done?"

Chapter Sixteen

As Hawke had hoped, he'd slept nearly all the way to Riggins, a four-and-a-half-hour drive through Lewiston and down the Clearwater River. He woke up just before Whitebird. "Want to see if there's a place to spend the night in Whitebird?" he asked, sitting up straight and scrubbing his face with his hands.

"I checked motel vacancies before I picked you up. There aren't any in Whitebird. But there were still some rooms at the Riverview Motel in Riggins." She glanced over at him. "I secured two of them."

"Good thinking." He hadn't really paid attention to Riggins on his previous trip. He'd been focused on getting to the area and finding White.

"Do you always snore when you sleep?" Dani asked, catching him off guard.

"I don't know. Why?" He studied her in the light from the gauges in the dash.

"I wondered if it was because you were so tired or

if you do it all the time."

The wistfulness in her voice had his gut squirming. This was why he'd shied away from asking her to bring him here in the first place.

"You'd have to ask Dog if I snore." He changed the tone of the conversation by bringing his pet into the discussion.

She laughed. "Yeah, I guess he knows pretty much everything about you."

"From the time I got him till now." They crossed a bridge, putting the river on their left. Up ahead square lights from windows glowed. They were getting close to Riggins.

They found the Riverview Motel on the left, after passing several rafting businesses. It was a two-story building with the hills on the other side of the river behind it. The office was located in a Quonset hut shaped building along the road.

"Are the rooms under your name?" he asked, reaching for the door handle.

"Yes. I'll get the keys." Dani slipped out of the car.

He followed. No way was he letting her pay for the rooms. He'd asked her to bring him here. Hawke reached the door before her, held it open as she walked through, then pulled out his credit card as she asked about the rooms.

"Will we be charging both rooms to the card on file?" the shaggy haired young man asked.

"No. They both go on this card." Hawke handed his card over and was glad Dani didn't say a word.

With the rooms paid for, instructions on where they were, and the keys in their hands, Hawke escorted Dani out of the office and over to the car. "I'll walk over to the other building." He needed more air and time to wake up.

Crossing the parking lot, he wondered where Ms. Cox had headed. Would she go back to work and act as if nothing had happened? He doubted it. She was wanted for aiding a convict's escape, being a witness to his murder, and a suspect in the murder of Sean Sheridan.

He had a feeling she was hiding out on the Idaho side of the Hells Canyon. But she couldn't do that the rest of her life.

What they needed to do was dig into her uncle's life and see if they could find a cabin or property that he'd owned. Chances were, if this whole escape and murder were connected to his death, she was staying where she felt close to him.

A car beeped. Hawke jumped.

"Hey, do your daydreaming out of the middle of the parking lot," Dani called to him from the window of her car.

He glanced around and realized he stood in the middle of the asphalt between the office and the rooms.

She stepped out of her car and popped the trunk. "You gonna grab your duffel, or do you want me to get it?"

He hurried over, grabbing his bag and shutting the trunk lid.

"Are you hungry?" she asked.

"Yeah."

"I googled and The Steak House has good marks." Dani walked up the stairs to room 210 and shoved the key in the doorknob. "Meet you out here in fifteen?"

"Yeah." He unlocked 211 and stepped into a small,

clean room. The bed was inviting, but his grumbling stomach overrode his desire to fall on the bed and sleep. How long would it take him to feel rested? Once he got back to Wallowa County, he'd load up Horse and Jack and head back this direction to look for Ms. Cox. He knew Idaho officials were looking for her, but he had a vendetta. No one kills someone and gets away with it, when he should have known something was up. He wouldn't be able to let this go until the woman was in custody.

《》《》《》

Hawke waved at Dani as she drove by when he turned off the highway onto the road leading to the Trembleys. He'd had a nice dinner with the woman last night. She'd realized how tired he was and didn't ask him to stay up visiting with her. He'd hit the bed and been dead to the world when she'd knocked on his door in the morning to see if he was ready for breakfast.

They ate, and she drove him out to Saddle Pit where he thanked her, climbed into his pickup, and headed home. She'd followed him all the way.

On the drive, he'd called Spruel. The sergeant told him they'd found both the shotgun and the handgun in the ashes. That meant Ms. Cox had another weapon or used the handgun on Sheridan and tossed it down to be ruined in the fire. No way to connect a weapon with her. She was clever.

After the sergeant updated him, Hawke asked for time off. Given the days and hours he'd put in the last week, the time off was granted. He didn't tell his superior where he was going. Sometimes it was best to keep that sort of thing to himself.

He'd also called Mathews at the Idaho County

Sheriff's Department and asked him for all records on Theodore Shoat and Tonya Cox.

He backed his truck up to the horse trailer. Dog ran out of the stables, his tail wagging.

Hawke stepped out of the vehicle and scratched the dog's ears. "Are you rested up? We're heading out again."

"Looks like you're going somewhere with the horses," Herb said, crossing from the barn, where he worked on farm machinery, to the stables.

"Taking some time off. Thought I'd go on a camping trip with Jack and Horse." Hawke wasn't lying. He was going camping with his horse and mule. Because he wasn't officially working.

"That's good. But I'd think you'd want to go rest with your mom or someplace that didn't require you sleeping outdoors." Herb studied him.

"You know me. I appreciate the wildlife and being in the outdoors." Hawke plugged in the trailer lights and headed to the stables. "Will you ask Darlene to take care of Boy while I'm gone? I plan to compensate her for all the extra work I've given her this month."

Herb waved a hand. "You know she doesn't expect anything extra from you."

"I still shouldn't be putting more work on her." Hawke stopped at the bottom of the stairs. "I'll pack and be out of here in an hour."

"Take care." Herb turned and walked out of the stables.

Hawke snagged his pack still sitting at the bottom of the stairs. He'd have to wash clothes somewhere. In his apartment, he dumped the contents of his pack onto the floor and sorted the food dropped to him by the helicopter and what little he'd had of his own. He shoved the dirty clothes into his pack and closed it. He'd wash these on the way out of town. Alder had a clean laundromat, and the woman who owned it would switch his clothes from the washer to the dryer while he went shopping for food.

He put the food he planned to take with him in a paper bag. There wasn't much. After writing a check for his rent and the stable rent, he put the checks in an envelope. He'd drop it off at the house on his way out. The rent would be due while he was gone. His simple life required he worry about few bills. He liked it that way.

Carrying the dirty clothes and bag of food, he descended the stairs and dropped the bag of food at his pack box and took the backpack out to toss in the back of his truck. Back in the stable, he put the food in the pack box after checking to make sure all his camping gear was in the box. Mentally, he calculated how much dog food and food he'd need to purchase to keep Dog and him filled up while looking for Ms. Cox.

He put the packsaddle and pack box in the storage area in the front of the horse trailer. When that was all stowed along with his saddle, bridle, and hay cubes, Hawke loaded up Jack and Horse.

Dog jumped into the pickup cab when the door opened. He wasn't going to be left behind.

Darlene strode down the walk from her house as he slowed to a stop. "Where are you going?"

"Time off. Going on a vacation." Hawke handed her the envelope with the rent money. "When I get back, I'll treat you to a day at the Lake Spa for taking care of Boy."

"You don't have to do that. You know I like that flighty appaloosa." She took the envelope.

"Doesn't matter if you like him. I keep giving you more work." He pulled away and headed the truck for Alder. If he was lucky, Mrs. Rochelle would get his laundry done quickly while he shopped.

Chapter Seventeen

Hawke pulled into Pittsburgh Campground after dark. He unloaded Jack and Horse and walked them around. It had been a long haul. After tying the animals to the side of the trailer, he took his collapsible and regular bucket to the water faucet under the tree down by the boat ramp and filled them. Back at the trailer he set the buckets in front of the horse and mule to drink.

He shoveled the horse manure into a corner of the trailer and set up a small cot he carried in the tack compartment of the trailer. This was where he planned to spend the night and head out first thing in the morning for an area Deputy Mathews told him had belonged to Theodore Shoat. The land had reverted to the Forest Service at the man's death. Hawke had a feeling he'd find Ms. Cox hiding there. The authorities had her description and photo all over the media in hopes someone would report her whereabouts.

《》《》《》

Dog led the way as Hawke, riding Jack and leading Horse, followed a faint trail north of Pittsburgh Landing toward Horse Ridge. Mathews discovered Ms. Cox's uncle had a mining claim in that area. Hawke had the coordinates to get him somewhat close, but it would be up to him to discover where the woman was hiding.

His phone vibrated in his pocket. Surprised he received a signal, Hawke glanced at it. Shit!

He slid a finger across the surface and answered. "Sergeant, what are you doing calling me on my vacation?" His superior must know what he was doing or he wouldn't have called.

"You know damn well why I'm calling you. You're lucky I haven't relayed what I know on to the lieutenant."

Hawke groaned. Not only was his butt on the line for this unofficial foray after Ms. Cox, but now his sergeant's was as well. "I got a lead on where Ms. Cox might be hiding."

"Lead? That's what you call asking another officer to send you information that you wouldn't need if you were really on vacation?" Spruel sounded more than irritated. An angry tone Hawke had never heard turned on him made him wonder if he should have gone to the reservation and visited his mother.

"I can't let this woman get away with murder. She played me, and I'm going to find her." Hawke felt his reputation was on the line along with his sense of justice.

"Then you shouldn't have asked for a vacation. Just said you were going to find the woman." Papers shuffled on the other side of the connections. "As of this moment you are no longer on vacation, but you damn well better take one soon. Keep me updated as best you can. I believe Mathews is also on the ground looking for the woman."

Hawke knew he shouldn't be pleased Spruel took him off his vacation to save both their butts, but he'd known the man would back him up. "I'll try to connect with Mathews." The sergeant said something else but the signal faded.

"Looks like we're back on the job," he said to Dog. "Good thing I have my badge and gun."

He was so used to wearing his badge on a chain around his neck, hidden under his shirt when out in the woods, he'd not bothered to leave it home. It was second nature for him to put it on when he was headed out with the horses. His handgun was a given no matter if he was on duty or off when he rode around in the mountains. The shotgun in his scabbard, that was more for warning off cougars, wolves, and bears than protection.

After contemplating the map of the area, he'd decided to follow West Creek to Horse Ridge. Somewhere on Big Canyon Saddle was a mine that had been staked by Theodore Shoat.

《》《》《》

Mid-afternoon Hawke stopped to give the horses and himself a break. He opened up a bag of jerky and tossed Dog a biscuit while he read the report on Tonya Cox. By all accounts she was an upstanding citizen. Though he did notice as a child she'd spent lots of time in this wilderness with her uncle. Her parents were killed when she was a teenager. Uncle Theodore, her mother's brother, had stepped in as guardian.

There were several copies of the letters she'd

written to White while he was in jail. They gushed with admiration for his love of the wilderness, specifically the Hells Canyon region. They had a similar attachment to the area.

He didn't see any mention of the claim in Big Saddle Canyon. She'd told the man nothing of herself. How had they instigated the escape? It should have been caught in the letters they'd exchanged. Had she met with him personally at the prison? But how did she make the whole escape happen? Was someone working on that angle? The next time he was on the top of a ridge, he'd see if he could get a signal to call and ask about that.

He wondered which direction Mathews would be coming to the area from. If they crossed paths it would be to their advantage.

"Let's go," he said to Dog, tightening the cinches on Horse and Jack. Hawke swung up into the saddle, and they continued along the forested river, slowly climbing in altitude.

《》《》《》

At dark, Hawke picked a spot that was still in the trees but at the bottom of the rock cliff they'd climb in the morning. On the other side of this ridge was Big Canyon Saddle.

Horse and Jack were high-lined between trees, munching on grass. Hawke leaned against the pack box, studying the map with his flashlight. The air was cooler this high up. He wore his jacket and was thinking about taking off his boots and sticking his legs in his sleeping bag that was rolled out underneath him.

Dog laid down beside him. Hawke put a hand on his head. "Since we'll be at the top to drop down into the saddle, I think we should do a back and forth sweep starting from the top."

Dog made a noise that sounded like agreement to Hawke.

"Now that that's settled, let's get some sleep." He flicked the flashlight off, set it and his boots next to where his head would rest, and slid into his sleeping bag. While he was determined to catch the woman, he wasn't thrilled to be out here again so soon after the last week-and-a-half. A sure sign he might need to think a little stronger about retiring. He was close to thirty years in the State Police. But he knew in his heart, he'd continue working for them until they kicked him out. He had nothing else to do with his time, and he enjoyed what he did most of the time.

His eyelids grew heavy.

The crack of a limb not far off, popped his eyes open.

Dog tensed.

Hawke put a hand on the dog's collar, holding him close. "Shh," he said before the vibration in the animal's body escaped as a growl.

Careful to not make a sound, Hawke eased himself out of his sleeping bag. He wasn't going to get jumped when his body was trussed up.

He listened.

No tap of hooves. It wasn't a deer or elk. It was unlikely a wolf or cougar would snap a branch while moving through the trees. They moved with too much stealth. The only thing he could think that would make a branch crack was a person or a bird landing on a weak branch. But there hadn't been the sound of a bird catching its balance.

He put his hand on the butt of his Glock. He always slept with it on when outdoors. Not wanting to give up his location, he stared into the dark shadows under the trees, one hand on Dog and one on his weapon, listening.

Another snap and the sound of brush scraping cloth. It was a person.

The sound grew closer.

Dog vibrated.

Hawke slipped his Glock out of the holster and pointed it the direction of the approaching person. He leaned down close to Dog's ear and whispered, "Stay."

With the hand that had been keeping Dog still, he picked up the flashlight, pointed it the direction of the person, and flicked the switch.

The beam lit up the area in front of Hawke.

A man stepped into the glow, his arm raised to shade his eyes. "What the…?" he said and Hawke recognized the voice.

"Mathews. What are you doing wandering around in the dark?" Hawke slipped his weapon back in the holster before the man knew he had been in the sights.

"I was camped about a quarter mile over and spotted your light. Thought I'd come see if it was you or Tonya Cox." He walked closer and dumped his pack on the ground.

"You make enough noise, if it had been Ms. Cox you'd be another casualty." Hawke held the flashlight as the man untied his sleeping bag and rolled it out.

"I thought I was being quiet. But I'm not usually in the wilderness as much as I've been lately." Mathews sat, untied his boots and slid into his sleeping bag.

"Why did they send you out here when there are

law enforcement trackers?" Hawke had wondered the same thing when Spruel told him about Mathews heading this way as well.

"I think for the same reason you are. This woman slipped by both of us at Sheep Creek cabin. It's kind of my reputation on the line. And I believe yours, as well, since she slipped by you more than once."

Hawke was pleased there wasn't any smugness in the man's comment. He was simply speaking the truth. "Yeah, that's why I'm here. To save face." He flicked the flashlight off and settled back in his sleeping bag. He'd have to figure out how they would work together. He knew for a fact Horse wouldn't do well as a mount for Mathews and they needed him to haul the pack boxes.

Chapter Eighteen

Hawke and Mathews worked out a plan. Since Hawke had the horse and pack mule, he'd zig-zag back and forth from the top of the saddle downward, looking for the mine and the woman. Mathews would use his GPS to try and find the mine with the co-ordinates he'd written down from what he could find from the survey documents. If one of them discovered the woman first, they were to radio the other person. They would apprehend her when they were both present and haul her out together.

Hawke rode along the top of Horse Ridge, using his binoculars to scan the area below. The underbrush wasn't enough to hide a person or a mine entrance. The pine trees in the area lay deteriorating on the ground from a fire years ago. He wondered what Shoat could have been mining. This area wasn't known for gold or silver like other areas, though thirty plus Chinese miners were massacred in 1887 for the gold they found on the Oregon side of the Snake River. Another culture that had been treated poorly by the Whiteman.

He shook his head and moved along the ridge. He was in plain sight. There was nowhere to hide, unless he crept along the other side of the ridge and peeked over with his binoculars. This was quicker and easier. If Ms. Cox saw him, he would think she'd try to hide or move out of the area. Then he would see her movement.

A thorough scan with the binoculars had him convinced the mine was hidden better than he'd anticipated or they were in the wrong area. He'd caught sight of Mathews on the south side of the saddle, making his way down into the basin. If he had the coordinates and was moving to the bottom, Hawke decided he'd best get to the bottom as well.

He gave Jack his head and let the horse make his way down the side of the rocky ridge. Horse followed behind, but jerked several times, balking and not agreeing with Jack's route.

Dog walked alongside. This trip he didn't run off and come back. He was still tired from all their hiking the week before.

Nearing the bottom of the ridge, the underbrush grew heavy. Hawke had to pay attention to the different bushes to make sure Jack wouldn't be scratched by thorns as they pushed through. The limbs scraped the pack box on Horse.

It was hard to hear any sound other than the scraping. With this noise he'd never sneak up on anyone. Besides the brush, the animals had to step over the decaying logs strewn about the ground like the game Pick-up-Sticks. They finally moved out of the taller, thicker brush and Hawke discovered a trickle of water, he'd not seen from the ridge.

This had to come from a spring. There wasn't a large enough patch of snow left on the rocky ridge to make a trickle of water this steady. Where the beginning of the spring came out of the ground could possibly be close to the mine.

He leaned down, watching Dog drink. Hawke dismounted and let the horse and mule quench their thirst. The direction of the trickle was revealed by a narrow, green, grassy path. Hawke studied the ground. The only prints were from wildlife.

Opting to take his time moving closer, he led the animals along the green path. Dog walked in the trickle of water. "You have sore paws, my friend?" Hawke asked softly and reach out to pat the dog on the head.

A sound caught both their attention. The steady drone of a generator meant there was someone up ahead.

Hawke tied the horse and mule to a downed log and continued on foot with Dog at his heels. The drone grew in volume. The noise the machine made would make it hard for a person to hear anyone approaching.

A camouflage net covered a small wooden hut near the base of the ridge wall. The green path of the spring water went alongside the hut.

From all appearances, Ms. Cox had planned well ahead to hide out at her uncle's mine. If this was his mine. He wondered if she even knew the land had reverted back to the state. From the look of the hut, it had been maintained after his death.

She must have carried or used a pack animal to bring in fuel for the generator and the supplies she'd need. Had she done it alone? She'd called Sheridan by his first name. Had they planned it all together and he'd become a threat rather than an accomplice?

Hawke motioned for Dog to sit. They had a good position to keep an eye on the place and make sure it was Ms. Cox before he called in Mathews and the authorities.

His stomach growled. He'd left all the food and water back with Jack and Horse. Dog glanced up at him as if he, too, wondered at Hawke's not grabbing at least water even though the animal could easily lap at the water trickling by them ten feet away.

The generator died. Still no sign of anyone. The trajectory Mathews had been taking, he should have shown up by now.

Hawke waited another thirty minutes after the generator died before slowly moving toward the hut in a flanking pattern. He didn't plan to walk right up to the door. He'd go toward it from the side.

There wasn't a window on the side he crept toward. Veering a bit to his right, he checked to see if there was a back entrance. Nope. It looked like the only way in or out was the front door. At the corner, he duck-walked to stay under the window. With one hand, he motioned Dog to stay behind him. He raised his arm, knocking up as high as he could reach on the door. If the woman had a gun, this would be a good way to tell.

No shots rang out.

Scuffling sounds and a muffled voice piqued his awareness of his surroundings. He pressed his ear to the wall. It was definitely a muffled cry for help.

On hyper-alert, he gave a yank on the rope sticking out the small hole in the door and shoved.

The door swung open.

Nothing.

The muffled voice grew louder.

He popped up to look through the window rather than walk through the door. Mathews was tied to a chair in the middle of the hut. No one stood in the dark corners.

Hawke hurried in and yanked the bandanna out of the deputy's mouth. "What happened?"

"She knocked me in the back of the head with something before I even saw this place. Must have dragged me in and tied me up." Rage or embarrassment reddened the man's face.

"Was the generator running when you approached?" Hawke was trying to work out a time line and where the woman might be.

A loud angry bray rang through the air. He knew exactly where the woman was.

"Fetch Jack!" Hawke ordered Dog. The animal flew out of the hut.

Hawke quickly cut the cord around Mathews. "She's taking off with my horse," he threw over his shoulder as he ran out the door.

The thorny bushes whipped his hands and face as he ran, not looking for an easy path straight for his animals. He leaped over downed logs, thinking only of his horse and mule. They, like Dog, were family.

He stopped so fast, his upper body leaned forward. He caught himself before he fell on his face.

Dog had Jack's rein in his mouth, holding the horse who stared at the body on the ground in front of his contrary mule.

Hawke was happy to see his animals safe but fearful Horse may have killed the woman. He walked up to the animal, crooning words of his ancestors to calm the agitated mule. Horse's eyes were wide and his nostrils flared as he stared at the body, nearly touching his hooves.

"Easy boy, back up," Hawke reached out slowly, grasping the lead rope and inching the mule backwards. The end of the lead rope pulled out from under Ms. Cox's body.

She moaned.

Thank the Creator the woman was alive! Hawke tied Horse to a log ten feet from the woman as Mathews appeared, scraping and thrashing through the brush.

"She alive?" he asked between gasps of breath.

"She moaned." Hawke knelt beside the woman. "Call on the radio and get a helicopter in here to pick her up."

"I don't—"

"The radio is in the pack box on the right side." Hawke felt the woman's arms. She moaned when his fingers touched a knot he was pretty sure was a broken bone.

"Ummm…" Mathews stood beside Mule, who had his head turned, his teeth bared, and long ears laid back.

Hawke stood and retrieved the radio for the deputy. He returned to the woman, probing her sides and legs. It appeared to only be her arm that was broke. But he didn't like the fact she wasn't waking up. Blood appeared to be seeping into the dirt under her head.

Mathews called in their location and the need for Air Medical Transport.

"Help me roll her over. She's got a broken arm." Hawke held the side with the injured arm, and they rolled her to her back. As he'd feared. She'd landed with her temple on a rock. It had cut the skin, which was bleeding.

He grabbed his First Aid kit from the pack box and went to work wrapping the wound without moving her head any more than he had too. When he finished that he placed his jacket over her upper body to keep her warm.

"What do we do now?" Mathews asked.

"We wait for the helicopter. And you tell me exactly what happened."

Chapter Nineteen

Hawke watched as the Air Idaho Life-Flight helicopter lifted into the air. Deputy Mathews went with them after the paramedic determined Hawke's bleeding on his hands and a couple of scrapes on his face were superficial. Now that the excitement was over, the scratches stung like a son-of-a-bitch.

He dragged his body up into the saddle. His legs felt like the long flimsy strips of leather his mother would cut to use as lacing. He hadn't hurdled that many objects since being on the high school track team. And that was forty years ago. No wonder his muscles were quivering like a newborn colt.

As he rode toward the hut, he contemplated what Mathews had told him about his encounter with the woman. She'd apparently known he was coming, or that both of them were, since she'd made good time finding his horse and mule. But why had she tied the man up and not killed him as she had Sheridan? This wasn't making any sense. If she was a ruthless killer, who had used him to find Sheridan, why hadn't she killed Mathews?

He dismounted at the hut, hanging onto the saddle horn to give his legs a chance to transition from dangling to walking. When he'd been running to make sure his animals weren't harmed, he hadn't thought about the obstacles and how at his age he shouldn't be sprinting and leaping. Now, he understood just how far he could push his body. The realization was hard to swallow.

Inside the hut, he scanned the small ten by ten room. It would be a comfortable place to recuperate from all that had happened. However, he wasn't here for a vacation. He had to discover more about Ms. Cox and how she and Sheridan became mixed up.

After searching the inside and finding her belongings, including a computer, he decided to spend the night here and get back to his truck and trailer in the morning. Hawke unsaddled the horse and mule, fed them the hay cubes from the pack, and tied them under the camouflage netting by the hut.

Dog plopped on the small cot and fell asleep.

Hawke found the generator but didn't start it. He also discovered a propane cookstove and helped himself to a can of stew and made a pot of coffee. As the food heated, he opened the computer.

Turning the device on, he was pleased to see it had a nearly full battery. The downside, it required a password to get to any of the files. He rifled through a notebook and small datebook in her pack. Nothing revealed a password.

He tried Shoat. Nothing.

Theodore. Nothing

Felix. Nothing.

White. Nothing.

He stared at the screen. A thought struck.

Typing Uncle Teddy, he had a sensation he was being watched. Hawke glanced at the window. Nothing. Horse and Jack were on the side of the building. They would have made a fuss if someone had sneaked by them after their earlier experience.

Hawke glanced down at the screen and the computer had opened. He was in.

The documents were all under files. He scanned the file names and saw one that was titled White. He opened it and many other files and documents popped up. Some were copies of the records he'd received for the investigation. Others were interviews with people who knew Felix White.

The coffee boiled, and he rescued it from boiling over. His mind was on the information in the computer. He poured a cup of coffee, turned off the gas to the stove, and sat back down.

All the interviews stated Felix wasn't a violent person. They couldn't understand why anyone would think he'd killed that family. Hawke didn't understand why the people were so adamant when his police record appeared to show an escalating tendency to violence.

He clicked on the police file on White. Tonya had highlighted the arrests and made comments in comment boxes in the margins of the documents.

The first altercation the police responded to was in January of the year he was first sent to jail. It was at a party in Boise. It appeared White had been attending college at Boise State for Environmental Studies. The police broke up the party and an intoxicated White had yelled profanities at them. Tonya's comment on the side: Felix wasn't in Boise on this date.

The next police report stated White had gotten into a fight with another student at a bar not far from the campus. Tonya's comment: Felix was at his apartment working on a project with another student.

The final document was a file on the arrest of Felix White for assault with a deadly weapon on a speaker at the college. He was given five years and when he was released, he went home and killed the people living in his shack along with Tonya's uncle.

Again, there was a comment on the side. Felix didn't have a quarrel with the visiting lecturer. He was in his apartment sick with the flu.

Hawke shook his head. This wouldn't be the first time someone was wrongly accused. But he wondered that Tonya was keeping it quiet and secretly helping White. He had a feeling everything on this computer would explain it all.

Even though it was one of the smaller, thin computer devices, he had the sense to know if she was digging into the truth, whoever railroaded White into jail would be looking for it. Hawke dug around in Tonya's pack and found a flash drive. He stuck it into the computer and opened it. The flash drive appeared to have all the same documents as the computer. With the exception of one that was titled "Bringing Down the Corrupt." He opened it and discovered a manuscript. That was why she was so determined to dig for the truth. She was writing a book about the events.

He clicked out of the flash drive, pulled it out of the computer, and tucked the drive into the bottom of the sheath in his boot where he kept his knife.

Picking up the pot of tepid stew, he ate, filling his belly and letting Dog have the rest. Tomorrow, he'd load Tonya's belongings onto Horse and head for home. He'd go through all of Ms. Cox's notes and see if he couldn't figure out how she'd discovered the information she did and why she hadn't gone to authorities other than the police. It was obvious the police had railroaded White. But why?

《》《》《》

Hawke breathed a sigh of relief as he walked Jack up to the truck and trailer at Pittsburgh campground. He'd nearly fallen off the horse twice, whipping his head around at a sound that made him think someone was following. Dog had appeared just as nervous. He wasn't sure if it was knowing two deaths had been caused because an innocent man was sent to prison or because there was someone watching them.

He was too tired and wanted to get the evidence he had back to the Oregon State Police, seeing as how there was someone in law enforcement in Idaho that couldn't be trusted to try and catch whoever might be following him.

Usually, he unsaddled the animals. Today, he set the pack boxes, including the one with Ms. Cox's belongings into the horse trailer first, then led the two animals in, loosening their cinches but not unsaddling them. He wanted on the road.

"Let's go," he said to Dog, holding the driver's side door open on the pickup.

Dog leaped into the cab.

Hawke slid behind the steering wheel, shut the door, and turned the key, waiting for the plugs to warm up. The lights went off. He turned the key farther to start the engine. Nothing happened.

Someone had sabotaged his truck. There was no other explanation. He'd never had problems with this engine. He kept it up to date with oil changes and any other mechanical thing that needed to be done.

Whoever had been watching and following him had a partner who'd messed with his truck. Did he dare step out and work on it, leaving his back vulnerable? Would they think he knew more than he did? Shit!

He opened his cell phone and called Sergeant Spruel.

"Spruel."

"Sarge, I'm sitting in my truck at Pittsburgh Campground in Idaho. Someone sabotaged it, and I'm pretty sure I'm being watched."

"Why are you being watched? I heard they air flighted the woman to a Boise hospital last night."

"You need to make sure she has someone keeping her safe." He told Spruel what he'd read on the computer and how he figured there were some corrupt officials involved.

"I have the flash drive in my boot sheath if anything happens to me. I just wanted you to know what I know before I step out and work on my truck."

"Be careful, Hawke. I'll see the woman gets protection and send a trooper your way." The connection went dead.

Hawke heaved a deep breath and opened the truck door after flipping the latch to the hood of the vehicle. "Come," he ordered Dog who had already fallen asleep on the passenger seat.

The animal stretched and slowly jumped out of the

cab.

Hawke placed Dog sitting with his back to the front of the vehicle. "Watch," he told the dog, scanning the three other unoccupied vehicles in the parking area before opening the truck hood and leaning under the hood to inspect the motor. He discovered someone had removed the fuel filter. Did the person take it or toss it?

If it was tossed, he could find it and be out of here quicker than waiting for someone to bring him a new one.

He left the hood up and raised his right arm. If he had taken the fuel filter off… He slammed the hood down with his left hand and threw with his right. Hawke kept his eye on the area his hand had pointed to when he threw. He walked to the area and started searching like he would when looking for evidence. After fifteen minutes, he found the filter.

Back at the truck, he opened the hood and replaced the piece. Within an hour of first trying to start his vehicle, he was pulling out of the campground. He called Spruel to tell him he was headed back and what route he was taking. As much as he wanted to check on Tonya Cox, he wanted to get back to Wallowa County and get the flash drive and computer into the hands of people he trusted.

Chapter Twenty

It was evening when Hawke rolled into Alder. His stomach growled. He hadn't stopped for food or coffee anywhere. His eyelids felt like lead gates wanting to lower. He'd navigated down Rattlesnake Grade and back up Buford Grade at a snail's pace to avoid going over the edge.

Parking the truck and trailer in front of the sheriff's office, he checked on Jack and Horse. The two had their hips cocked, half asleep. They were used to trailer travel.

He walked across the road to the Tree Top Café. The deputies and courthouse staff took meals along with the locals who wanted to know what was going on in the county. The door hadn't closed before he heard his name.

"Hawke, what are you doing in here this time of the night?" Ralph, the young county jailer asked. The young man spent all his off time in the café chatting up one of the waitresses who was old enough to be his mother.

"Getting something to eat." Hawke sat a couple stools down from where Ralph perched at the counter.

Janelle, a bleached blonde in her forties, slapped a menu on the counter in front of him. "Coffee?" Her smoker's voice was a turn-off for Hawke but it appeared to have the opposite effect on Ralph.

Hawke turned over the upside-down coffee cup on the counter in front of him. "Please."

She filled it and waited as he read through the menu. He didn't frequent Tree Top enough to know their menu by heart.

"I'll have the double burger and fries." He closed the menu and handed it to the waitress.

"You look tired," Ralph said, picking up his cup of coffee. "I heard you've been on special assignment in Idaho."

"Is that what you heard?" Hawke wasn't surprised the word had reached the county level. The law enforcement in this county worked closely together. They had to with the five-man State police, five-man city police in Alder, and six county deputies covering over three thousand square miles and giving aid to seventy-two hundred people.

"Yeah. You were looking for someone who escaped from a Boise prison." Ralph set his cup down. "Did you find him?"

Hawke nodded and set his cup of coffee down as Janelle placed a red plastic basket with a double burger and fries in front of him.

"Need any sauce or are you just a ketchup man?" she asked.

"Just ketchup. Nothin' fancy for me." He raised the burger to his mouth and took a big bite. This should settle his grumbling stomach and hopefully keep him awake the rest of the way home.

He'd eaten half his fries and burger when he heard what sounded like hooves banging the side of the horse trailer and Dog barking.

Hawke bolted out the door of the café in time to see a man push his way out from behind Horse, who hopped on his hind legs as if he were trying to kick the man.

"Hey! Stop!" Hawke yelled and ran down the street behind the thief carrying Tonya's computer.

A car raced up the street. The back door flew open. The man with the computer dove in and the car engine roared as the bumper aimed for Hawke.

He jammed his feet into the asphalt, stopping his forward momentum and lunged to the side. The car swerved, but he rolled behind a car parked along the street and the vehicle roared out of sight.

Ralph arrived at his side. "You okay?"

"Yeah, just too many athletics lately." Hawke cursed. The only thing he saw about the license on the car was the state—Idaho.

Horse was still carrying on, kicking the side of the trailer and braying. Hawke hauled his aching body off the ground and stumbled to the trailer.

There was a reason the mule was throwing a fit. Someone, most likely the man who swiped the computer, had tied the mule's back end to the side, curling his body in a small space.

Hawke sliced the rope loose, allowing his friend to straighten out not only his body but his attitude. After the animal calmed down, Hawke walked under Horse's neck to check on Jack. He wasn't as territorial as Horse. The person would have only had to push his rump to the side and walk around him or go under his neck. Horse was a threat from both ends. He kicked and he bit.

The pack box was open, the contents scattered as the man looked for the computer. Now he knew for certain someone had been watching him at the cabin, but they must not know he had a copy of the information on the computer.

He threw the scattered items back in the box, patted both Jack and Horse, and closed the back door on the trailer.

"Go finish your dinner. I'll keep an eye on the trailer and report this so they can look for the car," Ralph said.

"They won't be back. They got what they were looking for." Hawke patted the young man on the back. "But I appreciate you letting everyone know about the car." He walked slowly back to the café.

《》《》《》

The next morning, Hawke slept in, fed his animals, and headed to the State Police Office in Winslow. He wanted to get the flash drive in a safe place and read everything on it. He was moving stiffly when he walked through the door into the State Police half of the building.

"Moving kind of slow," Sergeant Spruel said, motioning for Hawke to follow him into his office. He closed the door and waited for Hawke to take a seat. "I've been told to stop digging into the White murder."

Hawke eased down onto the chair and nodded.

"After reading what little I have from the files Ms. Cox gathered, I figured we'd get our hands slapped for looking into it."

"Which means, you are going to stay on it like a ravenous dog." Spruel's sandy colored eyebrows rose.

"After the long week of hiking, hurdling logs, and just about getting run over last night when someone stole Ms. Cox's computer from my horse trailer—"

"I heard about the theft this morning. But I didn't know you were almost run over." Spruel stood up behind his desk, his hands splayed on the top. "Why didn't you call it in?"

Hawke shrugged. "I was tired. Ralph, the deputy at the county jail called in the car. Figured I'd fill you in this morning."

Hawke reached into his boot. "Raise a stink, but we don't need the computer." He pulled the flash drive out of his boot. "Everything we need to dig into these homicides is on here. If you don't mind, I'd like to keep this bit of informatino between you and me."

Spruel nodded. "Did you see who stole the computer?"

Hawke told him everything he remembered. "You might ask Ralph. He saw as much as I did since we both ran out of Tree Top at the same time."

"I'll send someone to take down his statement." Spruel scribbled on a pad. "I'm assuming you want that vacation again…."

A smile quivered on Hawke's lips. The word vacation had been used around him more than he'd ever heard it in his thirty years as a State Trooper. "Unofficially."

Spruel studied him. "Unofficially. Which means

you will check in with me before you talk to anyone, and you will update the files every night. I want to know who you are talking to and what they are saying."

Hawke nodded. "Someone has to have my back. It appears whoever is trying to keep this quiet has no qualms in killing anyone—including a police officer."

"That's why you will check in and keep me informed." Spruel slid the flash drive across the desk to Hawke. "Get what you need off of this then bring it back to me. I don't want it going missing from a state evidence locker."

Picking up the flash drive, Hawke peered into his sergeant's eyes. "You know this could get us both in a lot of trouble."

"We're just seeking the truth. I've never known you to back down from finding the truth behind anything." Spruel stared back at him.

"You have that right. I'll get this back to you as soon as I get it all printed out." Hawke headed to the door. "I'd rather work with paper than having to check something on the computer."

"Just don't let those files out of your sight." Spruel sat back in his chair.

"I won't." Hawke left the office and sat down at his desk. He turned on his computer and slid the flash drive in the port.

Fish and Wildlife Trooper Sullens walked by. "About time you got back into the schedule."

Hawke shook his head. "Every time I've tried to take a vacation it has been cut short. I'm taking it as soon as I get all the reports written."

Sullens slugged him in the shoulder. "We've been taking up your slack the last two weeks."

"I didn't ask to be sent after an escaped convict or the person who killed him." He shrugged. "I'm at that age where I need to rest up now and then." He hated to admit it to a younger trooper but it was the truth and it was something the younger man would relish knowing and be less likely to bother him about a vacation.

Sullens laughed. "You can out hike all of us younger troopers, and you know it. But if you want us to believe you need to rest, I'll pass that around when someone asks where your lazy ass is."

Hawke waved him off and logged into his computer. He pulled up his file on White, adding the fact he'd been nearly run over and lost Ms. Cox's computer. In between writing on the file, he opened files on the flash drive, copying them at the machine next to his computer. He stapled each file singly and by the time he finished his report he had about a hundred pages. This wasn't going to work. He carried the pile of papers into the conference room and found an old three ring binder. He punched holes in the pages, took out the staples, and put them in the binder.

Three hours after he arrived at the office, he placed the flash drive on Spruel's desk and left the building with the binder under his arm.

He called the Rusty Nail, ordered a ham sandwich and chips, and drove to the front of the café.

Justine walked the bag out to his pickup. "Any reason you wanted front door service?"

Hawke smiled. "Too tired to walk in and B.S. with all of you." He handed her a twenty and took the bag.

"Take care," she said, leaning back from the vehicle.

He nodded and pulled away from the curb. The

twenty-minute drive to home with the windows rolled down was exactly what he needed to refresh his mind.

In his apartment over the arena, he opened the bag Justine had handed him and pulled out the sandwich. Then he opened the binder and began reading what Tonya Cox had discovered and saved that pertained to Felix White being railroaded and eventually killed.

Chapter Twenty-one

Hawke made a list of the people he wanted to talk to and the first on his list was Tonya Cox. After another night in his own bed, he drove to Boise to talk with the woman who had started the investigation into the wrongful incarceration of Felix White. The person the Idaho courts said killed her uncle.

At the hospital, he ran into a small, feisty nurse who refused to let him talk with Tonya. "She's only allowed family."

He showed her his badge.

She stared at it and shook her head. "Idaho authorities are the only ones allowed in with the patient."

Hawke walked away. He'd learned the room number and had a plan. Mathews had seemed like a person who wanted to know the truth. Hawke had asked Sergeant Spruel to do a check on the Idaho County Deputy. He'd come back as clean as Mother Theresa.

That meant, Hawke could count on the deputy to help him get in to see Ms. Cox.

Spruel had also given him the number for Deputy Mathews. Hawke dialed the number.

"Mathews."

"This is Oregon State Trooper Hawke. Got a minute to listen?"

"Yeah. I'm on leave. Someone thinks my getting tied up needs to be looked into." The sarcasm in his voice, told Hawke all he needed to know.

"About that. I could use some help in Boise. Any chance you could run down here?" He wasn't going to say too much not knowing who could be listening to the conversation on Mathews end.

"I can be there in two."

The connection went silent. Hawke smiled.

《》《》《》

Mathews was true to his word. Two hours later he called and asked Hawke his location.

"St. Alphonsus Hospital. But let's meet at the sandwich shop on Curtis."

"Copy."

Hawke had left the hospital after his first call to Mathews and drove around, trying to figure out the best place for them to meet. He'd noticed the sandwich shop while returning to the hospital parking lot to wait for Mathews' call.

He headed out of the parking lot. A car that he'd noticed twice while driving around the area, pulled out of a slot three cars over as Hawke drove past. He was being tailed. Word would get back to whoever was in charge of the coverup that he and Mathews saw the Cox woman at the hospital. He'd like to keep their visit under the radar. And he'd like to keep his and Mathews' collaboration quiet for a while yet.

Hawke dialed Mathews. "I have a tail. I'm heading to the Grocery Warehouse off Shum Road. Wait for me behind the building."

"Copy."

Staying the speed limit and driving as if he knew where he was going, Hawke drove the mile and a half to the large bulk grocery store. He had a card to this chain of stores but rarely shopped here for anything other than clothing. The food all came in larger increments than he could use.

He parked in an area that let him leisurely walk to the store as if he planned to go shopping. The car tailing him had also pulled into the lot, but they were still circling. Out of the corner of his eye, he saw the passenger get out.

Once inside the doors, Hawke pulled his hat from his head and took his checkered, long-sleeved shirt off. He was down to his blue t-shirt. Wrapping the hat in his shirt, he walked briskly toward the back of the building using the tall shelving to hide him.

He walked through the large double doors into the area marked employees only.

"Hey, you can't be back here," a man in his forties and wearing a store badge said.

Hawke pulled his badge out from under his shirt. "Just passing through. You didn't see me."

The man stared at him as Hawke continued to the unloading zone and blinked at the bright sunshine.

He glanced both ways down the loading area and lights flashed on a vehicle to his right. Hawke hopped off the loading platform and jogged to the older

Mustang convertible with the top up.

"Glad to see you. We need to get away from here before whoever is following me figures out I ducked out the back," Hawke said, lowering his body into the small confines of the vehicle.

Mathews backed the vehicle and turned around. "Where to?"

"Far from this area." Hawke wanted to scan the parking lot as they drove out to see if the car that followed him was still there, but he didn't want to draw attention to them.

"Who do you think is following you?" Mathews asked, working his way to the interstate and heading west.

"I'm not sure. I don't even know who or why White's records were falsified."

Mathews whistled. "Falsified? What do you mean?"

Hawke studied the deputy. Mathews had proven to be reliable so far. Hawke hoped his instincts were right about the man.

He told Deputy Mathews everything he knew from being picked to find White to the information he'd discovered about White possibly being railroaded into jail and killed before he and Tonya could prove he hadn't killed the Goodwin's or her uncle.

"That's heavy stuff you're trying to prove." Mathews turned off the interstate and pulled into a fast food restaurant. "This place has outside seating."

Hawke liked the way the deputy thought. If they continued this conversation over lunch it was best others weren't in earshot.

They ordered and sat at a table the farthest from the

entrance.

After a couple of bites of his sandwich, Mathews asked, "Why did you want to talk to Ms. Cox?"

"To let her know I have all her information, see if anyone threatened her, to find out exactly what happened to White and Sheridan, and to see if she trusts us to look into who really killed her uncle."

Mathews set his sandwich down and stared at him. "That's a lot to talk about in a short amount of time. You know if someone started tailing you from the hospital, they are watching her."

"I know. And the nurse wouldn't let me in. Even with my credentials."

Mathews stared at him for several minutes. "Then maybe we shouldn't go see her."

Hawke thought Mathews was on the side of justice, now he was beginning to wonder. "I have to talk to her."

The man nodded. "Talk to her. Not see her. I can get a phone and a note to her without us going near the hospital."

"That's risky for the person and Tonya." Hawke didn't like bringing anyone else into whatever they were wrapped up in.

"My sister works for a flower shop. She could deliver flowers, a phone, and a note without anyone thinking anything."

"I like that idea," Hawke said.

"Finish eating and we'll go get a pay as you go phone and see my sister." Mathews smiled at him and continued eating.

Hawke grinned. This was the first time he'd worked with a partner. He liked having another person's input on things. Even though Dog had had many good ideas over the years.

《》《》《》

With the phone in hand, his number added to the list of contacts without his name, and the note he'd written asking Tonya to trust him and give him a call, they walked into a small flower shop in one of the outlying areas of Boise.

"Scotty! What brings you to the big city?" a woman clearly close in age to Mathews asked, giving the deputy a hug.

"Business," Mathews said. He motioned to Hawke. "This is a co-worker."

The woman released her brother and studied Hawke. "I see."

Hawke stepped up to the counter. "We'd like to purchase a flower arrangement for a friend in the hospital."

"Oh, no! Did an officer get hurt?" Mathews' sister exclaimed.

"No." Mathews moved closer to his sister. "We need to get a phone and a message into a patient that we feel is being watched." He handed the phone and Hawke's note to the woman.

"You want the flowers delivered personally by me?"

Hawke had to give the woman credit, she caught on fast.

"Please." Mathews said.

"Where and to who do you want the flowers delivered?"

Hawke rattled off the hospital, room number, and name.

The woman's eyes widened. "That's—"

"No one needs to know about this," Mathews interrupted her.

She nodded. "When do you want the flowers delivered?"

"Today if you can," Hawke said. He'd already reserved a room at a motel, but wanted to get information from Tonya so he knew what he was looking for.

"I'll take them out on my four o'clock delivery."

"How much do I owe you?" Hawke asked.

"If I do a standard get well bouquet it will be Thirty-nine-ninety-nine."

"Does that include a delivery fee?" He picked up a card and wrote, *We hope you get well soon, your hiking buddies*.

"That's another ten dollars."

Hawke paid for the flowers and he and Mathews left the flower shop. "Have you had your sister do things like this before? She seemed to go along with it pretty easily."

Mathews shrugged. "She sent flowers and a message to a girl when I wanted to meet her, but nothing work related."

"You know, if they discover the phone and realize the person who delivered it is related to you, you both could be in trouble."

Mathews stopped at the driver's side of his Mustang. "Our dad was a cop. He died on duty because his superior didn't think a situation was as bad as my dad told him. If I, we, can prove corrupt police or legal system, then both my sister and I are willing to do all we can."

Hawke nodded. Now he knew where Mathews stood and why he was willing to help. "Take me back to my pickup at the warehouse store. But just drop me off on a side street. Then meet me here." He handed Mathews one of the business cards he'd picked up at the motel where he was staying. "I'm room one-thirty on the end."

Chapter Twenty-two

Hawke sat in the motel room, watching Mathews read through the file. He knew hauling around the binder with all the incriminating evidence in it wasn't a good idea, but it was much easier to make notes and plan his next move with the paper rather than clicking through files on a computer.

After reading the last page of what Hawke considered evidence, Mathews stared at him. "If everything Ms. Cox dug up is true, White was incarcerated under false pretenses and possibly killed because he and Ms. Cox were working to prove it."

That statement started bells going off in Hawke's head. "If, as I believe now, Sheridan was working for whoever wanted White killed, why didn't he kill the woman at the same time if she and White were planning to prove the police in Boise were corrupt?"

"Good question. Because that would have cured their problem and with whatever clout it took to put

White in jail, I'm sure Sheridan would have been cleared of any wrongdoing."

Hawke stood and paced the length of the room. "It's not making sense. Any of it. If the people who put White in jail were worried about Tonya having information, which she does, they could easily kill her in the hospital." He knew Spruel had talked to the Idaho State Police. They were the ones guarding the woman, but there hadn't been any attempt on her life.

"You haven't seen the woman in the hospital room. She may not be there."

At Mathews' statement, the hair on the back of Hawke's neck tingled. "Your sister could be walking into a trap."

Mathews pulled out his cell phone and punched numbers.

Hawke glanced at the clock on the table by the bed. 4:15. They had to stop his sister from handing the phone or the note over to the woman until they knew for sure it was Tonya Cox.

"Sis, it's Scotty. Don't deliver the flowers. Or do, get a good look at the woman, but don't deliver the other items." He closed the phone. "It went to voicemail."

Hawke sat down on the bed. What would Spruel think of him if he got an innocent woman mixed up in this? He wished he knew which part of law enforcement was corrupt. They believed it was the city of Boise. That's why Spruel had asked the State Police to guard Tonya. If the State Police weren't involved, they should allow him access, especially if Spruel called over here.

He pulled out his phone and called Spruel. "I need

to get in and see Ms. Cox." He went on to tell how the hospital wasn't allowing him access and how he and Mathews had thought about getting a phone to her, but then realized the woman in the bed might not be Ms. Cox.

"I'll contact the person in charge and have them give you a call." Spruel disconnected.

Mathews phone rang.

"Mathews," he answered. He nodded. "Good. Hang on to it. Did you see the woman?"

He listened.

Hawke had a feeling the call was from Mathews' sister.

The deputy ended the call and looked over at him. "Cassie said the woman had brownish-blonde hair, was thin, hazel eyes, and seemed to be anxious to get out, but her eyes were glazed like someone drugged."

Hawke shook his head. "She shouldn't be that drugged. She had a head injury and a broken arm." He paced. "As soon as I get the call to go see her, that's what I'm going to do. And see about getting her holed up somewhere that no one knows about."

Mathews stared at him. "You're not talking about kidnapping her?"

"That's what it will look like to the people who want to keep her drugged, but no. I'll make sure the State Police are in on it." All he could do now was wait for Spruel's call to spur someone from the Idaho State Police to call him. In the meantime, he'd read the information Tonya collected one more time. Hawke grabbed the reports on White and read who had arrested him. The same city officer wrote up the reports.

"Do you know anything about this guy?" Hawke

pointed to the name.

"No, but we can find out. I'll go get my computer out of my car and we can look him up."

Hawke nodded.

Mathews left the room and Hawke's phone rang.

"Hawke," he answered.

"This is Trooper McCord with the Idaho State Police. I was instructed to let you know you can come over and talk with Ms. Cox," a female voice said.

"Thank you for calling so promptly. Have you been filled in on why you are watching her?" he asked.

"I have been fully apprised of the circumstances," McCord replied as Mathews came through the door.

Hawke watched Mathews set up his computer as he explained to the trooper his idea for getting Ms. Cox out from under the watch of those who might harm her.

"You do realize I'll have to let my superior know."

He couldn't tell by her tone if she disapproved or felt her superior would disapprove. "As long as you tell him afterwards and know I'm not telling anyone where the woman will be."

There was a long moment of silence.

"You do know that by knowing this ahead of my superior and not relaying the information could get me reprimanded."

He hoped she had some compassion for people who were unjustly charged. "I can't give you all the details because they aren't clear to me and my colleague just now, but one injustice has been done by law enforcement, and I'm trying to keep a second one from happening."

Again, the silence. Then a long drawn out sigh. "I'll do my best. But if my butt is kicked, I'll find you and kick yours."

Hawke grinned. He was looking forward to meeting this trooper. "It's a deal. How can I get Ms. Cox without being seen?"

They worked out the logistics of getting him in and the two of them out. "See you in forty-five." He hung up and found Mathews tapping keys on his computer. "Find anything?"

"The city cop who wrote the arrest files is retired and living in Arizona. That's a long way to send someone to ask him questions." Mathews glanced up.

"And a lot of paperwork. You come up with anything else?" Hawke was trying to think if he knew anyone in Arizona who might check up on the retired cop without needing to go through proper channels.

"I figure there has to be something to do with the White's family home that started all of this. Because Felix was the only survivor when he left for school. Why someone didn't just purchase the land from him rather than set up this elaborate scheme to frame him, I don't understand." Mathews glanced up. "You need me to help with snatching the woman?"

Hawke shook his head. "Just the keys to your car. The people watching me know my pickup."

The deputy dug into his pocket and tossed the car keys to Hawke. "I'll keep digging through the online stuff."

Hawke walked to the door.

"Is this where you plan on stashing the woman?"

Hawke shook his head. "Nope. I'll send you the address when I get there."

"Wait a minute. How far are you taking my Mustang?" Mathews gave his full attention to Hawke.

"I'm taking it across the state line. It will be easier to watch Ms. Cox and do our digging when we don't have to worry about interference from over here. And besides, we believe she killed Sheridan in Oregon, which technically makes her our suspect."

"Just don't drive too fast and check the oil every hundred miles. She's an oil guzzler." Mathews returned his gaze to the computer and called out before Hawke closed the door. "Hey! How am I getting there? Where's your pickup keys?"

Hawke stuck his head back in the room. "Leave my pickup here. I'll send someone for it later." He placed money on the end of the table by the door. "Have your sister take you to a car rental place."

《》《》《》

At the hospital, Hawke drove up to the Emergency Room doors. He'd asked Trooper McCord to escort Ms. Cox down to the Radiology area. He walked in the Emergency Entrance, scanned the area, and followed the signs to Radiology.

The emergency room was as chaotic as he'd hoped. He spotted Tonya in a wheelchair, with a hospital gown and a robe. A small Black woman dressed in a blue trooper uniform stood behind the chair, scanning the hallway.

Hawke walked up to the two. "Trooper McCord, I'm Hawke."

The trooper's eyes narrowed. "I.D."

He pulled his badge out from under his shirt and flipped open his wallet to show her his driver's license to show the picture matched the name.

"Badge was all I needed. Your Sergeant told me your badge number."

She'd been checking up on him to make sure she handed the woman over to the right person. He liked that. She was thorough.

Hawke nodded. He held out a bag with clothes he'd brought from Tonya's backpack. "Want to take Ms. Cox into a restroom and help her change? I doubt we'll get out of here with her in a hospital gown."

Tonya took the bag, peeked in, and looked up at Hawke. "These are my clothes."

"From the pack you left behind." He nodded to the hallway with a restroom sign. "Get changed. The longer we linger here the more apt we are to be discovered by the wrong people."

The two walked to the restroom.

Hawke placed the wheelchair beside another one sitting along the hallway.

By the time he came back to where he'd met the two women, they walked out of the restroom. The bandage was gone from Tonya's head. A bandanna he'd added to the clothes from his bag was tied hippy style around her head to hide the stitches. Her left arm was in a cast and a sling.

"Thanks again. If you get any trouble over this have your superior call Spruel," Hawke said to McCord.

"You can bet I will. Take care, Tonya." The trooper pivoted and headed to the elevator.

Hawke led Tonya out through the emergency room, into the parking lot, and had her settled in the Mustang before he let out the breath he'd been holding. He didn't fear the people he'd been avoiding seeing them, he'd feared the security at the hospital going after him.

"Where are you taking me?" Tonya asked, settling into the passenger seat and tipping her head back.

"Do you still need doctors care or any medicine?" he asked instead.

"They were going to let me go yesterday, but someone convinced them to keep me through today. I just have a slight headache. They said it was normal. I could take Ibuprofen if it gets too bad." She eased her head sideways and peered at him. "Where are you taking me?"

"Some place where we can piece together the information you've gathered and figure out who killed Sheridan." He put the car in drive and left the hospital, pulling onto the Interstate headed west.

"You must have found my computer if you're saying we need to dig deeper." She closed her eyes and continued. "You saw the evidence I'd gathered that proved Felix wasn't guilty of murder. He was a gentle man. He'd never kill anything. He told me the day he arrived at the cabin and found everyone, including my uncle bleeding, he tried to help them, but he was too late. He couldn't believe what he'd seen. He was in shock when they found him."

Hawke let her talk. He was curious about how much she had in her head that she hadn't put down on the computer files.

Her voice wavered. "Did you know they think I killed Sean? I didn't. I arrived in time to hear the shot. I peeked in the window, saw Sean lying on the floor, and figured I'd better get out of there before whoever did it saw me."

"I'm curious. If you saw Sheridan kill White, why did you go with him?" Hawke glanced over at the pale woman.

"Because he said if I didn't go with him, he'd tell you that I killed Felix and everyone would believe him over me. And, I thought he'd lead me to the person responsible for Felix's going to jail, and since Sean shot him, the person responsible for his death." Her head moved ever so slightly. "I should have gone to someone with what I'd found. Felix and Sean would both still be alive."

"If you did that you could be the one dead," Hawke said. "If you had taken your findings to the wrong person you could have ended up a missing person."

She shuddered. "I might as well be since my actions caused two deaths."

"Not your actions. The actions of the person who started it all. That's who we are going to go after." Hawke headed out of the Boise traffic anxious to cross the state line and be under the jurisdiction of his home state.

Chapter Twenty-three

Hawke only stopped the vehicle once to check the oil, add fuel, get some snacks, and let Tonya use a restroom. Five hours later, he pulled up to his mom's house on the Umatilla Reservation outside of Pendleton, Oregon.

He'd tossed the possibilities of where to hide Tonya around in his head on the drive and had decided, they'd need computer access. Going to Charlie's Hunting Lodge in the Eagle Cap Wilderness would make it hard for someone to sneak up on them, but they wouldn't have internet access. Here, he'd have the Rez police look out for unknown vehicles and they could use his mom's internet as long as he paid to up her data.

"What are we doing here?" Tonya asked. She'd slept the first three hours of the trip but had been reading all the signs since their pitstop.

"This is the Umatilla Reservation and this is my mom's house." Hawke slipped out of the car and stretched.

Two boys about seven-years-old tumbled out of his mom's house, rough-housing. They stopped at the sight of him. Or rather, the car. They ran over to the Mustang and put their hands on the hood.

"Cool car," one of them said, his eyes never leaving the lines of the vehicle.

"I'd say thanks, but it belongs to a friend, so don't drool all over the hood or you'll have to wash it." Hawke walked around to the passenger side and helped Tonya out.

The shorter of the two boys looked up at Hawke. "You Mimi's son? The one who's a cop?"

Hawke nodded.

The two yelled and ran around the side of the house.

Tonya chuckled. "I take it you've been here before."

"I have, but I've not met those two before." Hawke walked Tonya up the dirt walk to the cement steps and knocked once, before opening the door and pushing Tonya through.

His mom walked out of the kitchen wiping her hands on her colorful flowered apron. "Hawke what a wonderful surprise." She said this as she studied Tonya, speculation glittering in her eyes.

"Mom, this is Tonya. She and I will be staying with you for a few days." Hawke eased Tonya through the small, tidy living room and into his mom's favorite room, the kitchen.

"I see, for how long?" Mom hurried to the cupboard, pulled out two glasses and placed them on the table.

Tonya sat, her gaze slowly taking in the well-used kitchen.

Hawke hadn't really noticed the faded wallpaper and worn vinyl flooring until he looked at it through the eyes of a stranger. He should get someone to come replace the flooring. He'd purchased a new cookstove for her two years ago. She'd refused a dishwasher, claiming washing dishes kept a person grounded.

"How long have you two been seeing each other?" his mother asked, filling the glasses with iced tea.

Hawke raised his hands. "No, we aren't seeing each other. Tonya is under protective custody."

The pitcher hit the table with a thud as Mimi put her hands on her hips. "You brought trouble to my door again?"

"Again?" Tonya asked, her expression relaying she found this exchange interesting.

"There was never any trouble when I brought Kitree here," Hawke said, trying to figure out how to get his mom to warm up to the idea of using her house as a base of operations.

"And why haven't you brought her back to visit?"

The sadness in his mom's voice made Hawke feel like the small boy who hadn't been able to save her from his stepfather's blows.

"I promise, this summer, I'll bring her to visit. She's been asking when she could come see you again." His words brought the light back into his mom's eyes.

The back door banged open and one of the two boys that had run their hands over the Mustang stopped inside the door.

"What did you want, Phillip?" Mimi asked.

"Annie says we can't swing unless we give her a

carrot. Can Gray and I have a carrot?" The boy kept his eyes on Hawke as he talked.

Mimi laughed, "That Annie has become the queen of the backyard." She opened the refrigerator and handed the boy two carrots. "Tell her these are to allow you to swing the rest of the day, Mimi says."

The boy nodded and ran out the door with the carrots.

"Is that the same Annie I met several trips back?" Hawke asked.

"The one and the same." Mimi smiled.

"I take it her grandparents gave up on getting her from her father?" Hawke had remembered meeting the father and daughter before. The man had thought Hawke was there to take his daughter away.

"James managed to talk the grandparents into keeping Annie one weekend a month and not taking her completely away. But they spoil her and so does her father. She has become a handful." Mom sat down. "Tell me why you brought Tonya here."

Hawke only hit the high points. Tonya had information that other people wanted, and he, Tonya, and a friend who would be joining them, were going to work on finding everything they needed to keep her safe.

"I'm going to up your data on your internet so we can use your computer and service to do most of the digging." Hawke held up his hand before Mimi could say a word. "I'm paying for the upgrade and I'll pay this month's electric bill." He saw her glance toward the cupboards. "And I'll give you money to get groceries."

She smiled. "You're such a wonderful son. If only

you'd be as obliging with grandchildren."

Tonya laughed and picked up her iced tea when Hawke glared at her.

He'd texted his mom's address to Mathews when they stopped for gas. His phone vibrated. It was Mathews.

On the road. Should be there in four hours.

Settling in. Hawke replied.

"Did you bring clothes with you?" his mom asked.

"I'll run home tomorrow when Mathews is here and get some. I thought Tonya could borrow some of the clothes Miriam left behind." He knew his mom had saved everything he and his sister left behind when they moved out. And his sister had always loved clothes. There was a closet, dresser, and boxes of clothes, though outdated, they would fit Tonya.

"I'll show you to my daughter's room," Mom said, moving through the kitchen door.

Tonya stood but looked at him. "Is Miriam your sister?"

"Yeah. She doesn't live around here, so you can stay in her room and use her clothes. She won't care because they aren't the latest styles."

"That's a bit callous." Tonya didn't move toward the door.

"We have never seen eye to eye. Once she hit eighteen, she lit out and rarely comes home to see mom. You better go, or she'll be setting out clothes for you to wear."

She frowned and headed down the hallway to the three bedrooms. His mom's, his, and Miriam's.

Hawke went into the living room and walked over to the corner table with his mom's dinosaur computer.

He'd tried to buy her a tablet for Christmas the year before, but she'd insisted her computer worked for her needs. She kept up on the reservation news and committees, emailed some friends, followed Pinterest, and had a Facebook profile mainly to follow relatives and the people who brought their children for her to babysit.

He turned the computer on and waited for it to boot up. The tower next to the television-tube shaped monitor whirred to life. He hoped they didn't freeze up her computer using it to dig for information.

The sound of children playing in the backyard and the chatter of women talking down the hall were sounds he seldom heard. Living above the stable he heard, snorts, neighing, and foot stomping with the occasional sound of a vehicle coming and going. He hadn't realized how relaxing the sound of happy voices could be.

"I'll add extra potatoes to the pot," his mom said, stepping into the living room.

"Good idea. Hey, what is your password for your internet account?" He'd pulled up her account so he could upgrade it to more data and hopefully faster connection.

"Your full name and birthdate." She disappeared.

Hawke shook his head. He should have known she wouldn't use something no one could figure out. He typed the information into the password, making the first letter of each name uppercase and adding his birthdate at the end.

He was in. He upgraded and made all the changes to the account he thought they would need. He'd have to put it back down before the end of the month or his mom would be arguing with the internet provider when she received her next bill.

He opened the search engine and typed in Felix White. He wanted to know more about the man before he went to jail, if that were possible.

Tonya wandered into the room. "What are you doing?"

"Looking up the history on Felix White."

"That's in my computer," she said.

Hawke stared at her. "I didn't see it."

"It's in the manuscript." She sat in the chair next to the computer table. "Where is my computer?"

Hawke twisted in the chair and faced her. "Whoever wants to keep you quiet has it."

She glared at him. "That has everything we need."

He raised his hands. "I found the flash drive you had all the same information on. I gave that to my superior. And I have all of that in paper in a binder. I left it at the motel with Mathews. He'll be bringing it with him. Can you give me a quick overview?"

"Mathews? Who is that?"

"The deputy you hit over the head and left tied up in your uncle's cabin." Hawke studied her.

Her face reddened. "I thought he might be the person who killed Sean. I didn't want to wait and ask him who he was when I could knock him in the head and get away." She touched her temple where the stitches were. "Except your mule wouldn't let me get on the horse. He knocked me down and I hit my head. I thought sure he was going to stomp me into the ground before I blacked out."

"He's not vicious, just protective of Jack." Hawke studied her. "What did you plan to do at the cabin?"

"I was going to put all my evidence together in one report, I guess you'd call it, and submit it to the state police for them to investigate. I know it was the Boise City Police who falsified the documents on Felix."

Hawke nodded. "We're working with Idaho State Police. That's why Trooper McCord handed you over to me."

"I figured as much." Tonya leaned forward to see the monitor. "When will Mathews arrive with my information?"

"In about four hours. In the meantime, fill me in."

"I found evidence that Felix White wasn't anywhere near the places he allegedly was arrested. According to him the first time he was pulled in, was on the assault charge." Her face puckered in anger. "Which he didn't do. But there were witnesses who said they saw him."

"Why didn't he fight the charges? Didn't he have someone he could contact?" Hawke couldn't see how someone who wasn't even present could be sent to jail for a crime he didn't commit.

Tonya shrugged. "I don't know. He doesn't have any family he knows of, and he really didn't have any friends he could call." She sighed. "Until I started digging into his case to find out why he killed my uncle, he didn't have anyone who would listen to him."

Hawke was beginning to feel emotionally attached to the young man Sheridan killed. Instead of being a killer, he was a victim.

She continued. "He went to the homestead when he was released from jail after the assault charge because he'd hidden information in the cabin before he went to jail that would prove one of the water companies was using river water, and not processing it, for a subdivision that was built in two-thousand-and-nine."

Hawke whistled and leaned back in his chair. "White was sent to jail to keep him from spilling about water contamination?"

She nodded. "There were a lot of political people with money invested in the subdivision."

"Had he already approached someone about the water issue?" Hawke could see if White had pointed his finger and vowed to cause trouble, that someone paid the police to get rid of White without killing him. It was interesting that while the person had no qualms giving people who bought in his subdivision bad drinking water, he wouldn't resort to murder. But in the end, they had, killing the Goodwins and Theodore Shoat. Was that to frame White or was there another reason behind their killings?

"He had taken his findings to his professor at the college. In fact, Felix wrote his dissertation on *The Stealing of Surface Water to Hide the Dwindling Groundwater*."

"Did you talk to his professor? Did White name names in the dissertation?" Hawke could tell by the down turn of the woman's mouth something had happened to the paper.

"I found out the professor moved to another country and when I tried to find him, I didn't have any luck. When I asked about his papers at the college, they waved me to a room in the basement full of boxes. None of them were marked. It would take a hundred people a long time to go through those boxes and find any paper if it was there."

The paper and professor were a dead end. He had

another thought. "Tell me why your uncle was at the Goodwins the day they were all killed? Had White sold the cabin?"

She shook her head. "The Goodwins were one of the families Felix had talked to. They had a child that kept being diagnosed with giardia after moving to the subdivision. They were a clean family, no animals, the mother was a stay at home mom, so the child wasn't left at a day care. They had the water tested and that's when they started asking others in the subdivision about their health." She sighed. "My uncle had known Felix his whole life and had gone to the cabin to welcome him home when he was released. I'm not sure what the Goodwins were doing there. Maybe they had gone to do the same thing, since Felix was the only person who was helping them gather information before he was wrongly put in jail."

"Someone knew they were there, or someone had gone to the White homestead to kill Felix and turned the tables by killing the only people who believed in him." Hawke studied the woman. She had drawn her knees up to her chest, hugging her legs with her good arm. The woman sitting on his mom's chair didn't seem near as calculating and in control as the woman he'd met in Hells Canyon.

"Do you know which subdivision it was?" He needed to find out the names of the people involved.

Chapter Twenty-four

The Sunset Rose Subdivision was easy to find. Hawke had found all the landowners who profited from the sale of the land, the development company, and a list of management companies that ran the subdivision by the time Mathews arrived.

Hawke opened the front door and a brand new shiny blue Mustang convertible sat next to the older model. Mathews walked up the path to the front door, lugging a computer bag, a duffel bag, and the binder.

"It looks like you enjoyed the drive here," Hawke said with sarcasm.

Mathews' smile beamed even wider. "I still love my old girl but these newer models are fun to drive."

Stepping out of the way, Hawke motioned for the deputy to get inside. "I haven't had a chance to let the reservation police know who owns the cars and to keep a lookout. I'll do that once you're settled."

Tonya stood, wringing her hands in front of her.

"Deputy Mathews, this is Tonya Cox." Hawke introduced the two.

Mathews ran a hand across the back of his head. "I hope this time you don't hit me when I'm not looking." He deposited everything he was carrying onto the couch and held out a hand. "You can call me Scott."

"I'm sorry for hitting you. I thought you were the person who'd killed Sean." She grasped his hand and released it quickly before lowering back down in the chair and elevating her arm in the cast.

"You saw the person who killed Sheridan?" Mathews asked.

She shook her head. "I arrived when I guess the person was setting the place on fire. Because I looked in the window to make sure it was the place Sheridan was to meet someone. I saw him lying on the floor with blood seeping out from under him and ran back to Idaho. I didn't know about the fire until later."

"And who is this?" Mimi asked, walking into the living room from the kitchen.

"Mom, this is Deputy Mathews. He's helping me protect Tonya." Hawke motioned for Mathews to greet his mom.

Her brow was furrowed and her eyes narrowed. "Your name is Matthew or Mathews?"

"I'm Scott Mathews. You can call me Scott." Mathews held out his hand to shake.

Mom smiled at him. "Come on in, dinner is ready." She turned and headed into the kitchen.

"We've been summoned," Hawke said, motioning the other two into the kitchen where his mom had set the table she'd fed he and his sister on after she'd remarried.

The table had a plastic tablecloth with summer flowers. The woman had always used the plastic cloth because it was easier to scrub it down than spend the water and money washing a cloth one in the washing machine every other day.

Mom orchestrated where they sat. Placing Hawke across from her, Tonya on her left, and Mathews on her right.

"I hope you like soup. I added more vegetables when I realized I would be feeding more than myself and the children for lunch tomorrow." Mimi untied her apron, draped it across the back of her chair and sat.

"It looks good," Hawke said, grabbing a homemade roll. His mom had worked hard to figure out how to make yeast rolls. The last few years, she'd finally found the secret. He remembered years of eating rolls as hard and chewy as tennis balls. Now they were light and fluffy.

"Thank you for letting us stay with you, Mrs. Hawke," Mathews said, dishing up soup.

Hawke's mom snorted. "I wasn't asked. My son just showed up as if I am a motel who welcomes anyone any time. And call me Mimi."

Tonya stared at him. "You didn't even ask your mom if we could stay here? You've put her in danger without asking her permission."

Hawke glared at Tonya. He'd left out a lot when he'd arrived and said they were staying. He hadn't planned on his mom knowing about the danger, because he'd hoped to have this solved and be gone before it arrived here.

"Danger? You said Tonya was here for protection. Is someone going to come into my house and kill me in my sleep? What about the children? I don't want harm to come to any of the children I watch." Mimi stared at him as if she'd never seen him before.

"Mom, if I thought any danger would come to you or the children I wouldn't have come here. We needed some place no one would come looking. The reservation is the best place." He nodded to Mathews. "We're going to have a chat with the Reservation Police tonight and let them know we are here and to watch for vehicles with Idaho plates."

"You think I feel any better knowing our police are looking out for me?" She ripped the roll on her plate apart with her fingers. "Someone walked into Trixie Red Horse's place last week during the day and walked out with her new microwave and tablet. You know what the police said? 'You should have been more careful'. How more careful can you get than locking your doors?" She put up a finger. "Which until only a few years ago we didn't have to do. People knew to leave others belongings alone."

"You'll be safe with Mathews and me here. I promise. If I had thought trouble would actually come here, I wouldn't have used your house to hide a witness." Hawke dished up the soup. The best way to appease his mom was to compliment her cooking.

He sipped the beefy broth and bit into the perfectly cooked vegetables and told his mom it was her best soup ever.

The expression on her face and glint in her eyes said she knew he was trying to smooth things over, but she wasn't too angry to not accept the compliment.

The other two also commented on the tasty meal.

While Tonya helped his mom with the dishes, he

and Mathews walked outside. Hawke dialed up the Reservation Police station and asked for one of the officers on patrol to come by Mimi Shumack's place in Mission.

About ten minutes later a patrol car rolled down the street.

Hawke and Mathews had been discussing the new information Hawke had discovered and that Mathews had come to a dead end on White's family.

The vehicle pulled up alongside the rental Mustang. A short, thin man wearing the Reservation police uniform stepped out of the patrol car.

"These your vehicles?" he asked.

"Yes." Hawke stood and walked out to meet the man. The officer was in his thirties, narrow faced, dark suspicious eyes.

"Why did you call for a patrol man? You don't live here." The officer kept his hands on his utility belt.

"I'm Gabriel Hawke, Mimi's son." He drew the state patrol badge out from under his shirt. "This is Deputy Mathews from the Idaho County Sheriff's Office."

Mathews pulled his badge case out of his pocket and flipped it open for the officer to read.

"What are you two doing here?" The man still seemed skeptical. Bright was the name on his name tag.

"We wanted to let you and your force know that we are here protecting a witness and would like your cooperation in keeping an eye out for vehicles with Idaho plates and patrolling this neighborhood more in the next few days." Hawke stood with his arms crossed. Not to intimidate but to show they were counting on help.

"I'll have to tell the Tribal Police Chief. And let the others in this area know." Officer Bright said.

"That is what we'd like. As long as all of this doesn't go off the Reservation," Hawke said. "We don't want the people looking for our witness to get wind of where we are."

Bright nodded. "Will these cars be here the whole time?"

"I'll be taking the rental car tomorrow, but I'll be back by evening." Hawke needed to run get clothes, tell his landlords he'd be gone a little longer, and update Spruel.

The officer nodded and slid back into his patrol vehicle, a small SUV.

"He wasn't very friendly," Mathews said, as they walked back to the house.

"Everyone, especially the police, are leery of strangers on the reservation." Hawke had been following the growing rise in missing and murdered women on reservations.

"But you're one of them." Mathews stammered. "I mean if your mom lives here, you're Native American."

Hawke slapped the deputy on the back. "Yes, I am American Indian and I lived half of my childhood on this reservation. But that young officer has never seen me."

Inside, they found Tonya reading the binder with the printouts from her files. She glanced up. "You do have critical information in this binder."

Hawke sat down in the chair next to the couch, where the woman sat. "Did you name the stockholders and builder of the Sunset Rose Subdivision?"

She nodded. "If you'd had a chance to read this

manuscript, you'd see I named all the people who knew the water was being piped illegally from the nearby river." She flipped through the pages, stopped, and tapped a page before handing the binder to Hawke.

He scanned the page to the area where she'd tapped her finger. All the names were the same ones he'd pulled up on the computer except for one. "How did he get involved in this whole mess?" Hawke kept his finger under the name and handed the binder to Mathews.

"You're kidding me?" Mathews set the binder on the coffee table and pulled the laptop he'd been taking out of a bag onto his lap. "What's the password to get internet on my computer?"

Hawke stood up and unplugged the ethernet cable and handed it to Mathews.

"You're kidding." The deputy stared at him as if he'd just handed him a dinosaur egg.

"There's no modem. I tried to get her to put in a modem and use a tablet last Christmas and she said no. The computer works just fine for her."

Mathews dug around in his computer bag and came up with an adapter that he attached to the ethernet cable and plugged into his laptop.

"I do know that Childress was on the Boise Police force before he retired," Mathews said, waiting for his computer to boot up.

"Do you think he paired me with Sheridan thinking once the whole thing was over, I'd go back to Oregon and forget a man I'd been tracking was killed?" If the man had done his homework, he would have learned that the Oregon State Police Officer had a one-track mind when it came to finding the end of the trail, whether it was tracking, murder, or drugs.

"I'd guess that would be why." Mathews leaned back. "Here's his file."

Hawke drew his chair up beside Mathews and started reading.

Childress had amassed several honors.

The deputy put *Herman Childress, Boise Idaho* into an internet search engine and many articles and photos popped up. "Looks like he has his fingers in just about everything that has to do with police work. Head of the SAR organization in Idaho, Retired Police Officers, and on the Ada County Planning and Zoning Commission."

"That would be a conflict of interest," Tonya piped up.

"That it would." Hawke skimmed the articles as Mathews scrolled slowly down. "Wait, look at that." The name of the officer who had forged all the police reports was linked to Childress. It was his brother-in-law. "I think we have a clue as to how to find the officer who forged the arrest reports."

He wrote the man's name down. "Find out if the man is married to Childress's sister or is his wife's brother."

Hawke wrote all that they'd discovered so far onto the sheet of printer paper he'd pulled out of his mom's printer. It would have to do until he had a logbook. He'd left the one he'd been using in the glovebox of his pickup.

"It is his wife's brother." Mathews looked up. "We could have a trooper go to their house tomorrow and ask Mrs. Childress for her brother's information."

Hawke shook his head. "She'd tell her husband,

and he'd contact the brother to get lost." He studied Tonya. "See if you can come up with anything on the wife or the brother-in-law that Tonya could call and do an over the phone interview. While interviewing, she could ask for a way to contact her brother to get a quote from him."

Mathews and Tonya both smiled.

"That's a great plan." Tonya sat on the arm of the chair where Mathews was clicking away on the laptop keyboard.

They were reading through the files together when Mimi walked into the room. Hawke smiled at his mom. She hadn't changed much the last twenty years other than more gray hair and a few more wrinkles. She'd been seventeen when she'd become pregnant and had him. A young mother, but she'd been a fierce mother. Protecting him and finally giving his father the ultimatum to bring them here. She didn't want to be a widow to a man that was alive. They'd divorced, he'd brought her to the Umatilla Reservation, and they never saw him again.

She walked across the room and put a hand on his shoulder. "Where will Scott sleep?" she asked.

"I'm fine on the couch," Mathews answered. "I have a sleeping bag in my car."

"Will you three be up much longer? I'm going to take my tired body to bed. I have children arriving by seven in the morning."

"We'll be quiet and go to bed soon, too." Hawke gave his mom a one-armed hug. "Sweet dreams."

She peered at him. "It's been a long time since I heard that phrase around here."

"You said it to me and Miriam every night until we

moved out." He started to smile then stopped. She'd always made sure to come say that to them after her second husband had drank too much and been physically abusive. It was as if she wanted them to forget what they'd heard.

"The last few years I knew I didn't need to say it anymore, but it had become a way I could see you before the lights were turned out for the night. Make sure you were okay." She kissed the top of his head. "Good night," she said to the other two and walked out of the room and down the hall.

Tonya cleared her throat. Hawke pulled his attention from his mom's departure.

The woman studied him with interest. "What made you become a State Trooper?"

She wanted to understand his past after his mom's comments. "Because I wanted to help women and children like my family." He stood. "Did you come up with a way to interview Mrs. Childress and her brother?"

"It seems their father worked on the restoration for the capital building. There are several archived stories about him being one of the few people in the area who knew how to restore decorative plaster and oversaw the work in nineteen-ninety-eight." Tonya glanced up. "I could easily work that angle. He's dead. I could contact his daughter and his son to see what they remember about their father's work on the building." She plucked a piece of paper from the printer and started jotting down questions. "Scott, pull up a phone number for Mrs. Childress."

"I'll leave you two to finish up." He walked to the hallway and stopped. "I'll lock the back door. You do the same to the front after you get your sleeping bag."

Mathews waved as he rattled off numbers to Tonya.

Hawke had a feeling the three of them would get to the bottom of all of this. And hopefully without anyone, including innocent people like his mom, getting hurt.

Chapter Twenty-five

The sun was in his eyes as Hawke drove from Mission, over the tollgate pass to Elgin and on into Wallowa County. Mathews was right, the new Mustang drove like a dream, but it was uncomfortable for his six-foot frame.

He'd left his mom's house as she'd wandered into the kitchen to start a pot of coffee. Entering Winslow, he'd planned to go straight to the office, but his growling stomach wouldn't allow his foot to let up on the throttle. He drove by the station, headed to the Rusty Nail for breakfast.

Hawke parked behind the café so no one would see him get out of the fancy Mustang. He didn't need rumors spreading he was on the take because he'd pulled up in a car that was ineffective six months of the year in this county.

The door jingled as he walked in. The farmers around a table to his left, raised their cups of coffee in a salute. He nodded. The group of businessmen shoveling food in and talking at the same time, raised a hand, some holding a triangle of toast. His usual spot at the counter was empty. He wondered if anyone ever sat on the stool.

"Morning stranger," Justine said, pouring coffee in the cup on the counter in front of him.

"Morning," He sipped the coffee as she waited for his order. He should have stayed at home and breakfasted on his mom's mouth-watering pancakes, but he wanted to get his clothes, update Spruel, and get back as soon as he could.

"What are you eating this morning? The usual?" Justine asked.

"No, I'll have French toast and bacon." He smiled. That was one thing his mom never made right. It was either too soggy or too dry. He'd taste her pancakes tomorrow morning.

Justine relayed his order to the cook at the same time Merrilee, the seventy-something owner of the Rusty Nail, walked out of the kitchen.

"Hawke, there's been a guy in here twice looking for you." Her watery, faded blue eyes peered at him. "I thought you were on vacation?"

"I am." He wondered who could be looking for him. "Did the guy give you a name?"

She shook her head. Her orange tinted hair, that had been teased into a beehive-looking pile on her head, swayed. "He said he'd prefer to surprise you."

Hawke didn't like surprises. Especially, when he was a target for knowing too much. "Did you tell him to look for me at the Trembleys?" He didn't want trouble to end up on his landlord's door step.

"Nope. Told him to ask over at the State Police

building down the road." She smiled. "He didn't take too kindly to that suggestion."

He grinned. "Thanks, Merrilee. I don't think it was an old friend."

The meal arrived. Hawke ate it as fast as was polite, paid, and headed to the Mustang. Someone was looking for him. He had a feeling it had to do with the fact he and Tonya might possibly know something about the deaths of White and Sheridan, not to mention the Goodwins and Shoat.

He slipped into the Mustang and turned onto the highway running through Winslow. He followed the highway to the State Police office and parked behind with the official vehicles. Once he was inside the building, he breathed a sigh of relief. He had to figure out how to get clothing from his apartment without being seen. Just in case the person knew he lived at the Trembleys.

"Hawke, I didn't expect to see you." Spruel put a hand on his shoulder. "Come in my office."

He knew his superior wanted privacy for their discussion.

Inside, the sergeant closed his office door and said in a low voice. "Is the woman safe?"

"She's being watched by Deputy Mathews. We think we've figured out what started all of the murders." Hawke went on to tell Spruel about the subdivision, the water contamination, and the fact White had written a paper on it and was getting ready to share it with more than his professor when he was put in jail for assault.

"Tonya, Ms. Cox, believes the proof he had was hidden at the homestead. He'd gone there to get it when he found the bodies and hadn't had time to grab it when Sheridan arrived at the cabin." Hawke studied his boss. "I'd like to go back to the homestead and go through the rubble and see if I can find the information, but I just learned there's someone in the county trying to find me. From Merrilee's description, he isn't anyone I know, and he wouldn't give his name."

"You've got yourself wrapped up in multiple murders. It's not a good idea for you to go by yourself to such an isolated area." Spruel tapped a pen on the papers stacked in the middle of his desk. "Any way we could send someone else to look for the information?"

"No one knows what we are looking for. Not even Ms. Cox. She said White never told her where or how he'd hidden it." Hawke knew it was a long shot that they'd even find the evidence since the homestead was buried under the boulders and fallen roof. It would be easier to find all the people who had a part in the murders and question them one by one. "Do we still have the Idaho State Police working with us?"

"Yes. They are on stand-by for whatever help we need."

"Ask if Trooper McCord, and someone she chooses to go with her, can take a hike to the homestead and dig around." Hawke had a feeling the woman who had stuck her reputation on the line for him would do a thorough job looking for the evidence.

"That's the trooper who was watching Ms. Cox?" Spruel narrowed his eyes. "Why did you pick her?"

"Even though she seems like a by the book officer, she was willing to bend the rules a little to keep Ms. Cox safe and to find the truth. I believe she will dig until she uncovers whatever is there. And if the person responsible for all these murders is looking for me, she should be able to get in and out without anyone knowing she was there. It sounds as if no one but Tonya, and now us, knew about the information White had hidden."

Spruel thought on what he said a minute and nodded. "I'll make the call to the Idaho State Police. What is your next step?"

"Calling Herb to bring me some clothes since someone is looking for me, they might be watching the Trembley place. I'm in a rental car and don't want them to follow me back to the reservation." Hawke pulled out his phone.

"What are you doing about the investigation?" Spruel studied him.

"If Ms. Cox gets the number for the officer who falsified the reports on White, I'll call him, if he doesn't cooperate, I'll have you ask for him to be pulled in and questioned in Arizona. We also need all of the people, that I'll email you a list of, to be brought in and questioned in Idaho. But I think, the person who covered this up by manipulating the police reports is Childress. He seems to have his fingers in a lot of things in Idaho."

"Do you want the State Police to bring him in?" Spruel wrote the name on a piece of paper.

"Not until we have more than circumstantial evidence. But it wouldn't hurt to have someone keeping an eye on him. He's going to get nervous when all the people around him are being brought in to be questioned."

Spruel nodded. "I'll contact the Idaho State Police as soon as I get the list of people."

Hawke stood. "I'll keep you updated." He stepped out of the office and Trooper Sullens glanced up from his desk.

"For a man on vacation, you sure do pop in here a lot. You really need to get a life." The trooper studied him. "You don't look like you've been vacationing. You look stressed."

Hawke waved him off. "Vacation is more stressful to me than working." He left the building and sat in the Mustang. Rather than text Herb, he called the man's cell phone.

"You've reached Herb's voicemail. Leave a message."

Hawke didn't leave a message. He contemplated and finally called the house phone.

"Hello?" Darlene answered.

"Hey, it's Hawke. I need a favor." He hated asking her or her husband to bring him clothes, but he really didn't have any other choice.

"I thought you were on vacation?" Her voice held a note of worry.

"It's a long story, I'll tell you when you bring me three sets of clothes to Al's Café in Eagle." Hawke hoped she hadn't been getting ready for one of her social group meetings.

"I can be there in forty-five minutes. And I expect the full story." The line disconnected.

He sighed. There was no way he could give his landlord the whole story. It would be flying around Wallowa County and whoever was looking for him would go back to Childress and tell him they were on to him.

With forty-five minutes to kill, he started up the

Mustang and drove just under the speed limit to Eagle. He made a detour by the apartment over a garage where Dani stayed in the winter months, wondering why she didn't stay there when she flew in during the summer. A rental van sat in the spot where she parked her car and he understood why. The people rented it out during the summer months.

He drove back into Eagle and parked on the side street next to the café. Bart and Lacie Ramsey had purchased the café several years ago and never changed the name.

Lacie greeted him as he walked through the door. "Morning, Hawke. Here for breakfast?"

"Just coffee and a cinnamon roll." He was still full from breakfast at the Rusty Nail, but he always bought something. He was taking up a seat for a paying customer, and he was using their café for a business meeting of sorts. Since it wasn't his usual hangout, he didn't expect the person looking for him to be seated among the half dozen men scattered at the tables and counter.

"Coming right up."

Hawke glanced at his watch. Ten more minutes before Darlene would arrive. He picked up the local paper and scanned the headlines. There was a photo of Charlie's Hunting Lodge and Dani standing next to the plane she flew to haul patrons of the lodge in and out.

He was reading the story about how Dani had brought Charlie's Hunting Lodge to a new group of people when Lacie put the roll and coffee on the table.

"She is something. I think it's great a woman pilot is putting the lodge and this county on tourists' radar," Lacie said.

Hawke grunted. He was proud of Dani and this just proved while she might be a friend, it was ludicrous of him to think she would want to be linked to the likes of him. He'd best stamp out his crush on the woman and stay the hell away.

The door jingled, and he glanced over.

Darlene and Herb both walked through the door. They greeted Lacie and sat at his table.

"What's going on?" Herb asked in a low voice.

"Too much to tell you at the moment. Just you don't know where I am other than I went on vacation." He sipped his coffee and studied the couple who knew him better than anyone else in the county.

"Why didn't you take enough clothes when you 'went on vacation'?" Darlene asked, also in a low tone.

"Can I get you anything besides coffee?" Lacie asked, walking up to the table.

"Just coffee," Darlene said, pushing her cup across the table toward the waitress.

"I'll have what he's having." Herb pointed to the cinnamon roll.

Darlene glared at her husband. "You already had breakfast."

"It's wearing off," Herb shot back.

Lacie filled the two cups and hurried away.

Hawke set his cup down and sunk a fork into the roll. "I hadn't planned to be gone this long or have people looking for me." He glanced at the two people he called friends. "You need to tell anyone who asks about me that I'm on vacation and you don't know where."

"Are you in danger, again?" Darlene asked, her eyes darkening with worry.

"Not me, but the person I'm with." He peered into Herb's eyes. "If you see anything unusual call Sergeant Spruel at the State Police in Winslow. He knows what is going on."

His landlord nodded.

Lacie placed a cinnamon roll in front of Herb. "Will there be anything else?"

"We're good," Hawke said, shoving the bite in his mouth and chewing.

Darlene picked up the fork rolled up in a napkin at her spot and broke off a corner of Herb's cinnamon roll.

Herb stopped his fork halfway to his mouth, watching his wife.

"What? I can't taste it to see if mine's better?" Darlene asked, and popped the bite in her mouth.

Hawke enjoyed spending time with the married couple. It was the bit of relaxation he needed right now. "How are Dog, Jack, Horse, and Boy doing?"

"The horses and mule are fine but Dog is getting lonely. He's been sleeping on the front porch instead of in the stall with Jack," Herb said.

"I should have had you bring him, too."

Herb grinned. "We did. He's out in the pickup with your clothes. He wouldn't let us put the clothing in the vehicle without him."

Hawke laughed. "Then I guess he'll be going with me because you know there will be no way I can get away from him if he sees me."

"That's true," Darlene said, taking another piece of the cinnamon roll.

They finished their coffee and Hawke paid the bill.

At the Trembley's pickup, Dog started howling when he spotted Hawke.

Herb unlocked the doors and opened the back door.

Dog leaped out and straight into Hawke's arms. "Hey, boy. Did you miss me as much as I missed you?" The mangy mutt wiggled and cried.

Hawke set him on the ground, glad Herb had fastened a leash to the dog's collar.

"Here's your clothes." Darlene handed him one of his duffle bags. "Be careful," she added.

"Always. Thanks for doing this. It is safer for everyone." He hugged Darlene and shook hands with Herb.

He led Dog to the fancy car. While he placed the duffel bag in the back seat, Dog christened the back wheel.

Hawke laughed and told Dog to load up. He jumped in the passenger seat his eyes bright.

Behind the steering wheel, Hawke put the car in gear and they headed out of the county. On the way he talked with Mathews, asking him to put together a list of the people who should be questioned about the water contamination.

Before he pulled up to his mom's house in Mission, Spruel called and said Trooper McCord would be headed to the homestead tomorrow with another trooper.

Everything was set. Now to see if they could come up with the evidence that would corner the person responsible for all the deaths.

Chapter Twenty-six

Mathews and Tonya were seated together on the couch when Hawke walked in the house. They both looked up.

Dog walked over and sniffed them. He remembered them because his tail wagged at Mathews, but he planted his butt on the floor in front of Tonya and stared. He still didn't trust the woman.

"I'll put this in my room and then make the call to Mrs. Childress' brother," Hawke said, moving through the room and into the hall. He heard his mom's voice and a child's in the kitchen.

After dropping his duffel on the bed, he wandered into the kitchen. It was a year older version of Annie sitting in the chair at the table. Wet paths ran down her cheeks.

He pulled up a chair and grabbed one of the cookies on the plate. "Do you remember me?"

She sniffed and studied him. "You stole a cookie

from me."

Hawke laughed. "I did. But I brought you another one."

She nodded.

"Why are you so sad?" He bit into the cookie and watched her take a deep breath and glance at Mimi.

"She's learning it's not good to always be the one giving the orders," his mom said. "We were discussing how you need to treat people how you would like to be treated. Not like they are your slaves. That's bad karma. If you are nice to people, they will be nice to you. You aren't special. You may have gifts, like singing, drawing, good with numbers, but you yourself are no more special than the person next to you."

Hawke nodded. "That's true. We are all the same. It is how we treat one another that makes us special."

Dog wandered in the kitchen, sniffing. He by-passed the piece of cookie Hawke held out for him and walked up to Annie. He placed his head on her lap and she smiled, petting his head.

"Where did the dog come from?" the girl asked.

"He lives with me. His name is Dog." Hawke unhooked the leash dragging from the animal's collar.

Annie scrunched up her face. "He's too pretty and nice to be called Dog. His name is Prince." She slid off the chair and headed to the back door. "Can Prince play with us?"

Hawke shrugged. "If he wants to, but his name is Dog."

"Come on, Prince, let's play." Annie opened the back door.

Dog glanced at Hawke, then walked to the door and went out with the child.

Mimi laughed. "I think you need to change his name to Prince."

Hawke sighed and picked up the plate of cookies. "I'll take these in the living room for Tonya and Mathews."

His mom giggled. "They are becoming very close friends."

He was wondering the same thing from their body language when he arrived.

In the living room, he placed the plate of cookies on the coffee table and picked up the paper where Tonya had scribbled the notes from her talk with the woman and the phone number for the brother.

"Did Mrs. Childress say anything that gave you a clue she knew what her husband had done?" Hawke asked, catching Tonya's attention.

"No. She was excited to talk about her father. Said her brother knew more about the actual work, so that played well with asking for his phone number." Tonya pulled another piece of paper out from the pile on the table. "We did dig up the names of all the families living in the subdivision when the Goodwins made their accusations about the water." She smiled at Mathews. "I'm going to start calling them and asking about their children's health at that time and if the Goodwins or Felix contacted them."

"Good work," Hawke said, taking the paper out to the front porch where it would be quieter to talk on the phone. He dialed the number Tonya had scribbled on the paper. He wondered at the hard to read notes the woman had taken, that she could decipher it enough to write a story.

Three rings and the voice of a man who'd been

drinking answered. "Hellloo?"

"Mr. Trask?" Hawke asked, wondering what the man was doing being drunk at 2:30 in the afternoon.

"Yeah, who's askin'?" The man's tone was belligerent. Not a good sign for a conversation of this nature.

"State Trooper Hawke. Is there a better time to call you?"

"State Trooper? I ain't been drivin' around. I'm sittin' at home gettin' drunk where I can't hurt anyone. So stop harassin' me." The man slurred his way through the denial and slammed the phone down. Which meant he had a landline. No cell phone.

Hawke walked back into the house. "Mr. Trask have a wife he's living with?" He didn't like the idea of the angry drunk taking his call out on his wife.

Mathews shook his head. "Nope. Divorced. Two children, but they don't live in Arizona. Why?"

"He was drunk already." Hawke glanced at his watch. "A phone call isn't going to get anything out of him." He scanned his mom's living room. Sending someone else to do something he would rather do himself wasn't setting well with him. He gave in to McCord looking for the evidence at the homestead because he'd met her. He didn't know anyone in Arizona. But he did know someone who could pick him up in Pendleton and fly him to Mesa, Arizona and back. He just needed to get to a radio to contact her.

"If I can get a ride to Mesa this afternoon, can you keep an eye on Tonya until I get back?" He glanced toward the hallway where he heard the woman's muffled voice.

"When will you be back?" Mathews looked up

from the computer.

"Tonight."

The deputy whistled. "You can get to Mesa and back in the same day?"

"Yeah, but don't tell Tonya where I'm going." He studied the man on the couch. He hadn't shaved and his eyes looked bloodshot. "Why don't you take a break from looking up stuff and sit outside in the sunshine for a while."

"Why don't you want me to tell Tonya where you're going?" Mathews shoved the laptop from his lap to the coffee table and stretched.

"Gut feeling. She doesn't need to get so wrapped up in the investigation."

"It's what she does as a reporter." Mathews defended the woman.

"Well, she's involved enough that we have to hide her here. Best to just keep this between you and me. Okay?" He needed Mathews to see she was a civilian and while she'd been a help, she didn't need to know everything.

"Yeah. I'll make up something."

"Thanks." Now to radio Dani, and then tell his mom he was leaving two strangers with her for another night, only without him.

Without his work vehicle he had to drum up a radio to call the hunting lodge. Growing up there had been a man down the block who had a HAM radio. He found his mom at her usual place, in the kitchen.

"Mom, does Russell Temsee still have a radio?" he asked, walking over and standing next to his mother as she peeled potatoes.

"He's gone. But I think his daughter who still lives

there has the radio. Why?" She peered up at him.

"I need to contact someone by radio." He picked up a carrot coin, popped it in his mouth, and chewed. "And I won't be home for dinner. I'll be coming in late."

"You aren't going over to that tramp Linda's are you?" her eyes narrowed, and she pointed the paring knife at him.

"I told you, she is a friend. I don't buy sex from her. And no. I'm having a friend pick me up. I'll be back late." He headed to the back door and stopped. "What's Russell's daughter's name?"

"Hazel. She was only a year behind you in school." His mom studied him. "Who is picking you up?"

"Someone you would like." He swung the screen door open and ducked down the side of the house, heading for the road. At the end of the block, he didn't have any problem spotting the Temsee house. It looked the same as it had the last thirty years. Needing paint, the same pickup up on blocks as it had been since Russell had his driver's license taken away and his kids put the vehicle up so he couldn't go anywhere.

Hawke walked up to the door and knocked.

The sound of a television being turned down and then heavy footsteps, followed by the door opening and he was face to face with Hazel Temsee. He would have recognized her. She had the same round face, saggy jowls, and sad eyes as her father.

"Hazel, I'm Gabriel Hawke, Mimi's son."

She nodded. "Heard you were staying with her for a while."

He wondered how many other people knew. He should have remembered the reservation had a faster gossip wire than Wallowa County. "I was hoping I could use your radio to contact a friend."

Hazel looked him up and down. "Is this official?"

"Not really. I want to get a hold of a friend who owns Charlie's Hunting Lodge in the Eagle Cap Wilderness." He hoped she would allow him access.

"I guess it won't hurt any." She opened the door wider, allowing him access to the house. "It's in the back room."

He followed her wide backside down the hall to a room near the back door.

"You know how to use one?"

"Yes."

"I'll be in the living room watching my show." She motioned for him to step into the room and she disappeared.

It was apparent by the small bed and boxes that smelled like an old person, this had been her father's room until he'd passed.

Hawke sat down at the radio and dialed in the frequency for the hunting lodge.

"Charlie's Hunting Lodge, this is Hawke," he said into the mic and listened to the crackle of static. He repeated himself three times and was getting ready to give up when Dani's out of breath reply came.

"This is Dani. What's up Hawke?"

"I wondered if you'd be interested in flying me from Pendleton to Mesa, Arizona today."

"There's not much of today left," she responded.

"I thought you were a good enough pilot you didn't need to see the landmarks under you," he teased.

"Why you!" He heard the click of her releasing the mic button and figured she was cussing up a storm at his poking fun at her flying. The static cleared and she said. "I can be to Pendleton by five."

"I'll be waiting for you." He grinned and replaced the mic, turning off the radio.

He had a ride to Mesa with a feisty ex-air force pilot. Even if he came up empty with information from Trask, he'll have spent time with Dani in her element.

Chapter Twenty-seven

Hawke flashed his badge and walked out onto the tarmac as Dani taxied the Cessna 206H over to where a landing crew were waving orange wands. It was 5:15. He wondered if she'd run into trouble.

The propeller stopped and the cockpit door opened. Dani stepped out, wearing what looked like a flight suit. She talked to the crew as they put wedges behind the wheels.

Hawke walked up to her. "Need a pitstop before we take off?"

She shook her head. "I just have to file my flight plans."

That's when he noticed the papers in hand. "Mind if I get settled in the plane and wait for you?"

"Knock yourself out." She bumped him in the shoulder with her fisted hand and continued into the building.

He walked over to the plane, climbed into the passenger seat alongside the pilot's seat, and stared at all the gauges, knobs, toggle switches, and buttons. It would take him a lifetime to figure out what all they did.

Ten minutes later, Dani returned, settled in the seat, put the headset on, and motioned for him to put his on.

Hawke took his hat off and put the headphones on, listening to her talk to the tower and get access to leave.

Once they were in the air, she flipped a switch and her voice came through loud and clear. "Why are we headed to Mesa?"

"Working on a case." He wanted to tell her more but didn't want to get her mixed up in this anymore than he had.

She glanced over at him. "The one with the escaped convict? I thought he was dead. Why are you still looking into it?"

"I've discovered he didn't kill anyone and was put in jail unjustly." Hawke peered into her eyes.

"He was innocent? How can that happen?" Anger darkened her cheeks. He couldn't see her eyes because of the aviation sunglasses.

"Corrupt police." It was hard to get those words out. Over the years he'd run into a few corrupt police and it made his gut hurt every time he thought about it.

"That's why you're doing this, to get to the bottom of it?" Dani held out a hand.

Hawke placed his hand in hers and squeezed. She understood his need to right something that he hadn't caused but someone of his occupation had.

"Yeah. The convict had information that the people of Boise should have heard, but he was incarcerated and his voice stopped. I hope to get his findings released and his name exonerated."

"This trip will do all of that?" she asked, leaving her hand in his.

"Not all. But it will help me get information against the man I believe caused the whole thing. The one who had the most to lose if the environmentalist had been able to publish his findings." Hawke gave her hand another squeeze and released it. While he enjoyed holding hands with her, he felt better with her having two hands on the plane's steering apparatus.

"Do you want me to go with you to see the person?"

He was on the fence there. It would be good to have an impartial person along in case Trask did something stupid, but at the same time he didn't want Trask to tell Childress about Dani.

"I'm not sure."

She glanced over at him, again. "For my safety?"

"Yeah. These people have killed seven people to keep this information from coming out."

She shook her head. "That's a lot of bodies to cover up an environmental injustice."

"I agree. And that's why I'm hesitant to have you go along. But I also don't want to contact the man alone. It would be his word against mine." Hawke sighed. It was nice being able to talk about this with Dani, but he didn't want to drag her into the middle of it.

"I can go along and secretly tape the conversation with my phone." She smiled at him. "It's been a while since I did anything that got my adrenaline pumping."

He wasn't sure whether that was a come on or the woman was an adrenaline junkie. Hawke raised an eyebrow. "Really?"

Her cheeks darkened again and she flipped a switch. He heard her talking with the ground control at Mesa.

《》《》《》

Hawke rented a car at the airport. He and Dani drove to Trask's apartment and knocked on the door of apartment 217.

And waited.

"Maybe he isn't here? Maybe he went out to dinner?" Dani suggested.

"I doubt dinner is a high priority for this man." Hawke remembered the days when his stepfather would come home from an odd job already drunk, sit down in his chair, and ask Hawke or Miriam to get him a beer. After their mother had told him dinner was ready. A drunk didn't have a need for food. He got all his calories from the alcohol.

He pounded harder on the door and called, "Mr. Trask, I talked to you earlier today."

The door to 219 opened. A woman with dyed black hair and a pale white face stuck her head out. "He's down at Tony's Bar this time of night."

"Where's that?" Hawke asked.

"At the sidewalk, go right three blocks and you can't miss it." She started to pull her head back in and stopped. "You a relative?"

"No. Why?" Hawke studied the girl. She couldn't have been much over twenty.

"He was saying something about a relative coming to get him was all when he left. I passed him in the hall." She closed the door.

Hawke cursed.

"Is that bad?" Dani asked, running to keep up with

his long strides to the elevator.

"It is if it's his brother-in-law. It means Trask thinks he's next to die." At the entrance, Hawke turned right and strode down the sidewalk, holding Dani's hand to keep her up with him. At the bar, he released her hand and walked into the establishment. He didn't have a clue what Trask looked like. All he knew is the man would be shit-faced and belligerent.

He walked up to the bar. "What do you want to drink?" he asked Dani. She stared at him a moment and said a light beer.

Hawke waved the bartender over. "We'll have two light beers on tap."

The man nodded, wandered off to the tap, filled two glasses and returned.

Hawke paid him and asked, "Is William Trask in here tonight?"

The man stared at him. "Why are you asking?" His gaze darted toward the man at the opposite end of the bar.

"I wanted to see if he's okay. The young girl who lives next to him said he wasn't feeling well earlier." Hawke picked up the beers, handing one to Dani.

"Why do you care?" the bartender asked.

"I'm a family friend."

"He's been mumbling his brother is coming to get him. But if you don't know who he is, you can't be the brother." The bartender glanced past him to Dani. "You aren't his brother either."

"We're concerned friends that's all," Dani said, sipping her beer.

"He's the drunk on the end. I cut him off about an hour ago, but he hasn't left." The bartender moved off to pour another drink.

Hawke led the way over to the man sitting at the end of the counter. There was an open stool on his left. Hawke motioned for Dani to take the seat. She did and immediately pulled out her phone.

Moving to the man's right, he set his beer on the counter. "Mr. Trask?"

The man glanced up at him and squinted. The bar was dark, squinting in the bad lighting wouldn't have helped his sight any more than all the alcohol he'd consumed. "Yeah. Who are you?"

"I'm Hawke. I wanted to talk to you about Felix White."

The man started shaking his head. "I don't want to talk about that. Herman told me I'd never have to talk to anyone about that."

"Herman knew you'd falsified police reports about White, didn't he?" Hawke decided he'd just ask questions. The man wasn't in any shape to lie.

"He told me to write up the reports and what to put on them. I'd borrowed money from him for gambling and owed him so much I couldn't say no." He dropped his face into his hands and mumbled, "If Teresa ever finds out she'll have an attack and die."

"Who's Teresa?" Hawke asked.

"My sister. She's married to Herman. She has a weak heart." Trask noticed the beer. His gaze fixed on the glass. He licked his lips. "Who did you say you were?"

"Hawke. I'm a State Trooper from Oregon."

Trask dragged his gaze from the beer to him. "Oregon? Why are you asking about White and Herman?"

"Because I was tracking White when he was killed by Sean Sheridan." Hawke watched the man closely. It didn't appear the name meant anything to the drunk.

"Never heard of him."

"What about Tonya Cox?" Hawke believed the man had left Idaho before Tonya started her investigation into the wrongful incarceration of White.

"Tonya's a sweet kid. She's a newspaper reporter. Her parents were killed years ago. I was the policeman on her parents' case. Never did figure out why they ran off the road. If they were fighting, if her dad fell asleep. Never could figure it out." He licked his lips and his hand started to ease toward the beer on the bar. "I think that's why she became a reporter. To investigate."

Hawke slid the beer toward the man's hand. He didn't like drunks, but he wanted the man to keep talking. Being his friend by giving him a drink would help.

"Did she ever call and ask you about White?" She should have recognized his name on the police reports. Why hadn't she mentioned knowing Officer Trask instead of going through the ploy of calling Mrs. Childress to get the phone number?

"No. She wouldn't know about White. Those records disappeared right after White went to jail for killing that family." Trask drank half the glass of beer in one long gulped. Then he belched.

"What if I told you, she is the one who brought the falsified documents to me?" Hawke watched bewilderment and then fear misshape his face.

"She stole the records?" He focused on Hawke. "Who did you say you were?"

"I'm with the Oregon State Police."

"Shit! Are you taking me back? I can't go to jail. I'm a retired policeman." The man was practically crying.

"I'm going to call the Mesa Police and have them hold you for extradition back to Idaho. I'd like to have you tell the Idaho State Police everything you know about the records you falsified for your brother-in-law."

"He'll kill me if he knows I'm ratting him out." The man finished off the glass of beer. "I gotta go."

Hawke grabbed him by the arm and led him toward the entrance, glad to see Dani was right behind him.

Outside, he handcuffed the man and set him on a stone bench in front of the building.

"Keep an eye on him while I call the police," he said to Dani.

She nodded, and he looked up the city police on his phone.

《》《》《》

By the time Hawke talked the police into arresting Trask and then told them someone from Idaho State Police would be coming to get him, it was getting late. They walked out of the police station and both slid into the SUV Hawke had rented.

"I'd planned on heading back tonight but it's late." He studied the woman in the passenger seat. She didn't look tired, but she had to be. She'd told him she'd rose early that morning to help Tuck, her wrangler, build an addition to the corral.

"I wouldn't argue with you about staying the night and going back tomorrow."

"Your plane going to be okay at the airport overnight?"

"I just have to make a call." She pulled out her

phone.

"I need to call my sergeant so he can get the Idaho State Police down here quickly." He stepped out of the car and made his call to Spruel.

"This better be good Hawke. It's late."

"I have William Trask, the cop who falsified the records on White, being held at the Mesa, Arizona city police for the Idaho State Police to come get."

"How did you get to Mesa… Never mind, I don't want to know. I'll call Idaho and let them know. You better get this written up so I know what I'm talking about."

"I'll head to a motel room and leave you a long message on your phone at work. I'll be back in Oregon in the morning."

"How are you getting around so fast?" Spruel asked.

Hawke glanced at the woman sitting in the rental car. "I have my own pilot." Before the sergeant could ask any more questions, he dropped the connection and slid into the driver's seat.

"Did you happen to see any motels on the way to Trask's?"

"I'm sure if we drive back toward the airport, we'll find something," Dani said, putting on her seat belt.

Chapter Twenty-eight

The next morning, Hawke woke refreshed. He glanced at the woman in the bed beside him and while his brain told him he should have gone on to a motel that had two rooms available, his body was happy he hadn't.

She'd been at the counter with him when the clerk said there was only one room left. Dani had stared him in the eyes and said, one was fine. Just subtle as that and the next thing he knew, he was fulfilling a dream he'd had ever since meeting the woman.

Now, the morning after, and he didn't feel awkward.

She rolled over and smiled at him. "Did you make coffee?"

"Nope. Just woke up myself."

"I smell coffee." She raised up on one arm and stared at the unplugged appliance setting on the counter by the sink.

"It's not coming from this room." Hawke stood and dressed. "If you get dressed, we can go grab coffee and something to eat and get back to Pendleton. I left Dog with my mom."

"You dumped your dog on your mom?" she said, slipping out of bed and giving him a full view of her compact body.

"Also a deputy and a woman we are protecting." He didn't bother to look away as she dressed.

"I would say, *he* is protecting. You flew off for a quickie." She grinned and swat him on the butt as she walked by.

"That wasn't my intention when I called you," he said to the closing of the bathroom door.

His phone rang. Spruel.

"Did you get my message?" Hawke asked by way of a greeting.

"Yes. As soon as you can get that recording to me, the better. And McCord radioed that she thinks she found the evidence. She and the other trooper will be in Boise later today."

Hawke knew the trooper would get the job done. She reminded him of a younger version of the woman in the bathroom. "I'll have the recording sent to you as soon as I can. I should have done that last night but I forgot." The woman who had the recording had made him forget a lot of things. Including that he hadn't planned to get involved with her.

"Let me know when you're back in the state." Spruel disconnected.

Dani walked out of the bathroom. "Ready when you are."

He picked up the car keys and his hat and strode to

the door. "Let's go. I'm extra hungry this morning."

Dani grinned and walked through the door ahead of him.

《》《》《》

She flew him to Pendleton as if they hadn't slept together the night before. No awkward conversation, just the usual banter and him asking some questions about flying the plane. This was what he'd expected from the woman. No strings attached, each going about their lives as they had been before last night. But he saw a softness in her eyes when she looked at him that hadn't been there before.

"Mom wants me to bring Kitree over for a visit. You might let Tuck and Sage know I'll be contacting them about a time that works." He stood at the door of the plane, knowing he should walk away, but lingering, uncertain how to say he'd talk to her later.

"I'll let them know. Maybe you could come get her and stay the night." The wistfulness in her voice, told him what he wanted to know.

"Sounds like a plan." He closed the door and waved as he backed away.

It was the first time in a long time that he was looking forward to seeing a woman again. He strode off the tarmac, through the building, and out to the rental car. The first thing he wanted to do was question Tonya about knowing Officer Trask.

He drove back to his mom's and noted Mathews' Mustang was missing. Had he and Tonya gone somewhere? He shouldn't have left the woman alone. Not when she had so much contradictory information about her.

Hawke jogged to the front door and entered the

house. It smelled of pancake syrup and cookies. "Mom!" he called, heading to the kitchen.

Dog bounded out of the kitchen and planted his front paws on Hawke's stomach. "Hey boy." He ruffled the dog's ears and moved on by.

Mimi sat at the table with Annie and a little boy. The two children were sprinkling colored candies on cookies his mom was frosting.

"Why are you yelling? You stayed out all night. You said you would be back." The accusing tone in her voice had the two children leaning back in their chairs.

"I should have called. Things went later than I thought they would. I spent the night and came home this morning."

"You better not have been with Linda." She stood and sniffed him. Her eyes narrowed. "Children go outside."

The two headed to the door, though Annie moved much slower than the little boy.

"You were with a woman," his mom hissed. "I told you to stay away from Linda."

"It wasn't Linda. You would approve of this woman. Where are Mathews and Tonya?" He wasn't going to get into a long conversation with his mom about Dani. Not when he wasn't sure where they were headed himself.

"He got a phone call, and they said to tell you they were going back to Boise." She studied him.

Shit! "When did they leave?"

"About two hours ago." She sat back down. "I was happy to get my house back."

"Sorry I dropped them in your living room. But I need to call Mathews and see what is going on." He kissed the top of her head and picked up a cookie. She always appreciated when people enjoyed her cooking.

He paced the living room waiting for Mathews to pick up the call. His voice mail said to leave a message. "Where are you? Why are you going to Boise? This is Hawke. Call me. Tonya knows more than she's told us."

Frustration pounded in his temples. He didn't want to be driving all over trying to figure out what was happening. But his pickup was in Boise, he needed to return the rental car, and McCord had found White's evidence.

He strode back into the kitchen. "Mom, I'm going to get out of your hair, too. Thank you for putting up with us—me. I'll make sure to bring Kitree over for a stay soon."

"You make promises to your mother you better keep them," she called as he hurried to the bedroom and grabbed his duffel bag and Dog's bag of food and treats. "Come on, boy, we're going to Boise."

Once everything was stashed in the car, including Dog, Hawke dialed Spruel to update him on what he'd found when he returned.

"What do you mean you lost Ms. Cox!" Spruel boomed through the phone.

"I don't know who called Mathews from Boise that made him take her back there, but I'm headed there now." He pulled onto the interstate and pushed the accelerator down. "If you could make some calls and see who called him back, I'd appreciate it. Right now, he's not answering his phone. He should be between Baker City and Ontario if my mom was correct about the time he left."

"What is he driving?" Spruel asked.

Hawke gave him all the information he remembered about the vehicle.

"I'll put a request out for patrol cars in that area to look out for him and pull him over until you get there." The connection went dead.

"Thank you, Sergeant Spruel," Hawke said and scratched Dog's head. "Let's go as fast as the speed limit allows," he said, and then put the cruise five miles an hour faster. He was two hours behind Mathews and needed to make up time.

《》《》《》

Spruel called Hawke as he topped the hill and caught a glimpse of Baker City.

"A trooper has Mathews and the woman pulled over at the Huntington exit. Mathews tried to use his deputy status to get away, but I'd given orders for them to be held until you get there."

"Thanks. I just passed Baker City. I'll be going faster than the speed limit in a rental twenty-nineteen Mustang. You might let anyone else patrolling the area know." He ended the call and pushed the car up to ninety. The vehicle had the engine for the speed and the mobility. But he didn't like driving this fast without a siren to tell the other drivers he was a trooper not a sportscar nut disobeying the rules.

Nearing the exit for Huntington, he spotted the patrol car behind the older Mustang. Hawke pulled in behind the patrol car, rolled the windows down, and stepped out.

The patrolman had Mathews and Tonya standing with their backs to his car, facing the side of the road.

They both glanced his direction as he approached.

Tonya's eyes narrowed. Mathews glared at him.

"What's the big idea having us pulled over like this?" Mathews asked, stepping toward him.

The patrolman, put a hand on Mathews' chest, holding him in place. The deputy swat at the trooper's hand.

"Because you didn't answer when I called, and," Hawke stopped in front of Tonya. "Ms. Cox hasn't been telling us the truth."

She glared back at him, her lips pinched together.

Hawke faced Mathews. "Who called you?"

"Idaho State Police. They said we needed to come back to Boise." Mathews crossed his arms.

"No one at the Idaho State Police knew you were helping me. They shouldn't even have known you were with Tonya." Hawke moved his gaze to the woman. She stared at the name tag on the state trooper who pulled them over. "Who did you contact about where you were and who you were with?" Hawke wondered if the woman was really in danger or if she, indeed, was the killer of two men. One to keep him quiet about the information he'd found and the other to keep him quiet about her killing the first man.

When the woman continued to ignore him, he shifted his attention to Mathews. "Why didn't you answer my call?" Hawke pointed to the phone in the deputy's pocket.

"It didn't ring." He pulled it out. "It's turned off…" The deputy faced Tonya. "Why did you turn my phone off? To keep Hawke from contacting me?" Mathews took a step toward Tonya.

Hawke grabbed her by the wrist. "Ms. Cox you can ride with me to Boise. The evidence you say White had hidden in his family's cabin is now in Idaho State Police custody." Hawke nodded to Mathews. "You can lead the way or follow." Then he turned to the trooper he'd seen at a couple of trainings. "Johnson, thank you for detaining these two. I'll see that Ms. Cox meets up with whoever called Mathews from the Idaho State Police."

His comment caused the woman to flinch. It was obvious it hadn't been the police who called Mathews and she knew it.

"Not a problem, Hawke." The trooper headed for his vehicle.

Hawke led Tonya to the rental car and opened the passenger door. "In the back," he told Dog, who was sitting in the driver's seat. The animal hopped into the back seat, but had his eyes on the woman as she sat in the passenger seat.

"I'd not try anything stupid. Dog doesn't care for you and if you try to hurt me, he's going to intervene." Hawke closed the passenger door and walked around to the driver's side.

Once he was in the driver's seat, Hawke started the car and pulled into the fast-moving traffic. Mathews fell in behind him.

"Want to tell me why you neglected to tell us that you knew Officer Trask?" Hawke asked.

She stared out the side window.

"I guess I'll discover all of it when we get to the State Police headquarters. They must have information since they wanted you to come back there."

Chapter Twenty-nine

Hawke pulled into the parking lot at the Idaho State Police building in Meridian. Mathews parked beside him.

Rolling the windows down, Hawke told Dog to stay.

Mathews opened the passenger door and helped Tonya out of the car. "I can't believe I fell for your act of not wanting to come back to Idaho when you had staged the whole thing for me to bring you here."

Hawke studied the deputy. It seemed he'd thought about a lot on the rest of the drive to Boise without the woman in his car, twisting his thoughts. He stepped up and took hold of the woman by the upper arm and led her up to the doors of the building. They couldn't arrest her, with so little evidence. Only the knowledge she was with White when he was killed, though she said Sheridan killed him and she was at the cabin at the same time Sheridan was killed. And she had been lying about many things while also giving them information that was helping. He didn't know how to treat her anymore.

He was surprised to see Trooper McCord standing inside the door as if waiting for them. The small lobby had locked doors on either side.

"I'll take Ms. Cox to the interview room," McCord said.

Hawke held onto Tonya. "How did you know we were coming in with her?" While the trooper had brought the woman to him at the hospital and found the information that started all the killings, he was beginning to wonder if she was on the side of Ms. Cox and the people hiding their involvement in the subdivision scandal.

"Your sergeant called Captain Horton." McCord drew Tonya away from him. "He said you were bringing Ms. Cox with you and from what he knew of the investigation was worried someone who wanted her dead would be looking for her."

Hawke took pleasure in seeing the surprise in Tonya's eyes. Didn't she think there were people out to stop her from digging up the scandal?

"Can I see what you found at the cabin?" Hawke wanted to know everything. It was one of his downfalls when it came to getting caught up in a mess like this.

"Talk to our captain." She nodded for them to follow her. She buzzed them through a door.

Hawke motioned for Mathews to follow him. They walked down the hall to a door with the placard: *Captain Thomas Horton.*

Hawke knocked twice and waited for permission to enter.

"Just a moment," a deep voice called out.

Hawke glanced at Mathews as he waited patiently.

The deputy started fidgeting. Finally, he said, "What did you find out that made you suspicious of Tonya?"

"She knew Trask. The man I went to Arizona to talk with." Hawke filled Mathews in on the information he'd gathered from the man and how he was awaiting extradition to Idaho.

"You were busy!" He shook his head. "I still can't believe I thought every word out of Tonya's mouth was the truth."

"It turns out very little is," Hawke said as the door to the Captain's office opened.

A man in his forties, with a balding head, dark eyes, and a big nose stepped out. "Hawke?" he questioned, looking from Hawke to Mathews.

"I'm Hawke," he said, stepping forward and shaking hands.

"Mathews, sir," Mathews said, shaking hands.

"Let's go down to the conference room. That's where they are going over the information Troopers McCord and Wagner found." The captain led the way deeper into the building. At a door with a placard, *Conference Room*, he opened the door and three people, two with paper strewn about in front of them and one with a computer, sat at a long table.

"Reed, Stacy, and Rose, this is Oregon Trooper Hawke and Idaho County Deputy Mathews. They have been on this case from the beginning. I'd appreciate you sharing with them what you've learned so far." Captain Horton waved them into the room, joined them, and shut the door.

One of the two women had the blue Idaho State Trooper uniform on. The other two people present appeared to be civilians.

The woman in civilian clothes started. "I'm Stacy Clann. I'm a professor at the university in the environmental department. So far on the flash drive that was given to us, we found Felix White's dissertation on the effects of surface water versus ground water in relation to illnesses. He pretty much states that the Sunrise Rose Subdivision on the northeast side of Boise was using surface water without going through the proper cleaning methods. Yet, they were charging the property owners a high, water usage fee, stating it was due to the government regulated water purification methods."

"Does he name anyone in particular?" Hawke asked. He knew what had happened from Tonya's version, if she had told the truth about the paper. What he wanted was someone to pin the murders on.

"A corporation. No individual names." Ms. Clann flipped through some of the papers in front of her. "He shows tests he ran on the water from half a dozen homes in the subdivision and tests he did on the surface water. The tests were conclusive the water came from the Boise River."

He could tell the environmental injustice meant more to the woman than the murders. Hawke shifted his attention to the woman in the uniform. "Have you been able to pull up names on the people in the corporation?"

"I'm working on it. It appears the corporation was dissolved right after the murders in Hells Canyon." Trooper Oakley was the name on her pin, handed Hawke several pages.

The only name he knew was Childress. He hadn't been the lead in the development. A man by the name of Buck Bayle was the President of the corporation. "Who is this Buck Bayle?" he asked.

"Billionaire who owns half of Boise," Captain Horton answered.

"Any ties to things illegal?" Hawke asked.

"He tends to keep his nose clean."

"Which means you believe he is into illegal dealings but can't catch him." Hawke watched as both the captain and the trooper nodded their heads.

"Have you sent anyone to Arizona for Trask?" Hawke asked.

"I sent two detectives this morning." Horton faced him. "What did you discover?"

Hawke filled him in on the fact the man had been a part of the investigation into Tonya's parents' death, had falsified the police records on White, and was the brother-in-law to Herman Childress. "He's an alcoholic who will cave pretty easy once the booze is withheld. We might need to talk to him before you ask the people in the corporation to come in." He shrugged. Getting to the bottom of this today would simplify his life, but that wasn't going to happen.

"We can't hold the woman. We don't have any evidence that says she's committed a crime other than lying," Horton said.

"Then we need to ask Childress to come in after you talk to Trask and confront him with what we know. He seems to have manipulated his brother-in-law to implicate White in the murders. That means he knows who gave him the orders to take care of White. And I believe he picked Sheridan to go with me so the other tracker could kill White." Hawke put his hand on the doorknob. "While we wait on Trask and Childress, I'll see if Ms. Cox will talk to me."

Horton nodded.

"Mathews, stay here and see if anything I can use on Ms. Cox is found," Hawke told the deputy.

He nodded, obviously, grateful he didn't have to deal with the woman who'd twisted his thinking.

Horton led Hawke down the hall, back to where they'd entered and down another hall. "I believe McCord has the woman in an interview room." Horton stopped and faced him. "She needs to be booked and arraigned."

"I know. But I might be able to get more out of her if she thinks I'm a friend and not someone pushing her into jail. Any chance you can find the file on her parents' accident about fifteen years ago? It would have been with the City Police."

"I'll do my best. It's the room down there on the right." Horton motioned to a closed door at the end of the hall before pivoting and striding back the way they'd come.

Hawke stepped into a room with small metal table and three mismatched chairs. The sickening sweet stench of a drunk, the odor of unwashed bodies, and coffee met him as he walked in the windowless room.

He walked over to the only empty chair and pulled the single cup of coffee, sitting in the middle of the table, closer to him.

Tonya sat across him with a cup of coffee gripped in both hands in front of her on the wooden top.

Hawke smiled and leaned back in the chair.

Trooper McCord stood, when he walked in the

room. She held a cup of coffee.

"Take the other seat. This is a friendly conversation," Hawke said to the trooper and pushed the third chair toward her with his foot.

"Are you arresting me?" Tonya leaned back, as if by putting space between them he couldn't put her in jail.

He nodded. "Eventually, you will be arrested and arraigned for aiding in a prison escape. Right now, keeping you alive is more important. You know who killed White and possibly Sheridan. And you know all about the corporation who had them killed. Your buddy Officer Trask told me all about you and how you dug and dug because you didn't feel that your parents' deaths were investigated fully." Hawke took a sip of coffee. He'd caught the woman's attention.

"Trooper McCord found the evidence that White was after when the two of you took off to get away from Sheridan." He made as if he were deep in thought. "How did you and White know that Sheridan was going to kill him? That *is* why you shot at him through the window and then tried to bury him under rock?"

Tonya sat back down. She sighed heavily. "I knew Felix had information hidden that would help me get noticed in the investigative reporter world. I'd followed his trial, which went way to quick and had too much unclear evidence. So I started investigating who he was before he "snapped" as the prosecutor said over and over again at the trial." She sipped the coffee, made a face, and picked up a packet of sugar on the table near her. "All the information I found on Felix said he was a quiet, easy-going guy unless he felt there was an environmental injustice. I couldn't find anything that was environmental about the case. I mean, he knew the people who he'd supposedly killed, yet the prosecutor said they were strangers he found in his family home and killed them in a violent rage." She ripped the end off the packet and poured it in the coffee. "Nothing fit. So I kept digging and visited Felix at the prison. At first, he didn't say much. Then I'd start telling him things I'd found and asked him for clarification. That's when I realized he'd been put in jail to stop him from publishing his findings. But he wouldn't tell me where they were. He said if I could get him out of jail, he'd take me to them." She shrugged. "I figured out a way to smuggle him out of jail."

"Did you tell anyone about what you were doing?" Hawke wondered how Childress could have had a hitman sent after White so fast. And how he knew that Sheridan would do the job.

"The only person in on it was the guard I paid to look the other way when he shoved what was supposed to be an empty cooler out to the food delivery truck."

Hawke glanced over and saw Trooper McCord already had her logbook out, ready to write the guard's name down. "Who was the guard?"

Tonya clenched her lips together and shook her head. "I'm not snitching. He helped me get Felix out."

"And look what happened? Felix's life was cut short because of it." Hawke stared the woman in the eyes. He wouldn't need to get the name from her. All they had to do was ask which guard was on duty in the kitchen that day.

She flinched. "I was trying to help him."

"You got him killed. If you had gone to the proper authorities, you still would have had the story and

White would still be alive and out of jail—a free man."
Hawke drank some coffee, letting the words sink in.

Tonya brushed at tears in the corners of her eyes.
"Do you really think someone will harm me?"

He nodded. "You know too much. And you are the
one that dug all this back up. It had been forgotten with
White in jail." Hawke leaned forward. "Tonya, you
have to tell us everything you know and who all you
think is involved in the cover-up." He glanced at
McCord. The trooper had been writing down everything
Tonya had said

Tonya glanced at the trooper. "You're writing all
of this down?"

"You are wanted for the prison escape."

When the woman didn't say anything, Hawke
added, "Trask is on his way here. We know he was
used to push White into jail and from what he told me, I
believe he knows a few of the people behind the water
contamination. But I have a feeling you know everyone
involved and who the one could be that knows how
much you know."

A young trooper walked into the breakroom. He
dropped a file next to Hawke and walked out.

Hawke opened the folder. It was the report on
Tonya's parents' accident. He flipped through the
folder and a name caught his attention quickly. "You
didn't just want to help Felix White, you wanted to take
down the man who got away with killing your parents."

Her hands gripped the mug in front of her so tight
her knuckles turned white. Her face grew taut and red.

"This had nothing to do with an investigative story
and everything to do with revenge." Hawke slid the
paper across the table that stated Buck Bayle had been

cited for reckless driving and endangerment the same night as the accident where Mr. and Mrs. Cox were killed. No one could put the young billionaire at the scene of the accident, but he'd been cited not two miles down the road from the accident for driving while intoxicated. From the marks at the scene of the accident it appeared the Cox vehicle tried to swerve to miss something and ran off the road, catching the tires in the soft shoulder and the car rolled down an embankment, killing both occupants.

Tears trickled down Tonya's cheeks. She swiped at them with the back of one hand. "He came to my uncle and offered to pay for anything I needed," She glared at Hawke. "What I needed were my parents. I didn't want his guilt money. I wanted him in jail and my parents alive." She swiped at the tears and continued. "I told Officer Trask what I thought had happened and how Bayle had come to my uncle offering money." She leaned forward. "He told me that there wasn't any proof Mr. Bayle had caused the accident. That I should take the money and move on."

Hawke was getting an even poorer impression of both Trask and Bayle. It appeared the man had been in the billionaire's pocket for some time. He hoped not allowing the man any alcohol would make him turn on the billionaire who most likely made him an alcoholic with all his "favors".

"Instead, you spent your adult life collecting information on the man. Trying to dig up anything you could take to the police," Hawke said.

She nodded.

"How did you know he was mixed up in the White incarceration?"

"Officer Trask's name was on all the arrests. I knew he worked for Bayle." She pointed to the logbook McCord was writing in. "Make sure you put down all of this. I haven't been able to get anyone in law enforcement to take me seriously."

"Is that why you haven't been completely honest with me?" Hawke asked.

Chapter Thirty

Tonya opened her mouth to answer and a man with a briefcase walked in. "Don't say anything. I'm here to make sure you have legal representation."

Hawke saw the fear in Tonya's eyes and immediately stood, taking the man by the arm. "You aren't needed here. Ms. Cox isn't under arrest. You will be, if you don't leave this building."

McCord followed him to the door and grasped the man's other arm, leading him down the hallway.

"Keep your mouth shut!" the man hollered.

Hawke knew what he was doing. The man had come in just to warn Tonya not to make trouble. From her pale face and wide eyes, he'd say she knew the man and realized the threat was real.

Hawke sat down next to the woman. "Tonya. If you let us protect you, he can't hurt you."

She shook her head. "How did they know I was here?"

The file lay on the table in front of them. "I'd say when we requested this file from the City Police, word got out to Bayle that you were back in Boise at State Police Headquarters."

"If he got in here to see me, I won't be safe anywhere." She stood. Then sat back down. "I can't leave. They'll be watching." Her hands shook as she reached for the coffee mug in front of her. "I can't go to jail. They have people everywhere."

Hawke had been underestimating the breadth of Bayle's reach. He hoped there wasn't a Bayle man in the State Police. But how else did the man get past the high security at the front of the building? If there was, the best way to keep her safe was to work with Mathews and McCord on this. Right now, they were the only police in Idaho he trusted. She couldn't go to jail, yet. Not until they could figure out how to incriminate the billionaire.

He texted Mathews to come to the breakroom, and if he saw McCord, to bring her along with him.

"Mathews and I have stuck our necks out to keep you safe, and we'll continue. But we're going to need the help of Trooper McCord to get you out of here. We can't walk out with you knowing people are watching us to get to you." Hawke half stood and scooped up his now tepid cup of coffee.

"Why have you and Scott stuck your necks out for me?" Tonya asked.

"Because we both believe in justice, like most law enforcement officers. Unfortunately, we don't know which are the ones for justice and which are the bad cops on Bayle's payroll right now. Other than ourselves."

Mathews entered the breakroom followed by McCord.

"Close the door," Hawke said and motioned for the two to take a seat on either side of him and Tonya. He wanted to keep their voices low.

He studied McCord. "That man, if you haven't already figured it out, was sent here to scare Tonya and let her know they know where she is."

McCord nodded.

"How did he get past the security desk out front?" Hawke asked.

"I was wondering the same thing. I told Captain Horton. He's going to check the security cameras." McCord's mahogany brow was furrowed.

"What man?" Mathews asked.

"I'll fill you in later. Right now, the three of us have to make a plan to get Tonya out of here without anyone seeing her." He continued to watch McCord. "No one," he emphasized. "Is to know how or when she leaves."

"I can scrounge up some clothing from my car for her to change into, put her hair up and things, then take her out in a patrol car," McCord offered.

"I like that idea." Hawke thought about it. "Mathews, you go get in your car and head to where you rented the Mustang I'm driving. I'll leave fifteen minutes after you and meet you at the rental place. Then we can go pick up my truck at the motel." He shifted to see if Mathews was willing. The deputy nodded.

Hawke shifted his attention back to McCord. "You go about your regular routine. Give us a couple hours, then text me where to meet up with you." Hawke studied everyone. "Once we get Tonya, we'll stash her somewhere until we can get Bayle on all the charges." His gaze landed on Tonya. "Is this okay with you?"

She nodded. "I want to stay alive."

Hawke stood. "Get going. I'll be behind you about fifteen minutes."

Mathews saluted and left the room.

"Can you get her disguised without anyone seeing her leave this room?" Hawke asked the trooper.

McCord smiled. It appeared she liked doing the sneaky stuff. "I've got a plan. See you in about three hours."

Hawke grinned. "Looking forward to it." He left the breakroom, walked to the entrance, and out to the Mustang. He roughed up Dog's ears and started the vehicle. He was sure someone was watching him and would follow.

Two blocks and he noticed the vehicle following him. He drove straight to the car rental place and turned the Mustang keys over to the attendant. He and Dog stood on the sidewalk in front of the building waiting for Mathews.

The deputy parked in front of the building and pulled the passenger seat forward as Hawke opened the door. Dog jumped in the back seat and Hawke tossed in his duffel bag.

"I figured you'd be here before me," Hawke said.

"I was hungry." Mathews held up a bag from a fast food place.

Hawke's stomach started gurgling at the smell of greasy French fries. "Good thinking."

Mathews pulled out of the rental place and into a parking lot next door. They dug into the food, tossing

Dog fries and watching the cars go by.

Hawke nodded. "That one there followed me to the rental place."

"The green sedan parked across the street has been following me. We'll have to lose them before we can pick up Tonya." Mathews said.

"We will." Hawke finished off the burger and tossed the last fry to Dog. "Let's go get my pickup." They wadded up the paper bags and wrappers, and Mathews started his car.

At the motel, Hawke tossed the bag and papers in the garbage can by the motel office. He glanced down the empty parking spaces in front of the building and didn't see his pickup.

"Shit!" He shoved the Office door open and strode in. "Where's my pickup?"

The tall thin man behind the counter started mumbling in what Hawke thought was a middle-eastern language.

"Stop that. I know you can talk English. You did when I purchased a room here." Hawke pulled his badge out from under his shirt. "What did you do with my pickup?"

The man's eyes grew rounder. "I do nothing. A tow truck come. I know nothing."

"A tow truck? What was the name on the side of the truck?" He had a good suspicion it was a company in cahoots with Bayle.

"I don't read such good English." The man shrugged.

"No, you conveniently don't read such good English or speak it." Hawke spun on the balls of his feet and headed to the door. He stomped up to the Mustang, yanked the door open, and dropped into the passenger seat.

"Hey! This is a classic! Stop acting like it's a piece of junk," Mathews growled.

"My truck was towed." Hawke glared at the deputy. It wasn't the man's fault, but he didn't have anyone else to take his frustration out on.

"Impounded by the city?" Mathews asked.

"I don't think so. I think impounded by Bayle. The owner of the motel pretended he didn't speak or read good English. It sounds like someone told him to keep his mouth shut." Hawke waved a hand. "Take me to City Hall. I'll go see if Bayle has his hands in any towing companies. While I'm doing that you could do a drive by of the City Impound and see if my truck's in there."

"Okay. What about meeting up with Tonya?" Mathews asked.

"We'll have to play it by ear." Hawke didn't like not having his own wheels and how that might muck up their plan.

《》《》《》

Thirty minutes later, Hawke walked out of City Hall with the names of three towing companies Bayle owned. It seemed the man had a monopoly on the towing companies in town. He'd texted Mathews to come pick him up.

Standing on the sidewalk in front of City Hall, waiting for Mathews, he stared up the street at the Capital Building. This was a pretty town. But too big for his liking. He wondered what the car that followed them to the City Hall had done when Mathews dropped him off?

Scanning the streets, it didn't look like there was anyone hanging around waiting for him. It would be his best time to lose the tails.

He strode down the street and started walking with no particular place in mind. This was a test to see if he was truly not being watched. After four blocks and not being able to pick out a tail, he texted Mathews.

I've lost my tail. How about you?

Sitting at a stoplight, hoping I can cut to the right and down a side street before they see where I've gone.

If you can't shake them, find a motel and hang there until I call you.

Copy.

Hawke didn't have McCord's phone number to contact her. Looked like he had time to think about what they knew while he waited for her call. He found a coffee shop and went inside, sitting where he could see out the window but not be seen by anyone walking or driving by. Sipping a black cup of coffee and nibbling on a sweet roll, he pretended to read the newspaper that had been left on the table.

His phone rang. A number he didn't know.

"Hello?" he answered.

"It's McCord. We haven't been tailed that I can tell."

"I lost my tail." He told her the name of the coffee shop and the street it was on. "When do you get off duty?"

"I have about three more hours."

"Any chance you brought along Tonya's regular clothes?" He had an idea.

"She kept them on under the jumpsuit I gave her." The smile in her voice, told him she was proud of that

251

fact.

"Good. Have her slip out of the jumpsuit and drop her off at the coffee shop. We'll wander around, until I find a motel. When you get off duty call me back, and we'll meet up."

"What about Mathews?" McCord asked.

"He's still trying to slip the people following him." Hawke hung up and watched a city police car drive by. He wondered if they had been given his and Tonya's descriptions.

Fifteen minutes later, he saw a state police car park across the street.

Hawke picked up his paper bag and cup, tossing them in the garbage as he left the building. Outside, he glanced both ways and crossed the street. While he wanted Tonya to feel safe, he wasn't chancing her taking off to get out of the charges of getting White out of prison.

Tonya looked surprised when she stepped out of the vehicle and he stood three feet away.

He motioned for her to keep walking. Staying three steps behind her, he followed her into a store.

Tonya stopped halfway back and picked up a book. That's when he realized they were in a bookstore. He walked up to her. "You like to read?"

She peered up at him. "Yes. Reading and writing go hand in hand."

He shrugged. "I guess so. Want to buy that or go find a place to hang out?"

"I don't have any money," she said. All the woman had were the clothes she wore.

"Know any mid-range clothing stores around here?"

She studied him. "Why?"

"You need a few changes of clothes. I'm not sure when we'll be able to get to your things."

"They're in Scott's car." She replaced the book.

"He can't seem to shake the people tailing him, so we'll use him for a decoy." Hawke put a hand on her elbow, leading her to the door of the store. "Where is a clothing store from here?"

"A couple blocks that direction," She pointed to their left.

"Lead the way." Hawke walked beside Tonya, watching everything and thinking he might need to change into a different type of shirt. His usual plaid made him easy to find.

As they stepped into a store that appeared to be a secondhand clothing store, his phone buzzed. It was Mathews. "Go look around. I'll take this and find a shirt for myself."

Tonya nodded and started digging through the racks stuffed with clothing.

"Did you find someplace to roost?" he asked Mathews.

"Yeah. But I haven't been able to shake them." The deputy sounded defeated.

"Good. I want you to sit tight about an hour. Then get in your car, pick up some food, and deliver it to somewhere that might look like a good place to stash a person. I don't care where it is. You can keep them busy following dead ends while McCord and I get Tonya stashed someplace and I can get my pickup." Hawke had wandered to a rack of men's shirts. He found one the right size and pulled it out of the rest.

"Okay. What about your dog?"

"Is he a bother?" Hawke asked, knowing Dog wouldn't cause any trouble.

"No. Just wondered if you wanted him."

"Keep him with you. All the time. Don't leave him alone in the motel. I'll figure out a way for you to leave him with me." Hawke missed his mutt.

"Copy. Let me know what all you want me to do."

"I will." Hawke disconnected and glanced around the place for Tonya. Anger started to build when he didn't see the woman. Had she been stupid enough to slip out? He headed for the door when he heard his name called. She stood by the room where clothes could be tried on.

He hurried over.

"Were you leaving without me?" she asked, her tone reproachful.

"No. I thought you'd ducked out on me." He grabbed the clothing she had in her hands. "Are these what you want?"

"Yeah."

He took them up to the counter and paid for the clothing. Happy to see it all only added up to twenty bucks. With the clothing in a bag, he took the shirt out, handed the bag to Tonya and stepped into the changing room. He wasn't changing down to his skin, but he didn't want anyone in the store to see he was wearing his shoulder holster and Glock.

With the new dark green corduroy shirt on, he exited the room and found Tonya waiting for him by the door.

Out on the street he said, "Where's the closest motel?"

Chapter Thirty-one

Hawke's phone buzzed as he and Tonya returned to the room with food they'd purchased at a fast food place. It was McCord.

"I'm off duty. What do you want me to do?" she asked.

"We're in a motel, getting ready to eat dinner. I'm not familiar with the area, can you think of some place we can take Tonya that Bayle won't find out?" Hawke sat in the chair across the small table from Tonya. The woman was listening to everything he said as she pulled the skin off the piece of chicken she'd grabbed out of the bucket.

"I've been thinking about that all day. I know a woman who has a place out toward McCall that's like a commune. I don't think Bayle would look for her there. And they don't have any way to communicate. If they need help someone drives out to the nearest town and makes a call."

Hawke liked the idea. "How do you feel about taking her there tonight?"

"That's what I was thinking," McCord replied.

He told her the motel and street. "Make sure no one is following you before you even come close to here," he warned.

"I will. If you don't see me in thirty, it means I'm being followed."

The line went dead.

"Good thing you got those clothes today. McCord is taking you to a commune until we get Bayle for the deaths of White and Sheridan."

"And my parents." Tonya stared at him.

"I'll try. But that was a long time ago." He held up a hand when she started to speak. "The more murders we can pin to him the less chance his money will get him out of jail time. I promise, I will try to get him for your parents' deaths."

That seemed to appease the woman. She returned to peeling skin off the chicken piece.

Hawke picked up a piece and bit into it.

"How do you plan on getting him for Felix and Sean's deaths? You know he didn't do it himself," Tonya said.

"By proving he contacted Sheridan to kill White and finding a paper trail to prove he paid whoever killed Sheridan." Hawke knew it would take a lot of digging, but with Tonya someplace safe, he didn't have to worry about who followed him where.

A knock on the door after they'd eaten all the food and sat staring at the T.V. brought Hawke to his feet. He slipped over to the window and peeked around the curtain.

McCord.

He opened the door, and she slipped in.

"No tails?"

"I went different ways and backtracked and never saw the same car twice." She looked smaller out of her uniform. The top of her head came to his shoulder and her body was slender. Her curly black hair was cropped short. She wore jeans, athletic shoes, and a brightly colored button-up-the-front short-sleeved shirt.

Tonya stood. "I'll use the bathroom and we can go."

"Works for me." McCord watched Tonya walk into the other room and close the door. "How's she doing?"

"She just wants justice. But keep an eye on her. She's lied so much I don't trust her." Hawke said barely above a whisper.

McCord nodded as the toilet flushed.

He pulled out two of his business cards. He handed them both to McCord. "Keep one to give to the woman at the commune to contact me if Tonya disappears. Put the address of the place on the back of the other one, please."

McCord picked up a pen, setting on the table where they'd eaten, and scribbled on the back of one of the cards.

"Stay with her until backup comes. I'll call Horton and have him send someone up to relieve you. Tonya is a flight risk even though she knows her life is at stake."

The trooper nodded as she handed the card back to Hawke.

Tonya joined them.

"I hope you don't mind roughing it a bit," McCord said to Tonya.

"I grew up backpacking the Seven Devils. I don't mind roughing it," Tonya said, picking up the shopping bag with the clothes. "Thanks for the clothes," she said, as the two walked to the door.

"You're welcome. Take care. I'll contact you when we have something on Bayle," Hawke said, walking to the door. He watched the two get in an older Ford sedan and leave the parking lot.

Once they were gone, he called Captain Horton, requesting someone to make sure Tonya didn't run. Then he called Mathews.

"Stay where you are tonight, but in the morning come pick me up." He told him the motel and address and that Tonya was headed to a safe place.

"Where is she going?" Mathews asked.

"Better if not everyone knows," Hawke replied.

"How will anyone check up on her if something happens to you?" The tone in the deputy's voice was a bit belligerent.

Hawke wasn't sure if it was because the man cared about Tonya more than just as a lawman keeping her safe or he felt he should know everything.

"Enough people know. Get some sleep. I'd like you to pick me up by seven. We'll grab something to eat and hit the first tow truck outfit on my list." Hawke ended the conversation and dialed Spruel. His Superior needed to know what had happened since the State Trooper pulled Mathews over.

After getting the sergeant up-to-date and not telling him where Tonya was, Hawke stripped down to his underwear and climbed into bed. He'd hoped to fall asleep quickly but too many "whys" drifted through his head. Most of them he had no answers for and wondered if he ever would.

《》《》《》

Hawke was showered and sitting in front of the motel before seven, waiting for Mathews. He'd purchased a paper from the box in front of the motel office and read the front page. Bayle was going to be at the grand opening of a fitness center he owned at 2 pm. It might be fun to attend the event and see if Bayle showed any recognition when he and Mathews approached him. The thought had Hawke chuckling. The event would also give him a chance to watch Bayle and get to understand him a little better.

The old Mustang appeared at the parking lot entrance. Dog was riding in the passenger seat. Hawke waved and Mathews pulled up alongside of him.

"Hey boy, did you miss me?" Hawke asked, roughing up the hair on Dog's neck before waving the animal to the back seat and sliding into the passenger seat.

"He missed you." Mathews said. "I think he paced the room all night. I thought you said he'd be fine."

"If he was pacing the room, it's because there was someone outside your door or he saw someone messing with your car." Hawke wondered if Bayle would stoop to bugging their vehicles. Another good argument for Mathews not knowing where Tonya was. It wouldn't be brought up in any conversations. He'd have to be sure to not talk on the phone with McCord while in this or his vehicle.

Mathews caught on quick. He mimed, *Is the car bugged?*

"Could be," Hawke said. "I'm starving. Did you see any good places to eat?"

259

"I passed a couple." Mathews drove and they didn't say much of anything. He pulled into a Pancake House and as soon as they were out of the vehicle, Mathews dropped to the ground scrutinizing the bumpers and undercarriage.

"Don't worry about it now," Hawke said. "They just wanted Tonya. We won't be leading them to her and it might make them show their hands if they know where all we are going digging for information. But don't talk to anyone on the phone while in the car, just in case they did bug it." He entered the restaurant, and they took a booth where they could see the car and most of the parking lot.

Before they finished eating, the car that had followed Hawke the day before pulled through the parking lot and left. Yep. There was a tracking device on the car.

Mathews saw it, too. "They do have my vehicle bugged."

"Yep. This should be fun," Hawke said. "We're going to get my truck, do some sniffing around, and then attend a grand opening where Bayle is supposed to give a speech."

Mathews grinned. "That sounds like fun."

Chapter Thirty-two

His wallet kept getting lighter and lighter. Hawke grumbled as he pulled his pickup into a parking space near where the grand opening was going to happen. He was pretty sure the towing outfit charged him double the usual fee for towing and holding a vehicle. One quick inspection of the cab and he knew they had gone through it as well as any forensic team.

Mathews pulled in behind him. They'd been to the State Police headquarters to see if Trask was back in Idaho and if they had learned anything from him. He was back, but sleeping off the effects of the D.T.s from not having had any alcohol for nearly 48 hours.

"How do you want to do this?" Mathews asked, when he caught up to Hawke.

"Observe the man, until it looks like he's leaving. Then I want to introduce myself." Hawke grinned. This could either go well and make the man do something stupid, or it could go bad and the man could try and discredit he and Mathews.

They walked up to the entrance of the building. People milled around. From the cameras, microphones, and notepads, it looked like mostly media was present, very few of the general public. Hawke remained toward the back of the group of people, but where he had a good line of sight to the front. He found Bayle by the photo that had been in the paper. The billionaire was talking to what looked to be the Chief of the Boise City Police and Childress.

"What's he doing here?" Mathews asking, clearly meaning Childress.

"He is on several boards. I guess he's here to promote the opening." Hawke studied Mathews' narrowing eyes and distasteful curl of his lips. The deputy had a hard time hiding his dislike for someone.

"We stay away from him. All we're concentrating on right now is Bayle," Hawke said, putting a hand on Mathews' shoulder.

"Shouldn't Childress be at the State Police being questioned?"

Hawke shrugged. If he had been questioned, he didn't look the worse for it. "He probably clammed up and they had to let him go. Nothing to hold him on, until we get more proof."

Just then two men strode across the area between the parked cars and the men gathered near the ribbon that was to be cut. They went straight to Bayle. As they talked, Childress became agitated. Bayle started scanning the crowd. His gaze locked onto Hawke.

"I think his flunkies just told him we're here," Hawke said, staring back at the billionaire with a blank expression.

He knew as they stood here irritating Bayle, Spruel was talking Captain Horton into finding a way to look into Bayle's financial records. Specifically, for payments to Sheridan and whoever killed Sheridan.

The mayor stepped up to the microphone and announced how pleased he was to be a part of this event. He bragged about all the good things Bayle had done for the community and how this was one more of those magnanimous gestures.

Mathews coughed and one of the reporters near them looked over her shoulder.

"You don't believe everything the mayor is saying about Mr. Bayle?" she asked, studying them both before facing them.

Mathews glanced at Hawke.

Knowing the deputy might say more than he should, Hawke said, "We've been discovering things about Bayle that make us a little leery of any philanthropic acts by him."

The woman stepped closer. "Does this have anything to do with the fact Tonya Cox is missing and her last story in the paper had to do with Bayle owning the Boise City Police?"

Hawke exchanged a glance with Mathews. "What can you tell us about her accusations?"

The woman nodded to the Chief of Police and Childress shaking hands with Bayle. The billionaire had cut the ribbon and was getting ready to leave.

"Can you stick around? We'd like to visit with you." Hawke tapped Mathews on the arm, and they headed straight for Bayle.

The two men, who'd warned their boss he and Mathews were here, stepped between them and the billionaire.

Hawke didn't want to make a scene, but he wanted the man to know they weren't giving up. "Tell your boss, we know everything he's done from the reckless driving homicides to the contaminated water and the murders. And so do the Idaho State Police and the District Attorney."

Pivoting to walk away from the two, he bumped into the reporter.

"Is that true? The district attorney has the goods on Bayle?" The woman's eyes lit up like fireworks.

He hadn't planned for anyone to hear that but the two flunkies. Hawke grasped the woman's arm, leading her through the parked cars. Mathews was right behind them.

Hawke stopped in the middle of the parking lot where no one could hear what he had to say.

"If you report what I just said, Bayle will have you in court for slander so fast, you won't know what day it is." Hawke nodded toward Mathews. "We're trying to gather the information for the D.A. to send out an arrest warrant. At the moment, all we have is intimidation."

The woman's eyes narrowed. "What you told those men wasn't the truth?"

"Half of it was," Mathews said.

She shifted her gaze to the deputy. "What half?" Her pen poised over her notepad.

Hawke studied the woman. "I take it you aren't a fan of Bayle's."

"No. He stole my family's farm and turned it into a subdivision." The woman glared at Hawke as if he were the one to take the land.

"Where was this?" Hawke held his breath. If she

were angry over the Sunset Rose Subdivision, they'd have another ally who could dig up dirt for them.

"Sunrise Court." She spit the words out as if they tasted like the worst thing she'd ever eaten.

"Any connection to Sunrise Rose?"

She studied him. "Right next door. Tonya was digging up dirt on that subdivision."

Hawke nodded. "Do you and Tonya work for the same paper?"

"Until she helped Felix White escape prison. The owner of the paper canned her." She shook her head. "I didn't think Tonya would go that far to get a story."

"Why do you say that?" It was the words Tonya had said at first for why she'd helped get White out of jail.

"She seemed driven to right injustice. It seemed odd for her to do something illegal."

Hawke noticed the two men who worked for Bayle watching them. "I've got a lot to tell you, but not here. Can we meet this evening?" He glanced around. "Seven-thirty at that theater? Back row, far right corner."

She flicked her gaze from Hawke to Mathews and back to Hawke. "Anything you need me to look up between now and then?"

"We need to find a way to get Bayle's private financial records."

The woman smiled. "I'll have them for you tonight." She started to walk away and swung around. "Which movie?"

Hawke looked at the billboard. "Whatever's playing in number two." Both films were nothing he'd ever pay money to watch.

Mathews watched the woman walk away. "You should have told her two men have been killed and Tonya is in hiding. She may not have offered to help."

Slapping Mathews on the back, Hawke said, "She still would have helped. *She* is a reporter."

The woman, whose name he didn't know, had shown she cared for a good story and wanted to pull off one that would rock the city on its heels. She also seemed to have some kind of clout to be ballsy enough to say she'd have Bayle's financial records tonight.

«»«»«»

The rest of the day, Hawke and Mathews chased information. They learned where Bayle spent most of his time, who he hung out with, and what his schedule was for the rest of the week. With all this information, they planned to split up. Hawke would go by the City Police Department and start digging through Officer Trasks old files and see if he could find anything to connect Bayle, and Mathews would just hang out everywhere Bayle showed up.

After a quick dinner at a burger joint, they walked up to the theater at 7:15 and bought tickets for the movie playing in number two.

Mathews walked over to the concession stand.

Hawke wandered into the theater. The movie was already playing. He scanned the upper right side and noted one person sitting in that area. As he climbed the slanted aisle, he figured out it was the reporter. She was early.

He took a seat next to her and reached into her box of popcorn, filling his hand. "You never did tell me your name."

She tipped the box toward him. "Evelyn Gaines.

And you?"

"Hawke."

She shifted, peering at him in the dark. "Just Hawke?"

"Just Hawke."

Mathews plopped down next to him. "Here or the other side?"

"The other side." Hawke replied. "And this is Mathews."

"And you both work for…?"

"Law enforcement," Hawke said before the deputy gave too much away.

"I see. You aren't vigilantes, are you?" She righted her popcorn container.

"No. We have badges. We just don't want you to go sniffing around." Hawke was tired of the chitchat. "Did you get the financial records?"

She nodded. "My sister works in the office for Bayle's accountant. But you don't know where these came from." She slipped a regular-sized envelope out of her purse. Hawke took the envelope and slipped it inside his shirt, tucking it into his holster.

"Are you going to give me anything?" she asked.

"You'll have to quote anonymous sources," Hawke said, reaching across her to grab another handful of popcorn, this time out of Mathews' gallon-sized container.

"As long as they can't get me in trouble, I can do that." She placed the popcorn in the slot for a cold drink and pulled out her pad and pen.

"Bayle and the other members of the corporation that built the Sunrise Rose Subdivision piped contaminated water to the people who bought there.

The corporation saved money by not building a proper purification station and instead piped water straight from the Boise River into the homes. Many children in the subdivision became sick." Hawke stopped there. That was enough for the woman to start digging into. He didn't want to get her messed up with the murders. "You can find the evidence by talking to Professor Stacy Clann at Boise State."

"Hawke, Mathews, thank you for this. I hope what I gave you helps." She pushed to stand.

Mathews put a hand on her shoulder, lowering her back into the chair. "One of the two men who saw us talking at the grand opening earlier is out in the lobby. He followed us in."

"Then I suggest, we wait until the movie is over and then all three split up in the wave of people leaving." Hawke leaned back and closed his eyes. He had no desire to watch the movie.

《》《》《》

They made it out of the movie theater all going their separate ways. Only Hawke, Dog, and Mathews went to the agreed upon motel, and Hawke pulled out the papers Evelyn had given him. He'd asked for personal records thinking the man wouldn't want any transactions to hitmen to show up in his business records, but it would be easier to hide a payment here and there in the business records rather than the personal.

"Is Bayle married?" Mathews asked.

"I don't know. Google and find out." Hawke continued to slide his finger down the column of names of payouts.

"Yes, he is. And she's a looker. Don't understand

why he'd be spending so much money at the Gentlemen's Club." Mathews turned his phone toward Hawke.

The photo of the woman standing next to Bayle looked hot enough to be one of the strippers at the club. "That is interesting." He glanced at the clock. "Guess we could go check it out."

Mathews whooped, then gathered himself together. "Have you been to this place?"

"Nope. You?"

"My cousin's bachelor party. It's classy with some really nice-looking women. Not like the one across town, that's more like a bar with drunk women on stage." Mathews picked up his car keys. "You driving or me?"

"We'll take my vehicle. That way Dog can go and wait for us in the pickup instead of here." He could leave Dog here to make sure no one got in to put a bug in the room, since Bayle's men knew every where they went, but he'd rather know Dog was safe.

At the club, they paid to get in and found seats at the bar. You could learn more about a place by chatting up the bartender. And this one was not a problem to visit with. She was a busty, brunette with a wide smile, and big brown eyes.

Chapter Thirty-three

"What are you drinking tonight, boys?" the bartender asked in a soft voice.

"Two beers," Hawke said.

When the woman placed the two glasses on the counter, Mathews twirled his finger. "I'm going to cruise."

Hawke nodded and watched the bartender. She was efficient, talked with everyone at the bar and kept her eyes on the women serving drinks as well as the ones on stage dancing. He grinned. She would know everything that went on at this establishment.

She wandered back to his end of the bar. "What are you smiling at?" She wiped at the bar, but her gaze rose over his left shoulder as she watched something.

"I see you are a people watcher. It's one of my favorite pastimes, too." Hawke sipped his beer.

Her dark brown eyes landed on him. "What makes you say that?"

"Twila, I need refills," a small strawberry blonde called from the middle of the bar.

"Hold that thought." Twila hurried to the taps and filled four glasses with beer and made two mixed drinks that she placed on a new tray. She took the tray with the empty glasses and placed the glasses in a sink of soapy water, washed and rinsed the glasses, and put them in a rack to dry. Before returning to him, she refilled two drinks at the bar and took money from a man paying his bill.

She strolled back his way. "Where were we?"

"Discussing our mutual hobby of watching people." He spun a bit to his right to see more of the dark interior of the establishment. A small, too pretty man was on the stage introducing the next dancer. Whoops and whistles rang out.

He caught the slightest narrowing of the bartender's eyes before she said, "Don't you want to watch Sugar dance?"

"Nope. I didn't come here to watch the women dance."

She stared at him. "You don't give off any vibes you like your own kind."

Hawke laughed. "No, I'm definitely a man who likes my bed partners with curves and all the other womanly attributes."

Twila scanned the bar, then leaned closer. "Who are you here watching?"

"I was wondering why Buck Bayle spends a lot of time here?"

She straightened, walked down the bar, filling drinks, and setting up drinks on a tray for the red-headed waitress.

He sipped his drink, wondering if she'd figured out he was a cop and wouldn't answer his questions. Establishments like this, even the clean ones, usually had something illegal or immoral happening somewhere on the premises, which made all the people who worked there leery of the law.

Twila returned, taking his half full glass and putting a full one in his hand. "Buck bought this place after he married Ginny. She was the main attraction until he set his eyes on her. He bought the place to make sure she didn't work here anymore."

"Why does he still drop by? To make sure things are being run correctly?" Hawke asked with as much restraint as he could. He wondered at a man purchasing the place a woman worked so he could marry her.

The bartender's face grew dark, her mouth puckered in anger. "He comes by to get a lap dance from the flavor of the month. This month it happens to be Sugar."

From the anger and venom in the words, Hawke couldn't help by ask. "Were you the flavor of the month at one time?"

She pulled his beer away from him and raised her hand to call the bouncer. "No. I'm Ginny's friend. He's scum, and I tried to tell her that. But all she saw was his money."

"Hey, I didn't mean to demean you. I think we both have something in common."

She shooed the bouncer away when he arrived. "Sorry. Miscommunication." When the man left, she nodded to the waitress waiting for refills. "I'll be back."

Mathews arrived back at his side. "There are four rooms in the back. Three for lap dances and one that takes a code to get through. Four men have gone in and no one has come out."

"The bartender doesn't like Bayle, who, by the way, owns this place. His wife worked here before he bought it."

Mathews eyebrows rose. "I told you she was a looker."

Twila returned. She refilled Mathews' drink and he wandered off again.

"What's your friend doing?" she asked.

"Trying to find a way to get into the backroom without a code."

"That's a high-stakes poker game. I'd love someone to catch him playing." Twila wiped the counter.

"I'd like to catch him at something worse than gambling. Have you seen him in deep conversations with anyone here at the club? I mean other than the usual people?" Hawke picked up his beer and sipped.

"About three weeks ago he had his body guards block off one of the lap dance rooms while he had a conversation with an older man and a younger cocky guy. The older man left as soon as the meeting was over but the younger guy hung around." She nodded to the men at the bar waving their empty cups.

Hawke wished he had a photo of Sheridan. He did an online search and there was a photo of him. It made sense the man who was full of himself would have a blog about tracking.

Twila returned. Hawke showed her the blog with Sheridan's photo.

"Was that the man?"

"Yeah. That's him. Not much of a tipper for all the

puff he talked about himself." She grabbed his half empty glass, dumped it out, and gave him a refill. "The way he talked, he'd been in here before. Kept asking me about a Tina. I told him as far as I knew there wasn't a Tina dancing."

He was glad he wasn't drinking all these glasses of beer he'd be paying for. "Did he happen to mention why he was talking with Bayle?"

"Something about a killer getting justice and dollars for him." She stopped, grabbed Hawke's phone and opened the link back up. "This is the guy who was killed after the guy who escaped from prison." She studied him. "Did Bayle have something to do with that?"

Hawke couldn't say no, but he also couldn't say yes. Not to someone unofficial. "That's what we're trying to figure out."

"Do you have a card?"

He pulled out one of his cards, setting it on the counter by his glass.

She glanced down before staring at him. "Oregon wants him? What about Idaho?"

"He's wanted for murders in both states."

She nodded. "I'll see if the security cameras have the two men meeting with Bayle. If they do, I'll give you a call tomorrow."

Hawke smiled. "I like the way you think. I better mingle so someone doesn't say something about me monopolizing your time." He picked up his beer and spun on the stool as a new dancer was being introduced. The timing was perfect. He also noticed one of the men who'd kept him from speaking to Bayle standing by the door, scanning the room. Good thing he was getting away from Twila.

He found Mathews at a table and sat. "We may have something tomorrow. Twila is going to look on the security tapes. Sheridan and Childress were in here about three weeks ago with Bayle."

Mathews grinned. "That would go a long way to getting the Prosecuting Attorney to press charges."

"That's what I thought."

Chapter Thirty-four

The following morning, Hawke headed to the Boise Police Station to see if he could find anything in Trask's files that would help them connect the retired city policeman with Bayle and Childress. Hawke flashed his badge and asked to look at archived files. No one asked which file. They only asked that he write down his name and badge number. Then he was escorted to a back room that had three older computers, a lot like his mom's, and boxes.

"We have reports to two-thousand in the computer system. If it's any older you'll have to look in the database to see where to find the file," the young woman dressed in a uniform told him before she left him alone in the room.

He wasn't sure when Tonya's parents had their accident. He pulled out his phone and looked it up online. Once he had the date, he popped that into the computer and started scanning the reports for that day.

He'd had the files sent over that were from Trask's file on the accident, but Hawke had a feeling those had been carefully vetted to send only certain information.

Bingo. He found the file and there was considerably more information than had been sent to the State Police. Hawke studied the information. In this report, it noted something blue had side-swiped the Cox vehicle, causing it to veer off the road.

Hawke called McCord. "Hey, can you look up what color car Bayle was driving on nine-six-two thousand two?"

"Sure can. Call you back."

Hawke took a photo of the screen showing the information about the car being hit. This was the original report. Nothing doctored.

His phone buzzed. McCord.

"Hawke."

"It was a cobalt blue metallic, two thousand and two, Porsche, nine-eleven, G T two." The awe in the trooper's voice revealed she knew the car.

"Any chance that fancy paint would look blue when it scratched another car?" he asked.

"What did you find?" McCord asked, with more excitement than he thought the discovery warranted.

"The full traffic report on the Cox's accident. Any chance Bayle still has that Porsche?" Hawke didn't know what good it would do if they didn't have anything to compare it with.

"Let me look."

While he held for McCord to look up Bayle's car registrations, he scanned more of the report. There was an evidence box number. This piqued his interest. If there was an off chance someone scraped the paint flecks into an evidence bag, they just might have him.

"Yes. He does still own the car. Along with half a dozen older ones. What do you want me to do now?"

Hawke grinned. He knew what it was like to be pulled from patrol and get to "work" a case instead of leave tread all over the interstate. "Nothing, until I dig some more." He started to hit end and thought of something. "Hey, can you pull up all the forensic information they have on the White shooting? I never did see that. And check to make sure my sergeant sent over all the info on the Sheridan shooting."

"Will do." She ended the call.

Jotting down the evidence box number, Hawke closed out the computer and returned to the front of the building.

"Where do I find evidence obtained by the City Police?" he asked the young woman who'd escorted him to the old files room.

"They're kept at the Ada County Sheriff's Department." She looked up from the computer she was typing on. "But you have to go through our office or the County Prosecutor."

"Thank you." He left the police station, talking on the phone to Captain Horton. Hawke scanned the parking lot. There was one of the cars that had been following him since he arrived in Boise. He got into his pickup, drove to a park that allowed dogs, and let Dog out for a pitstop. While he and Dog walked around, his phone rang.

"An assistant prosecutor will meet you at the Sheriff's Office," Captain Horton said. "And what you find better be good, because Ms. Rutledge wasn't happy to lose her assistant."

"I'll have information she's going to like," Hawke said. He disconnected the call and put Ada County Sheriff's Office into his GPS. The building looked easy enough to find.

The car that tailed him sat across the street. Hawke loaded Dog back in the pickup and headed to the Ada County Sheriff's Department.

The one-story building spread out over half a block with other social services also using the structure. Hawke left the windows down and strode up the walkway and steps to the main entrance. He liked the trees and landscaping. It made the building feel more approachable.

Inside the doors, a young man paced, looking at his watch. No doubt the assistant prosecutor.

Hawke walked up to him, holding out his hand. "Trooper Hawke, glad you could help me out with this."

"Taylor Jones. I understand you're digging up an old case. My boss is interested in how this affects the White case?" The man pushed heavy rimmed black glasses higher up the bridge of his nose.

"If we find what I think we will, you'll see." Hawke motioned for the man to go ahead of him. The assistant prosecutor knew the routine and the sheriff's department employees.

They walked down that corridor and came to a woman dressed in the county uniform, standing behind a wall with a window.

"Mr. Jones. Do you have the proper paperwork?" she asked.

"I do, and Trooper Hawke will be helping me find what I'm looking for." Jones signed his name and motioned for Hawke to do the same.

She slid a book towards him. "Sign here along with the time. If you bring anything out, you'll need to have it recorded."

Hawke nodded and signed his name along with his badge number and the time.

The door next to the window opened.

"Follow the signs to the end of the corridor, push the button, and I'll allow you access." She picked up the ringing phone.

Hawke wandered down the hall behind Jones who was clearly in a hurry. His fancy shoe heels clacked on the floor louder than Hawke's cowboy boot heels. At the door marked evidence, Jones pushed the button beside the door. When the whirring of what sounded like the door unlocking ended, the prosecutor turned the handle and walked in.

Before the door closed, Hawke pulled out his phone and turned it on as Jones groped for the light switch. The overhead fluorescents added shadows in the room. The walls of shelving and boxes smelled of must, dust, and odors he didn't want to think about.

"What are we looking for?" Jones asked, staring down the aisles of shelving.

"The file said it is in evidence box seven-six-zero-nine." Hawke watched as the assistant prosecutor walked down to the fifth row.

"It should be in here somewhere."

They each took a side of the aisle, looking for the number. Hawke found two boxes with numbers on either side of the number. "Damn, someone destroyed the evidence."

"Why? How old is the case?" Jones shoved his

black-rimmed glasses up his wide nose.

"Two-thousand-and-two. Cops on the take." Hawke stared at the empty spot between the two numbers.

That only seemed more damaging. If they had removed the evidence there must have been something that proved Bayle was guilty. Something stuck out from under the box on top. A large envelope.

Hawke blew the dust off the end of the envelope sticking out and recognized the file number. This was the evidence.

He raised the box and pulled the envelope out. His hands shook as he opened the envelope. This could help them bring down the man responsible for so many deaths. Inside the envelope was a copy of the report he'd read on the computer. The real report. Also included was a small paper evidence envelope with what looked like paint scrapings.

Adding this to the report about Bayle being cited for driving while under the influence, should help Tonya's case that the billionaire be charged with manslaughter.

"This should help prove Buck Bayle killed Mr. and Mrs. Cox in Two-thousand-and-two and prove that there were several city policemen who were and still are on his payroll." He handed the evidence over to Jones. "We need to take this to your boss."

"I'd say so, if it does do what you claim." Jones tucked the envelope in his briefcase and they left the evidence room and walked back up to the front.

They signed out and left the building. Hawke said good-bye to Jones at the door and wandered toward his vehicle. His mind was on so many other things, it took him a second to realize he wasn't alone.

"Mr. Bayle would like to see you," the man behind him said.

"I'm busy at the moment, but I can see him in about an hour," Hawke said, not breaking the stride carrying him to his vehicle.

A hand grabbed his arm and jerked him around. "He said now."

Hawke spun, stuck his leg out, and knocked the man to the ground. "I said later."

Not waiting for the man to get off the ground, Hawke ran to his pickup and peeled out of the parking lot. Dog whimpered and sniffed, checking to see if he'd been hurt.

"I'm fine," Hawke said, rubbing Dog's head and driving toward the county courthouse.

He pulled into the county parking lot and his phone buzzed. The number was unfamiliar, but since he'd given his card to several people lately, he answered. "Hawke."

"This is Twila, we met last night."

"Yes. Were you able to find anything?"

"I was. Can you meet me at a coffee shop on West State Street?" She went on to tell him the name and address.

"I can be there in fifteen minutes." He disconnected, pulled out of the parking lot, and checked to see if he was being followed. So far, he wasn't. He didn't want the gorilla that tried to deter him at the Sheriff's office to show up when he was talking to Twila.

For that reason, he parked two blocks from the coffee shop and ducked through two stores before walking into the coffee shop. He spotted the woman easily. She wasn't wearing the makeup or seductive clothes she had the night before, but her facial features were distinctive in a good way.

He ordered a coffee and sat down at the table she occupied in the corner. "You could get in trouble for this."

She shook her head. "Barry, the person in charge of the security cameras, is my boyfriend. He hates the way Bayle treats all the women who work for him. But Bayle pays good money for security." She handed him a brown paper bag. "It's the tape for the night I told you about and then a couple nights later when he met with just the old guy again."

That piqued Hawke's attention. "Any chance the room where they met had a camera?"

She shook her head. "Those rooms are private."

"I appreciate you doing this. I'll keep your name and your boyfriend out of this if I can."

Twila stood. "I'd appreciate that. Not that I care about my job, but I know Mr. Bayle can play nasty." She walked out of the coffee shop.

Hawke finished his coffee, picked up the brown bag, and walked back to his pickup. He called Mathews. "Meet me at the D.A.'s office, ASAP."

Chapter Thirty-five

Waiting in the reception area for Marcia Rutledge, the Prosecuting Attorney for Ada County, Hawke filled Mathews in on the fact there was possible evidence of Bayle's involvement in Tonya's parents' death and that he had a security tape of Bayle talking with Sheridan and Childress at the strip club.

The door to the attorney's office opened and a woman in her forties of average height, with highlighted blonde hair, stepped out. "I'm Marcia Rutledge." She held out a hand.

Hawke grasped her long fingers and palm. "I'm Oregon State Trooper Hawke." Her grip was firm without trying to prove she had balls.

"I'm Idaho County Deputy Scott Mathews." Mathews shook hands.

"You're both a long way from your usual territory. Come in." She walked into her office and they followed.

When she was seated behind her desk, Hawke sat in one of the chairs in front of her. Mathews sat in the one beside him.

"In case you're wondering, I do know a bit about why you are out of your territories, Captain Horton came to see me this morning about a retired city cop named Trask who he wanted indicted for providing false information. He said you," she nodded at Hawke, "brought this man to him. And my assistant brought me evidence that could put Buck Bayle in jail for manslaughter. You've been busy."

He nodded. "The evidence your assistant brought you is part of that false information." Hawke went on to tell her about the accident, who was involved, and the fact he found the original report and the evidence at the Sheriff's Office. She was writing as fast as he told the story.

Ms. Rutledge glanced up at him. "You're saying you think the evidence that was falsified will show Buck Bayle is responsible for the death of Mr. and Mrs. Cox?"

"Yes. And we," he motioned to Mathews, "have reason to believe he also had Felix White killed to keep quiet the fact he sold houses and property that had contaminated drinking water."

The prosecutor leaned forward on her desk. "Tell me more."

Hawke told her all about who asked him to find White, who went with him, and what happened, while Mathews filled in more of what they'd learned.

"This is interesting. Do you have any proof Bayle was behind the deaths?"

Hawke held up the brown bag he'd carried into the

courthouse. "If the person who gave this to me is correct, this may be enough to pull Bayle and Childress in for questioning."

Ms. Rutledge picked up her phone. "Alison, bring one of the televisions with VHS into my office, please." She replaced the phone. "Tell me everything you know about this. I've wanted to get something on Bayle since I took over this office. My predecessor tried but didn't have any luck."

Mathews told her what he'd seen at the strip joint. The coded door and the men who went through the door.

"The bartender said it was a high stakes poker game," Hawke added.

There was a knock, the door swung open, and a television on a cart was rolled in.

"Thank you, Alison." Ms. Rutledge plugged the television into a socket and reached out for the tape.

Hawke handed it to her.

She turned the T.V. on, shoved the tape in the rectangular opening, and waited.

"I'm not sure how many hours are on this tape," Hawke said, leaning forward, his forearms on his thighs, studying the angle of the camera and trying to figure out where it was located.

"I saw that camera," Mathews said. "It's in the hall that leads to the private rooms and the one that needed a code."

Every once in a while, a woman and a man or a woman and a couple would wander down the hall, be off camera for half an hour, and return back to the main area. The time on the tape grew later and later. Several men wandered down the hall alone. Then Bayle,

Childress, and Sheridan followed by one of Bayle's bodyguards walked down the hallway.

Hawke jumped up and stopped the tape. "That was Childress and the man who was helping me track White. He shot White, then ran and was killed in Oregon."

Ms. Rutledge picked up a notepad and wrote down the day and time, then the three names. "Where was this?"

"The Gentlemen's Club on Eighth Street. Bayle owns it."

Her eyebrows rose. "What doesn't he own in Boise." She put the notepad down and pressed play.

Twenty minutes later the three, followed by the bodyguard, walked back down the hall toward the main part of the building.

"I wish we could have seen an exchange of money," the prosecutor said.

"We checked his personal financials and couldn't find a payment to Sheridan," Mathews said.

Ms. Rutledge shifted her gaze to the deputy. "How did you manage that?"

Mathews squirmed.

"We happened to talk to a newspaper reporter who had connections." Hawke kept his eyes on the television. "According to my source at the Gentlemen's Club, Childress came back in a few days later. I'm thinking it was after Sheridan killed White but left a witness."

The woman stopped the tape and picked up her notepad. "Who is the witness?"

Up to this point, Hawke had left out any mention of Tonya. "Tonya Cox, the daughter of the people Bayle might have killed in the car accident. She is also a reporter—"

"And the woman who helped Felix White escape." The prosecutor stared at him as if he were on trial. "Where is she? She needs to be held accountable for her part in the escape of a prisoner."

"Even if that prisoner was being held on trumped up charges?" Hawke studied her. He'd told her how Trask, Bayle, and Childress had railroaded White into jail for something he hadn't done.

"She still broke the law. Where is she?"

"We have her someplace Bayle can't find her." Hawke wondered if Tonya contacted Bayle if he would come talk to her. That might be away to get something on the man. "But I have an idea."

《》《》《》

It took a lot of fancy talking and concessions from Hawke and Ms. Rutledge, but they'd agreed to having Tonya call Bayle. She would tell him if he brought her twenty-thousand dollars she'd disappear and not tell anyone how she knew he'd paid Sheridan to kill White. She'd also promised to hand White's research papers over to him.

Hawke also had to call Evelyn Gaines and ask her not to approach Bayle or let any whispers of the story she was writing about the contaminated water leak out. They needed the information to lynch Bayle. She was more than happy to sit on the story if it meant the man would get what he deserved.

Mathews and Hawke drove to the commune. They found Tonya working in the garden.

She smiled and walked toward them. "I forgot how fulfilling it was to work with dirt."

"You look rested." Hawke peered over her head. "How many are here?"

"About twenty. They kind of come and go throughout the day, so I'm not sure." She led them over to a bucket of water with a ladle for drinking. "I like it here, but I'd like to go home. Have you locked Bayle up yet?"

Mathews shook his head. "That's why we're here. We need your help."

She put the ladle down and stared at them. "How?"

"We, meaning us and the prosecuting attorney, would like you to call Bayle and tell him you want him to bring you twenty-thousand dollars. You'll promise to disappear and not tell anyone you know he paid Sheridan to kill White and you will give him White's research papers."

She glanced back and forth between them. "You have all this information?"

"We know he had a meeting with Sheridan before you broke White out. He had to know what you were doing in order to get Sheridan sent to find him and kill him. But I think Sheridan was supposed to blame the killing on you, and he decided to try and get more money out of Bayle, which is what got him killed. Again, this is only speculation." Hawke studied the woman. Why was she hesitating to do something she'd wanted all along?

"And Felix's papers?" Her hands twisted together in a wringing motion.

"You know we have them. A friend of yours at the newspaper, Evelyn Gaines, is picking up the story. She's holding it until we can get Bayle to come here to see you. We'll be here to grab him when he pays you to keep you quiet. You'll have a packet of copies of White's research."

Mathews stepped forward and put a hand on her arm. "We also have evidence that might prove he did kill your parents."

Her head snapped up. "What did you find?"

"The original police report saying your parents' car was sideswiped by a blue car. There are flecks of the blue paint in evidence. The prosecuting attorney is having it analyzed to see if it matches the type of car Bayle was driving that night." Mathews dropped his hand. "We've done all this work for you. Will you help us catch Bayle?"

She nodded her head. "What do I need to do?" Hawke pulled out a one-time use phone they'd brought with them and the list of demands.

Chapter Thirty-six

Hawke, a technician, and Ms. Rutledge sat in the state police van hidden in the trees behind the main house at the commune. Everyone but Tonya had been evacuated. Several troopers and county detectives were dressed in everyday clothes, meandering around the place as if doing jobs and enjoying themselves. There were listening devices and cameras in every room in the main house.

Tonya had sounded believable when she'd called Bayle on his private number, that Evelyn's sister had given them. Bayle had said he'd meet her at three in the afternoon. She'd told him not to bring any of his bodyguards or she wouldn't see him.

It was two. An hour until the man was to arrive, but they had wanted everyone in place to not alarm him if he sent someone to check things out before he arrived.

"You're sure she's going to be able to pull this off?" Rutledge asked Hawke again.

"She is very good at lying to people." Something that nagged at him. She had done a lot of lying for a newspaper reporter trying to get a story. As far as he knew the legitimate ones, didn't lie.

A voice in their headphones said, "There's a car approaching. It's stopping. A man in the back seat is getting out."

"Someone make sure he doesn't get to the main house," Ms. Rutledge replied.

"Copy."

"The car is proceeding. Looks like there is someone driving and someone in the passenger seat." The voice added.

They'd also set-up a camera in a tree that gave them a view of where the car would park. The car came into view.

"I only see one person in the car," Ms. Rutledge said. "Did it stop?"

"Someone is hiding. Probably going to sneak out once Bayle is in the house," Hawke said.

"Make sure that man is contained," the attorney said.

"Copy," came another voice.

Bayle stepped out of the driver's side of the vehicle with a backpack. It looked like he'd brought the money. Or at least made an effort to look like he did. Hawke wasn't sure if the man would actually pay Tonya or try to kill her given the men he'd brought with him.

A couple of the undercover police waved at Bayle and continued hoeing and working in the garden patch.

A woman walked around the side of the house with a basket of laundry. "Welcome," she said, smiling.

Bayle smiled back and continued up the steps to

the front porch.

There was a woman detective in the house with Tonya. Hawke focused his attention to the two women as Bayle knocked on the front door.

The detective stepped into the kitchen. Tonya walked to the front door.

The door opened and Bayle stood for a moment staring at Tonya. "Ti—."

"Get in and shut the door," she cut him off.

He did as he was told and faced her. "You have the research papers?" His question wasn't demanding, more inquisitive. As if he didn't believe she had the incriminating file.

"Do you have the money?"

"How do I know you won't show up in six months or a year and shake me down again? Because you apparently can't be bought off." He had the backpack slung over a shoulder.

Hawke was getting a lump in his gut. Something was off.

"You want me to sign a paper saying I won't tell people how you had Sean kill Felix, then you paid someone to kill Sean."

Hawke noticed the slightest rise of her eyebrow. Almost as if she was challenging Bayle. But what was she challenging him about?

Bayle dropped the pack down off his shoulder and shoved a finger at Tonya. "That's why I thought the voice sounded familiar. You're shaking me down to get paid twice."

That's when it clicked. Hawke couldn't sit still.

"What's wrong?" Ms. Rutledge asked.

"She killed Sheridan. I knew it but couldn't figure

it out." Hawke wanted to arrest her, but knew he only had circumstantial evidence. What he couldn't figure out was why she went along with this sting.

"I don't know what you're talking about. Show me the money and I'll get the research papers." She motioned to the backpack.

Bayle listened as if he expected his bodyguards to rush up the steps outside. When nothing happened, he unzipped the top of the pack and slid his hand in, instead of pulling the top back.

"No!" Hawke said as the man brought a gun out of the pack.

The detective in the kitchen shoved open the door, but before she could say "Police, drop the gun," a shot rang out.

Hawke was shoving out of the van and charging toward the house. Everyone had headed to the house at a run at the sound of the shot.

He rushed through the open door and was surprised to see Tonya standing. It was Bayle wiggling on the ground whimpering. Tonya had a small caliber pistol in her hand.

Mathews ran over and took the weapon from her. Hawke moved behind her, cuffing her.

"What are you doing?" Mathews asked.

"She more or less admitted to killing Sheridan." Hawke said, handing the woman over to one of the county detectives. "Hold her to stand trial in Wallowa County for the death of Sean Sheridan."

Ms. Rutledge picked up the backpack and smiled. She pulled back the top and revealed stacks of one-hundred-dollar bills. Bayle had planned to pay her off. That was pretty good evidence that he wanted to keep his hiring Sheridan, the contaminated water, and the incarceration and killing of White out of the news.

Hawke pulled out his phone and dialed Evelyn Gaines. "You can run with your story. If you meet me for dinner, I'll give you another story."

Mathews stood in the middle of the living room with him. Everyone else had left, including the prosecuting attorney. "I can't believe she killed Sheridan," Mathews said.

"All of her lies were eating at me. You know what I think?" Hawke headed for the door.

"What?" Mathews trailed behind him.

"I think she has been trying a very long time to bring down Bayle."

"Why do you say that?"

"Because when we told her about the evidence yesterday, she didn't act overjoyed or say she knew it all along. She only said she'd call Bayle. She wanted revenge on him, for something other than her parents. And when she opened the door, Bayle had a jolt of recognition. He started to call her something other than Tonya." Hawke replayed the moment in his mind. "Ti. Tina! I bet Tonya worked at the Gentleman's Club as Tina. Twila said Sheridan had asked about a Tina when he was in the club. He might have recognized her and that's why he didn't kill her with White."

"Want to get a beer?" Mathews asked as they walked through the trees to where Hawke had parked his pickup with Dog.

"I have a dinner date. I'll drop you off at your vehicle, have dinner, and head back to the county. I need to check in with my sergeant and take care of my horses."

《》《》《》

Hawke and Dani were walking the path that ran from the side of Charlie's Hunting Lodge around through the trees and came out by the shower house behind the lodge.

"It's been a month since you tied up that business over in Idaho," Dani said. "Can you talk about it now?"

He'd arrived that afternoon to spend the night and take Kitree out with him to spend a week with his mom.

"Yeah. Turns out the woman newspaper reporter we thought was on the side of good, was using us to bring down the man who not only killed her parents in a car accident but also canned her from a job she had to try and get information on him. She was legitimately trying to help the young man wrongly incarcerated by Bayle. She did all the planning to break the man out and get information to bring Bayle down. Only Bayle had other plans for the young man and sent a hitman after him. A man who couldn't stop boasting. It turns out he knew the newspaper woman from when she'd danced at Bayle's strip joint. But when he told her how much he'd received for killing the young man and how he had plans to use that against Bayle to get more money to set him up for life, she made him think she wouldn't tell anyone and they'd go off together." Hawke plucked new growth off a pine tree. "She in turn killed Sheridan. She wanted Bayle dead rather than just discredited and in jail."

"No 'hell hath no fury like a woman scorned'," Dani quoted.

Hawke laughed. "Tell me about it! I don't plan on ever making a woman that mad at me."

She studied him a moment. "What about your ex-wife?"

"She got over her mad when her brother stole from her. But she still believes I shouldn't have turned family in." He sighed. "I can't help it if I believe in justice."

Dani wrapped an arm around his and leaned her head on his shoulder. "That's one of the things I like about you."

Hawke's heart pounded in his chest. He could get real used to having this woman make his world seem right.

Thank you for reading book four in the Gabriel Hawke Novels.

Continue investigating and tracking with Hawke as his series continues. If you missed his other books they are:

Murder of Ravens
Book 1
ISBN 978-1-947983-82-3
Mouse Trail Ends
Book 2
ISBN 978-1-947983-96-0
Rattlesnake Brother
Book 3
ISBN 978-1-950387-06-9

While you're waiting for the next Hawke book, check out my Shandra Higheagle Mystery series.

Paty

About the Author

Paty Jager grew up in Wallowa County and has always been amazed by its beauty, history, and ruralness. After doing a ride-along with a Fish and Wildlife State Trooper in Wallowa County, she knew this was where she had to set the Gabriel Hawke series.

Paty is an award-winning author of 43 novels of murder mystery and western romance. All her work has Western or Native American elements in them along with hints of humor and engaging characters. She and her husband raise alfalfa hay in rural eastern Oregon. Riding horses and battling rattlesnakes, she not only writes the western lifestyle, she lives it.

You can follow her at any of these places:

Website: https://www.patyjager.net
Blog: https://writingintothesunset.net
FB Page: https://www.facebook.com/PatyJagerAuthor/
Pinterest: https://www.pinterest.com/patyjag/
Twitter: https://twitter.com/patyjag
Goodreads:
http://www.goodreads.com/author/show/1005334.Paty_
Jager
Newsletter- Mystery: https://bit.ly/2IhmWcm
Bookbub - https://www.bookbub.com/authors/paty-
jager

Windtree
Press

Thank you for purchasing this Windtree Press
publication. For other books of the heart, please visit our
website at www.windtreepress.com.

For questions or more information contact us
at info@windtreepress.com.

Windtree Press
www.windtreepress.com

Hillsboro, OR 97124